IDA AND THE UNFINISHED CITY

CAROLYN COHAGAN

Published 2020, Girls With Pens Press, Austin, TX
Printed in the United States
ISBN: 978-0-9995624-9-9

ALSO BY CAROLYN COHAGAN

Time Zero

Time Next

Time's Up

The Lost Children

Creative Writing Journal: Clever Prompts for Clever Children

For my nephews, Liam and Kailen Cohagan, who were children when I started this book. By waiting ten years for a sequel, they learned an important lesson: ten years is a long stinkin' time.

PROLOGUE

After Vernon Lyon bent down and hammered in his last nail, he straightened up and surveyed his work with pride. This roof was strong, probably the best he'd ever made. Last month when he'd spread the tar, he'd been afraid he wouldn't finish the house in time, but, as usual, he had managed to get everything completed precisely on schedule.

His lower back ached, and his knees popped when he stood. Vernon was no longer a young man, and sometimes he wondered how much longer he'd be able to build houses. He looked out to the sea, inhaling the salty air. He was filled with the satisfaction and deep hunger that comes from a job well done.

Packing up his bag of tools and provisions, he checked his wallet for the picture of his departed wife. When he saw that he still had it, he left the small house and walked toward the hill. By midday, he'd climbed to his usual spot in the meadow. He put down his heavy bag, kicked off his shoes, and sat down in the grass. He ate a cheese sandwich he'd prepared the night before. From this viewpoint, he could see his entire beloved town, the Unfinished City. The ocean spread out in front of it like spilled paint. He frequently imagined placing an enormous level upon the horizon to see if the land were as even as it appeared.

Every citizen of the town sat or stood on the hill around him. They huddled in family groups with their pets, and some had herds of goats or cows. Someone waved, and Vernon grunted. There was little chance anyone was waving at him.

The sea was no longer blue. The sky overhead darkened as the wind picked up. Vernon put on his wool sweater, preparing. The sea churned and spat as it reflected the blackening sky. Lightning struck far on the horizon, and teenagers standing nearby whistled and cheered. Waves crashed onto the shore while a ripping sound tore through the sky. Water soared toward the dock as cold wind whipped through Vernon's remaining hairs. It was time.

The smaller waves parted, making way for a much larger crest that rose up like a bucking stallion. It lifted its foaming head and slammed through the dock as if it were made of tissue paper. Vernon gasped as if he were seeing it for the first time, awed by the water's strength and majesty, at the pure nature that would not be contained.

The tidal wave quickly moved through the city, crushing trees like blades of grass. Fences, walls, and houses were casually plucked and added to the pandemonium. Vernon saw the roaring beast lurching toward his own house, the last nail of which he had lovingly placed only hours ago. Despite bracing himself, he felt the wind knocked out of him as the wave embraced and demolished his home.

Eventually, the swell turned in on itself, laying a hand of rising water over the land. He watched the flood cover the city until nothing was visible and the water became as still as a pond, finally sated. He marveled at the beauty of the sea merging seamlessly with the sky, both the same shade of slate gray. He felt a lump in his throat, recalling that this moment had always been his wife's favorite.

Before long, the entire body of water seemed to inhale and push itself off the base of the hill. It receded humbly, leaving the city to reunite with the sea. The destruction it left behind was astounding—every building and home had been razed to the ground. The city's walkways had disappeared, apart from some jagged pieces of wood. The land had become one massive pit of mud, with plants, trees, and furniture all mixed in. All that remained standing was a marble statue smack dab in the middle of the town square.

The locals cheered and sobbed as they reacted to what they'd seen. Vernon breathed in the air, which was cleaner and fresher. He gathered his things. His body felt lighter and less sore. A beam of sunlight pierced through a cloud and illuminated the city. He took off his wool sweater, checked his wallet once more for the picture of his wife, and walked down the hill to begin rebuilding his home . . . for the forty-seventh time.

I

When the door to the tavern opened, the miners put down their drinks and stared. Standing alone in the doorway was a child who looked to be around eleven or twelve years old. She wore a sweet frilly dress with a green bow carefully tied at the waist. Her emerald eyes and enormous eyelashes were framed by tight black curls.

Without a word, she walked into the pub. Several patrons kept watching the door, expecting a parent to follow, but none did.

Not many strangers passed through this part of the land. Lollup was a rough mining town whose beauty could only be found three miles below ground. Its chief export, the Honey Stone, provided fuel for most of the country, but coaxing it out of the hard clay that lay underneath the mountains was brutal work. In Lollup, days were long and lives were short. Few dared to enter such a mountain community.

The strange girl walked confidently toward the bar, causing several large men to make way for her. She carried a worn leather bag that was incongruous with her pristine patent leather shoes. She found an empty stool and, not without effort, hoisted herself upon its wobbly seat. Silence filled the sticky air. The bartender, Harry Ickman, watched her closely, assuming that a customer's wife had sent this child to fetch a husband for dinner, but she was looking at him expectantly, and he realized that she wanted to be served. "Yes, ah, miss. What can I get you? A glass of milk?"

She smiled. "Strawberry juice, please."

Harry uncorked a large bottle, poured a glass, and placed it on the bar. Taking a long, slow sip of her drink, the girl spun on her stool and surveyed the rest of the tavern. She studied the tired faces of the miners, still sooty from their day in the mine, until her eyes came to rest on a group of men sitting at a table in the corner.

"Oooh, cards!" she chirped, jumping off her stool and almost spilling strawberry juice down her dress. She approached the men, who were so engrossed in their game that they hadn't noticed her entrance.

She looked over the shoulder of a wide man with oversized sideburns. Squinting at his cards, she declared loudly, "I wouldn't play that if I were you. I would go with the ten."

The men burst into laughter, and the one with the sideburns turned to glare at her. "Mind your business, ya brat!"

A man with ashy skin and a beard said, "Maybe you should listen to her, Yusef. You haven't won a hand all night." The other men chuckled.

Scoffing at them, Yusef played the card he'd originally intended: a seven.

The player to his left was called Tippo, who was known for his poor mining skills and taste for uncooked rabbit. Sneering, Tippo played an eight, placed his dirty thumb on the seven, and dragged it toward himself. "That would be a dead man's lock, my friend. You're out."

Cursing, Yusef handed Tippo a gold coin.

Tippo then turned to the girl and asked, "Who taught ya to play 'Black Thumb' little girl? Yer daddy?"

"Oh no," the girl said sweetly. "It's a kids' game. I just learned from watching."

"Ho ho," Tippo guffawed. "Did you hear that, Yusef? It's a *kids'* game!" He had eyes like a weasel's.

"I'd like to see her play *you*," Yusef said bitterly, standing to go to the bar.

"I'd love to!" Before anyone knew what was happening, the girl was sitting in Yusef's empty chair.

"Uh, wait a minute, young lady," Tippo said. "This here is an adult game. We're playin' for gold."

"Oh. How embarrassing." She held up her leather bag and shook it, and the sound lit up the men's eyes. "I only have twenty coins. Is that enough?"

Twenty coins was more than any of the miners made in a week. Tippo winked at the two other men sitting at the table. "Twenty coins is just about the perfect amount," he told her. "It's Reginald's deal. One-eyed jacks are wild."

Gulping down the rest of her juice, the girl belched loudly. She wiped her mouth with the back of her hand. "Fun!"

Reginald shuffled the cards slowly, not sure how he felt about gambling with a child, but twenty coins! Imagine how happy his wife would be if he came home with that! "Ante up," he announced, and everyone, including the girl, put two coins in the center of the table. Reginald dealt at lightning speed.

The girl looked at her cards and then waited for the man to her right to begin. He was older and seemed to have difficulty seeing his cards. Finally, he threw down the four of hearts. Smiling sweetly, the girl threw down the three of hearts. Then Tippo and Reginald put down the seven and ten. Reginald won the hand.

He dealt again, but before anyone could pick up their cards, Tippo said, "I raise the pot five coins."

The old man put down all his cards. “I fold!”

The girl looked confused. “So . . . if I lose this game, I’m going to lose my two coins *plus* another five coins?”

Tippo knew he had to handle this just right. “Yes, darlin’. But if you win, you’re goin’ to get seven brand new shiny coins!”

The girl’s eyes widened. “Seven coins! Golly, that's a lotta peppermint sticks!” She added five more coins, and so did Reginald, who appeared nervous. Tippo grinned.

Everyone looked at their new cards. The girl frowned, and Tippo could feel his heart racing. She put down a two of clubs. Tippo couldn’t believe it. The silly child had just led with the lowest card there was! He put a queen of clubs on the table, trying to suppress his giddiness.

Reginald scowled, “I’m out.” He put his cards face down on the table.

Reginald put his thumb on the jack and queen, adding them to his pile.

Tippo smiled at the girl. “Lookin’ like it’s just you and me.”

A crowd had gathered, curious to see how the girl would do.

Tippo signaled to Reginald to deal the last hand. When Tippo picked up his cards he kept a straight face, but inside he was dancing. He now had two red aces, two red kings, and a wild card. It was a “Red Thumb.” He tried to read the girl's face. She looked befuddled.

There was no way he could lose.

Looking more at his audience than at her, he said, “I raise you thirteen coins.”

The crowd gasped. It was an unheard-of amount to gamble, let alone win from a child.

The girl stayed steady. “Okey-dokey." Without batting an eye, she placed her entire satchel of money in the middle of the table.

Fifty-eight coins, almost a month's wages, was now at stake. Everyone held their breath.

Smirking, Tippo placed all his cards on the table. "Red Thumb!" Clapping his hands, he whooped with delight. He was reaching for the money pot when the girl said innocently, "Don't I get to show everybody my cards?"

"Of course you do, sweetheart. You go right ahead," he said.

The girl placed her cards on the table. She had two black aces, two black kings, and one black jack. It was a "Black Thumb" with no wild cards—the highest hand you could get. Tippo's jaw fell open. The odds of the girl getting that hand were . . . were . . . Tippo sank in his chair as he realized how much money he'd just lost.

The people in the bar laughed and clapped, happy to see the little girl beat Tippo, who'd won money from almost everyone in Lollup.

Leaning forward, the girl scooped money into her bag. "This was so exciting! I can't wait to teach my brothers and sisters!" Standing, she put the bag over her shoulder, the weight of it making her lopsided. "I have to go meet my mother now. She's visiting my aunt and she'll be worried about me." Before anyone knew what was happening, the girl had scurried to the entrance.

As she opened the door, she turned back to the bar. "Thank you, gentlemen. It was a pleasure. And please don't use this evening as an excuse to teach your children to gamble. Gambling with children is wrong." She smiled wickedly and was gone.

Tippo finally came out of his state of shock. He jumped up from his seat and ran after her, sure that the girl had swindled him, even if he couldn't explain how. When he got outside, she was nowhere to be seen. She'd disappeared as mysteriously as she'd arrived.

Shaking his head, Tippo returned inside to a roomful of men laughing at him. He said loudly, “Tell y’all what. I promise to buy y’all a round a drinks, and y’all promise to never talk about this here little incident ever again.”

The men just laughed harder.

2

By the next morning, Ida Dorrington was several miles south of Lollup. She'd learned over the years that it was best to get as far away as possible after she'd hit a card game, lest the locals decide her visit was not as charming and funny as they'd originally thought. This tended to happen after a man went home to his wife and tried to explain his light wallet.

She'd been walking since midnight, and her feet throbbed with pain. Surveying the thin forest, she found not a soul in sight, so she sat down on a rock, took off her patent leather shoes, and sighed with relief. After she'd wiggled her toes for a while, she opened up her satchel and dumped the contents onto the dirt. She knew how much she'd won, but she counted it anyway, each coin filling her with more satisfaction. *Fifty-eight coins.*

She smiled. It was enough to get her back to the Institute. She could buy provisions for the journey and still have enough for new socks, which, let's be honest, she should have bought months ago. She could be at the Institute within a fortnight. As she happily pulled her frilly dress up over her head, five playing cards fell to the ground—Ida's original hand that she'd hidden during the game. Ruffles hid a lot. She'd walked into the tavern with a perfect Black Thumb hidden within her petticoats.

She snorted as she thought of Tippo's face when she'd won all of his money. She'd met swindlers who felt guilty after they pulled a job. Not her. Life had dealt her a very bad hand, and it was only fair that she rearrange things in her favor when she could.

She had also taken the hardest thing in her life and turned it to her advantage: Ida could *never* grow old. She looked like a sweet twelve-year-old, but she was in fact sixteen years of age. Since one horribly fated day four years ago, her cropped black hair hadn't grown an inch, her feet had not elongated a millimeter, and her rosy cheeks would not give up the baby fat of childhood. She was stuck at four feet eight inches tall, and her hand was only wide enough to hold a small plum. The only thing that might give her away were her eyes. If she let you get close enough, which she probably wouldn't, you would see that her sharp green eyes held the wisdom she'd gained and the hardship she'd endured.

She counted among her virtues intelligence, wit, and a flawless complexion. Her vices included fighting, stealing, and a pure delight in telling a really good lie. She was also foul-mouthed, proud, and a perfect shot with a pointed rock. And over the last four years, she'd become one heck of a hustler.

She'd experienced and seen things that most of us couldn't imagine, even if we lived to be a hundred, but even with all her adventures, Ida *longed* to be sixteen. She wanted to be friends with people her own age. She wanted to be trusted with the responsibilities that her age allowed (she was sick of being treated as if she were as incapable as a cow patty), and one day she wanted to become an adult, like normal people did.

She didn't like to discuss her past. Who would believe her? She'd been buried alive next to a beast from the underworld who fed off the vitality of children. Anyone who had provided nourishment to the monsters, known as the Brothers, would never age again. The one time she'd dared to share her story, the woman she'd confided in had been so horrified that she'd run Ida out of her house with a broom, as if Ida were some sort of rodent. Ida had learned that people were very frightened of things they didn't understand, so she kept her history to herself.

Her life was now about one thing—finding a cure for herself and for the other children who had been sacrificed to the Brothers. She'd spent the last four years traveling far and wide, sampling various miracle cures, tonics, and pills. She'd eaten a raw egg from the nest of the purple tern, spent three days in the heat of the Yurelian Desert Caves, and paid a sorceress to dip her feet in wax made by white bees, all the time supporting herself with gambling and the occasional theft. But none of the cures had worked, and time was ticking by. She had finally decided that she was looking in the wrong place—that is to say, she had decided that perhaps she was looking in the wrong *world*.

In the orphanage where she'd been raised, The Higgins Institute for Wayward Children and Forsaken Youth, a magic doorway existed, a passage called a "Brokhun's Crack." Ida's friend Josephine had told her that the special door would take you *wherever you needed to go*.

Ida suspected that if she went through the doorway needing to find a cure, the door would send her to the right place. It was flawless logic in Ida's mind, and she chided herself for not having thought of it sooner.

Ida ran her fingers through her hair, pulling out the curls that she'd created with fabric rolls the night before. She grabbed her regular clothes from her bag and pulled on cotton pants, a simple shirt, and a decent pair of walking shoes. She forced her black bob into a hat until, from afar, one couldn't be sure if she were a girl or a boy. She took out a small flask, taking a grateful sip of water, scooped the coins back into the satchel, and shoved her frilly dress on top. She didn't want to waste any more time. She'd spent the last eight months traveling from town to town, slowly but surely making her way back to the Higgin's Institute. She was now so close she could taste it.

3

After she'd restocked her supplies, Ida spent the next two weeks traveling through forests, climbing rocky hills, and hiking across plains covered with long grass that tickled her legs like feathers. The journey gave her time, maybe too much time, to think about her destination and what lay ahead.

She'd been born just outside of the town of Gulm, where she'd lived in a beautiful cottage with her parents. They had died when she was very young, murdered by soldiers sent by the evil Master who ruled the land at that time. She'd been forced to grow up in the orphanage where she was headed now. The only light in that dark place had been her best friend Fargus, who helped her plan pranks against the nasty women in charge, Kitchen Maggie and Stairway Ruth.

They had finally escaped with the help of a new girl named Josephine, who later taught Ida about the magic doors. Ida, Fargus, and Josephine had parted ways several years ago. They each had their own important path to follow. Ida ached to see them again, but she'd vowed to herself that she wouldn't look for them until she had her cure. She'd had no idea it would take so long.

The sun lowering to the west told Ida that late afternoon was approaching. The grass of the plains had gone from long and straw-like to short and green. A few strange trees clustered in the distance—they had white trunks, flat tops, and leaves as purple as grapes. *She was close.* Nowhere else looked like this. She walked across the open country, marveling at her ability to cross the land without worrying about the Brothers, whom Josephine had helped return to the Dark World. The Brothers—huge bear-like beasts covered in black quills—could run on their hind legs and smelled like rotting meat. They had been the nightmare of Ida's childhood.

She traveled another hour before she finally spotted the enormous, gloomy building where she'd spent half her life. The Institute stood alone in the middle of the grasslands, an abandoned ship in a green sea.

As she approached, she saw that the towering front doors had been obliterated. She hollered, "Hello! Anybody here?" with a mixture of panic and fear.

She waited, and then waited some more, but no one answered. She exhaled, scolding herself for being such a coward, then puffed up her chest and walked inside. The first thing she saw was the remains of a long dining hall. The table and chairs were in splinters. Upturned bowls lay on the floor, their contents lapped up long ago by rats. Cobwebs and dust covered the walls.

She couldn't believe it. It had only been four years, but the Institute was in ruins. The place now felt frail and harmless. Ida couldn't believe that this was the same place that had held her prisoner for half her life.

Passing through the dining hall, she saw that the door to the kitchen had also been destroyed, and all that was left was a gaping hole. The stairway to her right was still intact. She crept up the stairs, feeling the familiar banister under her hand. When she reached the top of the landing, her hand was black with dust. She slapped it against her pant leg in disgust. Stairway Ruth would never have let things get so dirty. She would've had orphans on their knees polishing that banister every day.

Ida bristled at the thought of Stairway Ruth, a woman who'd terrorized her throughout her youth. She couldn't help but wonder if she would still be frightened of her now. After all, there was a big difference between being sixteen and being twelve. She decided that she'd be able to defeat Stairway Ruth with a few well-placed insults and a quick right hook. Her defense skills had improved noticeably since her days in the Institute.

The upstairs had escaped whatever devastation had hit the ground floor. She rounded the corner and saw the boys' bedroom. When she saw Fargus' old bed, she smiled, remembering when the two of them had put glue in Kitchen Maggie's hair tonic. Maggie's hair had stuck straight up as if she were permanently frightened by a mouse.

After they'd left Gulm, Ida and Fargus had traveled together for a year searching for Fargus' parents, but Ida had left him when she'd heard about a cure that was a *sure thing*. The cure had turned out to be a sham, and Ida hadn't seen Fargus since. Her stomach fluttered with guilt. She quickly left the boys' room, since she liked to pretend she never had regrets.

She crossed the hallway into the girls' room. It was still full of beds with mattresses thinner than a slice of toast. Sitting on her own old bed, she looked around the room. It was so strange, but Ida actually felt some nostalgia for this horrible old place. Well, maybe not for the place itself, but for the time in her life when everything had been simpler, and her future had still been a blank page. She removed her bag from her shoulder and lay down on the mattress. She was still small enough to fit in the bed perfectly. She looked down at her tiny hands and feet. How many times had she lain in this bed, staring at the ceiling and imagining herself as an adult?

The room was so quiet. The emptiness felt as if it might consume her. She hadn't expected her return to be disturbing, and yet the rapid deterioration of the Institute only served as a reminder of how little she herself had changed.

Shaking her head to dispel the self-pitying thoughts, she stood up from the bed. *Enough of this pathetic, wood-headed lamenting*. It was time for action.

She marched back down the stairs and into the kitchen, which had been smashed up just like the dining room. The wall to the cellar no longer existed, and the stairs leading down were in a broken heap. She'd have to climb down. *No problem*. She considered herself quite athletic and coordinated.

She sat down on the edge of the kitchen floor, now a ledge, her feet dangling above the jumble of broken stairs. Twisting, she lowered herself onto the wreckage until she found a foothold on the wood and debris. Once she was close enough to the floor, she jumped the rest of the way.

Landing, she stumbled backwards. She was glad no one else was there to see it. Ida liked to do things right the first time.

She examined the old cellar. The pile of flour bags where Ida had first found Josephine hiding was no longer there. One remaining sack had been torn open, and the flour had merged with the dust. Barrels were turned on their sides, and the whole place had a depressing musty smell. Most upsetting to Ida was that, although there were logs of wood scattered all over the room, there no longer appeared to be a *woodpile*. The only thing she knew about the magic door was that Fargus had said it was behind the woodpile.

She approached the corner where she remembered the pile

had been. From her pocket, she took out two timepieces. One was a fancy pocket-watch she'd nicked from an obnoxious headmaster who'd tried to force her to go to school. The other was a simple wristwatch that she'd bought for a few gold pieces. Both worked very well and were precise to the second. Of this, Ida was sure.

She held one in her right hand and one in her left. They both read three thirty-five and twenty-two seconds. Ida walked in a small circle to her right. The clocks stayed perfectly in sync. When she'd completed her tiny circle, she began again, but made the circle a little bigger this time. Using this method, she figured she would not miss a single inch of the room.

Ida had learned that wherever one found one of Brokhun's Cracks, one would discover a spot where time was inconsistent between two spaces only one foot apart. This was because when the door opened, it would leak a bit of the time from another land or era into this one. The best tool for finding these spots was a claganmeter, but the only one Ida knew of belonged to Josephine.

On her fourth rotation, she saw the second hand on the pocket-watch twitch ever so slightly. She glanced at the wristwatch, which was ticking along the same as always. When she looked back at the pocket-watch, she saw that it was now running one second behind the wristwatch. *This was it.*

Ida took a quick step backwards, not wanting to get sucked through the door without concentrating very carefully on where she was going. What if she happened to have a fleeting thought about food and ended up in some strange land made of ham?

Putting the timepieces back in her pocket, she adjusted her bag. She took a deep breath and, while exhaling, she thought of herself looking sixteen, then twenty, then thirty, and then finally, she imagined herself as an old woman. "Take me to a place where I can finally age," she whispered.

4

Cold wind whipped through the cellar. Flour sacks and logs flew through the air. Ida ducked, desperate to keep her mind focused on her goal. She stepped forward, causing a loud cracking noise and a bright light. Suddenly she was not standing, but falling into pure darkness. She screamed, but there was no noise. Unable to breathe, she was sure she would suffocate. She reached frantically all around her as she fell, but there was nothing to grab hold of—just dark space.

Just when she thought she would die from lack of oxygen, she landed with a squishing sound in what felt like dense mud. She lay motionless, waiting for the pain of the fall, but it never came. She felt as if the breath had been knocked out of her, but her limbs and head felt fine. She was grateful for the soft landing.

When she sat up, the mud made a squelching noise that sounded like a big burp. She was filthy from head to toe. *So much for my clean socks.*

A plank of wood landed beside her. A deep voice from

above said, "Blasted!" which was quickly followed by, "Oi! Look! Someone fell in the mud!"

Ida was in the middle of what appeared to be a construction site. People traipsed around on wooden walkways built on stilts. The walkways, barely wide enough for two people, were ten feet above the ground, and it was no wonder—the ground was pure mud as far as the eye could see.

A short, squat woman yelled down, "Do you need some help, girl?"

At least they speak the same language as me, Ida thought. "No!" she yelled back. "I'm fine. I just slipped!" She stood, showing them she was all right.

"Over there," the woman pointed. "There's a ladder."

"Thank you!" Ida carefully scanned her surroundings for a landmark. When she wanted to get back to her world, she'd have to come back to this exact spot and use the clocks again. Distinctive features were difficult to find in a sea of mud. Finally, she noticed a sign above the woman's head that said, "Farnucci Brothers' Glass Blowing Shop." That would do.

The woman waved good-bye and went on her way, but the deep-voiced man shouted with a smile, "Think you could bring me my plank?"

Ida nodded. She pulled her bag out of the thick mud, hoping the contents were still dry and safe. Hitching it over her shoulder, she picked up the plank of wood. She put it under her armpit and climbed up the ladder.

She couldn't believe no one had seen her bizarre materialization out of nowhere, but she soon realized that the air was filled with the enormous racket of sawing and nailing, and that it would take something dramatically loud to break through the commotion.

When she reached the top of the ladder, the man took his plank and gave her a hand onto the walkway. "Ta," he said, studying her. "Are you Kunker's little girl?"

Ida had to think fast. "Yes, uh-huh."

"Tell your father I said hello and that I expect to see him at the feast tonight."

"Yes, sir," Ida answered, grateful for all the mud that covered her features. No need to alert the locals that a strange girl was in town, not yet anyway.

The man climbed another ladder that went up to yet another walkway. Ida scurried off before she could give herself away.

Everywhere she looked, men and women were constructing buildings, and they were all on stilts, just like the walkways. Most the structures appeared to be houses, but some seemed to be businesses or government buildings. The workmen had designed an elaborate pulley system that allowed them to lift and lower tools and wood to each other. The construction and the walkways continued as far as Ida could see. Perhaps this was a newly discovered land and the people had just settled here?

What was odd was that all the people looked so pleased with themselves. They were working as hard as ants building a new hill, but no one seemed tired, and smiles appeared on every face. Mixed in with the sawing and hammering, Ida could make out raucous laughter.

Where in the world had she landed?

She could smell salt in the air, so the sea couldn't be far. When she reached a spot on the walkway where no houses blocked the view, she saw that the town hugged a large bay. In back of her, a hill rose in front of mountains. The locals had snuggled their new town pretty tightly between the ocean and the mountains.

She continued walking for a good ten minutes on the walkway, weaving past people, never making eye contact, and eventually entering what looked like a marketplace. The shops, simple square structures with sawdust floors, looked as if they'd been built in a day. They were precariously balanced, with their fronts attached to the walkway and their backs held up by stilts. They looked like huge bugs that had alighted there for a rest.

Ida realized she hadn't eaten lunch or dinner and that she was starving. She passed a butcher's shop, a lovely flower stall, and a fruit and vegetable stand. The vegetables were robust and tantalizing, and the fruit was practically bursting at the seams with sweetness. Ida's mouth watered, but she had no idea what these people used for money. Gold coins? Silver? *For all I know, they use cashews.* She needed to watch a customer purchase something.

Entering a bakery, she felt dizzy from the scent of fresh bread. A jittery woman came inside who was in a hurry. Asking the brawny woman behind the counter for two loaves of bread, she pulled a coin purse out of her dress pocket. Just as she reached into it, Ida bumped into her, causing the change to spill into the sawdust.

"Oh my! Oh goodness! I'm *ever* so sorry," Ida mock-fretted. She was on her knees immediately, grabbing at the money.

The woman looked down at the cute, black-haired girl who seemed the picture of innocence. "Oh no. I'm sure it was my fault."

Ida managed to slip two coins into her bag while she gathered the spilled change. She handed the rest of the money to the woman. "I'm afraid two of the coins slipped through a crack and down into the mud." She forced a small crocodile tear.

The woman took the remaining coins, smiled, and patted Ida on the shoulder. "Don't you fret for one moment, dear. Two lost coins is one new acquaintance." Winking at Ida, she handed her money to the baker, got her loaves of bread, and was on her merry way.

Ida smiled wickedly but then noticed that from outside the bakery a man stood and stared at her. He was tall and blond, with blue eyes that sparkled with mischief—and he was smiling at her like he knew exactly what she'd done.

5

Ida scuttled out of the bakery, determined to hurry away from the strange man. She kept checking over her shoulder to see if he was following her, instinctively putting her hand inside the pocket of her bag where she always kept two sharp rocks.

What if he told the police on her? Did they have police here? It wouldn't be the first time Ida was snagged for picking pockets.

Once the man didn't appear to be following her, Ida slowed down, allowing her heartbeat to return to normal. She found herself standing in front of a shop that sold only sponges. *Only a pigsty of a town like this one would need a* sponge *store.*

Looking more closely, she had to confess the sponges were quite exotic. One near the bottom shone an emerald green and appeared solid, like a jewel. She reached out to touch it, and when she did the tower of sponges began to fall. She reached up to stop the avalanche, but it was too late. Dozens of sponges tumbled onto her head. The last one bounced off her nose. *At least they weren't teacups,* she thought.

The landslide of sponges revealed a very small, very angry

man standing inside the shop. He had luscious black hair, olive skin, a teal silk suit, and a perfectly groomed beard that only covered his chin. He had his hands on his hips and his face was glowing red; however, he had a hard time looking intimidating, as he was only four feet and eleven inches tall.

Ida smiled, batting her eyelashes and giving him her best "I'm as dumb and innocent as a baby seal" look. "I am *so* sorry, sir! I saw that pretty, pretty green sponge and it reminded me of the brooch my grandmother used to wear. She used to sit me on her knee and tell me stories about the old times when people were forced to eat dirt—"

"I do not give a soggy grain of rice what your grandmother used to say! It took me all day to arrange those sponges, and now I have to do it again! For the love of sweet wine, get out of my way." Stomping in front of the display shelf, he began collecting the sponges in his tiny arms. He had a strange accent, barely opening his mouth when he spoke, as if he had a sweet on his tongue he didn't want you to see.

"Let me help you." Ida began to gather sponges, wiping off any sawdust and placing them back on the shelves.

"No, no! You're doing it wrong!"

She stopped immediately.

"I did not say to stop picking them up!" the man admonished. "Pick them up, hand them to me, and I will place them correctly." Producing a little ladder from underneath his shelves, he started to place the sponges in a row, exactly as Ida had done.

"You must always put the cheap sponges on the bottom of the pile and the expensive ones on the top, because only an *imbecile*," he stressed the word, looking at Ida, "would take a sponge from the bottom!"

Ida sheepishly handed him another armful.

"So are you going to buy a sponge or not?" the man asked. With the entire display back in order, he hopped off the ladder.

She hesitantly told him that she had no money, which was almost true.

The man ran his hands through his thick locks. "You make my hair hurt!"

"Sorry." She truly was. "You should probably go yell off a mountain."

"What did you say?" he asked, assuming she'd insulted him.

"When my anger and frustration get to be too much, I find a high place, like a cliff or a mountain, and I just yell and yell, until I don't feel like yelling anymore. You should try it sometime."

The man was completely taken aback by this odd girl. "What brings you to the Unfinished City? Where are your parents?" He looked around the marketplace, assuming they were near.

The Unfinished City? So that's where I am. "How do you know I don't live here?" she asked.

The man pointed to her filthy clothes and face. "Because only tourists fall in the mud."

Ida wanted to laugh. There was something amusing about this angry little man, and for some reason she trusted him more than all the smiling, laughing people she'd seen. She decided to take a risk.

"I'm lost actually. I got separated from my father when we arrived here."

Eyes widening, the man's manner changed completely. "My name is Dunkin. My mother, delirious with the aftershocks of childbirth, named me Wee Dunkin, but if you please, I prefer just Dunkin."

"I'm Ida." She offered him her hand.

Dunkin shook it, inquiring, "All alone? At your age? Come inside, child."

Ida followed him inside his tiny shop, which was empty except for some crates and a chair in the corner.

"Have a seat. Would you like some milk?" He opened a crate, bringing out a bottle of milk. "I have no cups. I wasn't expecting guests." He offered her the bottle.

She chugged down the milk greedily.

Taking back the empty bottle, he said, "I'm sorry there is no food, but I eat lunch at my mamma's house. If you like, you could join us for dinner—"

Belching, she asked, "Dunkin, why is it called the Unfinished City?"

"I'm amazed you don't know. Tales of our miraculous town usually reach the furthest reaches of Venn."

Venn. Ida made note of the name.

"We are called the Unfinished City because every year the goddess Aquacious blesses us with a flood. And every year we rebuild our city."

Ida blinked at him. This was the most dimwitted thing she'd ever heard. "You rebuild your houses, and then the flood comes and knocks them down again?"

"That is right." Dunkin's face shone with pride.

"Why don't you just . . . move?"

Smile disappearing, he spoke to her as if she were three. "The flood is a *gift* bestowed upon us. We are the happiest people in Venn. To *question* the flood—well, it is like questioning why the sun rises and sets every day!"

Ida smiled and nodded, humoring him. "Your sponges must be very popular after the flood."

"Ah, yes!" His eyes shone. "My Motvian sponges are the most absorbent in town."

"When is the next flood?"

"In one month."

She hoped to be long gone by then.

She wanted to ask her big question. Should she push her

luck? "My father is . . . well, he's ill, and we've been traveling all over . . . Venn," she said, trying out the new name. "Are there any famous *cures* in the Unfinished City?"

She thought she saw a flash of panic in Dunkin's eyes.

Grabbing a broom, he began to frantically sweep the floor. "Time to go, dear. I must clean the shop." Putting a hand on her back, he scurried her out to the walkway.

She was desperate not to be ignored. "What did I say? Was it about the cure?"

Dunkin shook his head, keeping his eyes on the ground. "No, no, not at all. I just need to get back to work. Now run along. Go find your father."

"Okay, Dunkin. Thank you for the milk." She backed slowly away, convinced that he had information for her. Frustrated and annoyed, she was concocting a new strategy when she noticed that the strange blond man from before was standing not ten feet from the sponge shop. Once again, he was staring at her and smiling as if he had a secret. Ida scampered away in the opposite direction.

ONCE THE GIRL HAD GONE, Wee Dunkin stopped sweeping and leaned on his broom. His panic gradually subsided. He felt sorry for the girl's father who was ill, but Dunkin would let his feet be consumed by water bugs before he would be the one to tell the girl about *the Treatment.*

6

Ida wandered around the walkways for another hour. Unfortunately, the coins she had stolen were not worth very much, and she was only able to buy an apple. She chomped it down hungrily but it somehow just increased her appetite.

She'd studied the coins before she spent them. They looked as if they were made of gold, and they were embossed with the image of a strange creature—it had the body of a seahorse and the head and arms of a beautiful woman, as well as a coronet, back fins, and a long spiraled tail. In tiny letters around the edge of the coin, Ida could read "Aquacious Loves & Protects Us."

Dunkin had mentioned "Aquacious" a few times in their conversation. He'd even called her a "goddess." He seemed to think she was responsible for causing the yearly flood. Ida thought it was all a bunch of rubbish. Floods occurred because of weather patterns and wind, not a woman with gills.

The sun had just started to set when she smelled something delicious, like grilling meat. The scent pulled her forward like a hook. She became giddy with it. Looking down from the walkway, she saw what looked like the town square—and it was mud-free! People were milling about, chatting, and laughing, and they were all eating from huge tables full of food. There was a band on a small stage playing a jig for couples dancing in the twilight.

Ida studied the scene, wondering if she could blend in and grab a quick meal. Sure enough, she saw several children running around, zigzagging through the adults. She knew it was a risk, but the smell was too overwhelming to resist. She climbed down the nearest ladder, joining the crowd with the confidence of someone who'd lived in the Unfinished City her whole life.

She reached the first banquet table. She extended her hand to grab a leg of what looked like mutton when she felt a hand on her shoulder. "Just a minute, young lady."

Maggot dirt. Why couldn't I be caught after *I've eaten?*

Turning, she saw a jolly-looking man with sauce all over his shirt. "Better wash up first! Over there—use the fountain!"

Breathing a sigh of relief, she remembered the dried mud that was caked all over her skin and clothing. She followed the man's instructions, walking toward a fountain in the middle of the square. In the center of the fountain was a statue of the same creature who was on the coins: Aquacious. The statue was immense, as big as a packhorse, and the creature was more majestic in three dimensions. Her mysterious eyes gazed toward the ocean, her arms stretched out wide to the people in the square, while her regal tail spiraled around a crushed tree. She wore a coral crown on top of a coronet that became long flowing hair. She looked very much like royalty of the sea.

Approaching the pool of water at Aquacious' feet, Ida dunked her hands. She washed off the encrusted mud and rinsed her arms. She was about to lift a scoop of water to wash her face when she thought twice. Better to stay incognito. The good thing about being a kid was that people expected you to be dirty most of the time.

A red-haired woman with coral in her hair and a green tail sewn to her dress walked up to the fountain and threw in a coin. Looking up at the face of Aquacious, she said, “May the flood be bountiful this year.”

Ida felt sorry for the lady, who obviously thought that with the coral and the tail she looked as majestic as the statue. She looked less like a mystical sea horse and more like a festive tadpole. Noticing Ida, the red-haired woman said, "You are a darling girl. You'd be so much prettier if you smiled."

Ida scowled. She'd heard this same pointless remark from countless people, and its repetition was one of the worst torments of appearing to be a twelve-year-old girl. Ida told the woman, "You are a *darling* woman. You would be so much prettier if you *used your brain*."

The woman gasped in indignation, which *did* make Ida smile.

Ida returned to the banquet tables and greedily grabbed a leg of meat in each hand. She wasn’t sure what the meat was, but it tasted gamey, like rabbit. She walked away taking bites from each leg in turn, feeling she might moan from the deliciousness of the succulent meat.

She moved on to the next table, which held all sorts of legumes and gourds in shapes that Ida had never seen before. She grabbed a plate and dug in. These people might be bonkers, but they sure could cook.

She was drooling over a third table full of exotic pastries and cakes when she noticed the red-headed woman whispering to a spindly old woman wearing spectacles. They were watching her. *Uh-oh. Better scram.*

Grabbing a large piece of what looked like spice cake, Ida began casually walking away. But the spindly old woman was quicker than she looked and was suddenly blocking Ida’s way.

She had wiry gray hair pulled back into a severe bun and wore several layers of long clothes despite the mild weather. On her feet were clunky black loafers that looked like shoeboxes attached to her ankles. The woman grabbed Ida's wrist, pulling her in so that Ida was only an inch away from her face. Her breath smelled of coffee and sour pickles, and she had a mole above her lip that sprouted a thick black hair.

"And where do you think you're going, young lady?" she hissed.

"Let go of me!" Ida was ready to bite her but didn't want to cause a scene with so many people around.

The woman sprayed spittle as she squawked, "I've never seen you before. Where are your parents?"

Ida looked up through her eyelashes sweetly. "Golly, ma'am. I was just going to meet my father. We're just passing through town for a few days."

Frowning in suspicion, the woman opened up the left side of her long coat and showed Ida a badge. "My name is Wilemina Neely, and I'm the truancy officer for this sector." Ida watched the mole bob up and down. "I make sure that all children are enrolled in school." She sniffed disdainfully at Ida. "And I keep vagabonds off our streets."

Ida blurted, "I'm no vagabond, Mrs. Neely—"

"Did I say I was *married*?" she spat.

"Ms. Neely."

Picking bits of meat out of her teeth, Ms. Neely studied Ida. She still had her hand firmly around Ida's wrist. Ida didn't struggle; she stood there smiling insipidly, waiting for the old bat to let her go.

Ms. Neely's eyes narrowed. "You'd better come with me." She pulled Ida away from the square.

Ida started to panic. "No, really. I need to meet my father!"

"Tell it to the judge." Ms. Neely managed to yank Ida to a ladder. Before Ida knew what was happening, she'd grabbed

Ida's bag. "You're going to climb up that ladder, and when you get to the top you'll wait on the walkway, or I'll keep this bag, got it?"

Ida nodded, doing a quick assessment of how important the contents were. She climbed slowly up the ladder, thinking: *Clothes, rocks, a few gold coins from my world, and the two timepieces.* Fig. *I need those clocks to get back to Gulm.*

She reached the top of the ladder and, to her surprise, a teenage boy stood there grinning like the devil. He reached down and yanked her up, placing her on the walkway next to a small gang of kids. A girl of around eleven or twelve pulled Ida to her side. The first boy snapped his fingers, and ten-year-old twin boys with white-blond hair crawled on their stomachs toward the ladder.

As soon as Ms. Neely's pruney head popped up, one of the twins grabbed Ida's bag while the other one gave the ladder a shove backward. Ms. Neely shrieked in horror. "Don't you dare, you little—" but it was too late. The ladder was falling and so was Wilemina Neely. She screamed all the way down, and then there was a great crash.

Creeping to the edge of the walkway, Ida saw that Ms. Neely had landed right in the middle of the cake and pie table. She was covered in jam and icing, and she struggled like a flipped turtle. A large upside-down cake had broken her fall. *Lucky, that.*

The children surrounding Ida howled with laughter. Ms. Neely looked up at them, croaking, "You heathens! You heretics! I'll get you! I know where you live!"

The young girl grabbed Ida's hand. "Let's get out of here!"

Ida sprinted away with the strange gang, each child barely able to see, their eyes blurred with tears of glee.

7

Ida was breathless when they finally stopped running. They seemed to be on the outer edges of the city, and Ida had no idea where they were. She didn't really care. She was just so happy to have escaped Ms. Neely.

One of the twins was the first to speak. "Did you see her face, Punch? It was priceless."

The other twin said, "I bet she wet her old pants when we tipped that ladder!"

More laughter erupted. The twins had the whitest hair Ida had ever seen, and their eyebrows were so fair that you could hardly see them. When they laughed together, they were so identical, you felt like you were seeing double. Ida found them a bit disturbing.

The oldest boy, whom the twin had called Punch, said, "Give the girl her bag."

The second twin handed Ida her things. Grinning, she said to all of them, "Thank you for that."

"No problem." Punch was tall, with sandy brown hair, blue eyes, and freckles. He wore a pair of circular wire-framed glasses atop a sun-burned nose. He had a lopsided, mischievous grin and was probably around sixteen. "We've all had our run-ins with Ms. Neely."

Ida raised an eyebrow at him. "Because you're vagabonds?" Each member of the group wore patchwork pants made of random, clashing fabrics.

The twins snorted. One of them said, "No, dummy. Because we aren't enrolled in her backward school."

Ida didn't like being called dumb. She felt her fist ball up, but Punch intervened. "I'm Punch, and the twins are Dag and Trak. Good luck telling them apart. That's Hilda." He pointed to the girl who'd grabbed Ida's hand and was now sizing Ida up. She was a little taller than Ida, with long brown hair tied back in a ponytail. She had steely eyes and high cheekbones, and you could see she'd be very pretty one day.

"And that's Georgie." Georgie could only have been about seven. He waved shyly.

Ida relaxed into a stance that told the world she didn't care about anything. "I'm Ida."

"We should bring Ida home with us," Georgie squeaked.

"Why?" Dag asked, or maybe it was Trak.

"Where's your family?" Georgie asked.

"I'm meeting my father here . . . in a day or two," Ida said.

"We can't leave her here all alone. It'll be dark soon." This was Hilda.

Punch shook his head. "No strangers."

"Do you have somewhere to sleep tonight?" little Georgie asked her.

"Uh, no," Ida muttered. She wasn't sure how she felt about all this. She usually preferred to operate on her own. She didn't want to waste time concocting lies and stories for a pack of delinquents. Still, the idea of a bed was nice. Otherwise she might have to sleep down in the mud.

"It'll be fine," Hilda told Punch, who was definitely in charge.

Punch got a very serious expression—so serious that it made Ida want to roll her eyes. “I’m willing to take you back to our headquarters," he said, "but on one condition.”

Here we go. The condition.

“You can never talk to anyone about what you overhear there, okay?”

Ida was intrigued. “Okay. That sounds easy.”

“Spit and shake.” Spitting in his hand, he put it out for Ida to grasp. She was a little grossed out, but she wasn’t about to let him see her flinch. She looked him straight in the eye as she spat in her hand and reached for his. She shook it with force. Punch seemed alarmed at her strength.

“Right," he said. "Let’s get a move on, then.”

DARKNESS HAD FALLEN, and a crisp breeze wafted across the walkway. As Ida felt the night air grow cold, she reassured herself she'd made the right decision about accepting shelter. Twenty minutes later they approached a series of red cliffs at the base of a small mountain. The construction of the Unfinished City was far behind them and no houses or buildings could be seen. *I’m going to be very annoyed if their shelter is just some freezing cave at the bottom of a cliff.*

But as she got closer, she saw that these were no ordinary cliffs—a series of houses were carved into their sides. At least ten structures jutted out of the rock, sculpted into precise squares with windows and open doorways and even little flower boxes. Ida couldn’t believe real people lived in them. *They look more suitable for birds.*

The homes hung two stories above the ground. How would they would reach them? She must have been standing with her mouth agape, because Punch said, “Pretty impressive, huh? Wait ‘til you get inside.”

Standing underneath the houses, he put his hands on either side of his mouth. He produced a strange noise that was a mixture of a screaming cat and a teakettle. Suddenly, a rope ladder swung down from a window and landed at Punch's feet. Grabbing hold of it, he confidently began to climb. Halfway up, he turned back and yelped, "Hold the bottom and send Ida up!"

The twins grabbed the end of the rope ladder to keep it from swaying, and Ida shot them a look. "Don't bother," she said, determined to climb up without help, just as Punch had done. They let go, giving each other knowing smirks.

Throwing her bag over her shoulder, she grabbed the ladder. She took the first two steps and realized that it was going to be tougher than Punch made it look. Keeping your balance was hard when the wind was blowing the ladder to and fro. But Ida would eat worms before she'd let these kids see her struggle. She gritted her teeth and took two more steps up, then two more and then three, and she never looked down, only up at Punch, who had by now reached the top and was standing with his head dangling out a window, a smug smile on his face.

"Be careful!" he taunted. "It's a doozy of a fall!"

That arrogant lice-train. Finally, after what felt like forever, Ida swung her leg over the ledge of the balcony where Punch stood. Proud, Ida placed both her feet on the solid surface and tried to catch her breath. The other kids piled after her, evidently having no trouble with the ladder whatsoever. Ida's instinct was to climb back down immediately and do the ladder over and over again until she was just as fast as the others.

A plump woman with frizzy hair and a toothy smile walked onto the balcony. She wore a dress in the same patchwork pattern as the children's pants. "Welcome home, children. Dinner is waiting." She spotted Ida and asked with surprise, "Who's this?"

Punch answered. "That's Ida, Mrs. Brown. We just rescued her from Ms. Neely."

Mrs. Brown scowled. "That frightful woman. I can't believe she has nothing better to do than bully children." She gave Ida a look of concern. "Are you all right, dear?"

Ida nodded.

"We were just about to eat our dinner. Won't you join us?"

"Yes, Ma'am." Despite the banquet, Ida was still quite hungry.

Mrs. Brown led Ida through the house, where the floors, walls, and ceilings were all carved from rock. The house was chilly and filled with the smell of cut granite. A set of rock stairs led to the higher rooms. *A rabbit must feel this way in his warren.* You could see that an effort had been made to make the rooms more cozy. Handwoven rugs lay on the floors, topped with hand-carved furniture. Ida couldn't imagine how they'd lifted it all inside. All in all, Ida thought it was one of the most fantastic places she'd ever been.

Mrs. Brown led her to a dining room which held a huge table with place settings for ten. The plates and cutlery were mismatched but sparkling clean. Mrs. Brown hollered into the next room. "Mrs. Gauge, we have a guest. It will be eleven tonight!"

"Ah!" Ida heard from the next room. "Well . . . wonderful."

The other children washed their hands in a large basin of water near the door, so Ida washed hers, too. They took their seats while Mrs. Brown found an extra chair. She placed it next to Georgie, signaling for Ida to take a seat. A brown-haired petite woman emerged from the next room carrying a huge steaming pot. Mrs. Brown made an introduction. "Ida, this is Mrs. Gauge, and it's her turn to cook tonight. Mrs. Gauge, this is our new friend Ida."

"Hello, sweetie. Lovely to meet you. I do hope you like fish stew?"

"Yes, ma'am." She noticed that the children had become quiet and well-behaved, nothing like they'd been outside.

Mrs. Brown discreetly handed Ida a damp cloth. "Perhaps you'd like to wash up before you eat?"

Remembering her grubby face, Ida took the moist towel and wiped the grime away.

Two men entered the room, talking seriously. Mrs. Brown interrupted them. "Gentlemen, I'd like you to meet our dinner guest, Ida."

The men looked up from their conversation. The first one said, "Hello, Ida. I'm Mr. Brown." Bald with a potbelly, he held a tiny pipe in his hand.

"I'm Mr. Gauge," the second man offered. Ida nodded at him. He was taller than Mr. Brown, and he had curly brown hair and an optimistic smile.

Sitting down in a chair, he kissed Georgie on the head, who giggled and said, "Hello, Poppa."

"Sorry I'm late, lovelies!" A third man entered the dining room. "Something smells deeeelicious." He was tall and blonde and had unsettling blue eyes.

Ida froze. *Son of a beetle dung.* It was the same man who'd been staring at her this morning when she stole those coins! *Of all the rotten luck.* She tried not to blanch as she waited to see how he'd react to her.

"Mr. Loor," Mrs. Brown said. "This is our dinner guest, Ida."

Studying her, Mr. Loor circled the table. While Ida held her breath, he took her hand. Would he yank her up and shake her until the stolen coins tumbled out?

"Ida, what a lovely name." He shook her hand with enthusiasm. "Welcome to our dinner table!"

She breathed a sigh of relief.

As Mr. Loor returned to the head of the table, everyone stood up, so Ida did, too. They joined hands while Mr. Loor spoke. “Good evening, my dear family and our new friend Ida."

He gave Ida a quick wink.

"We eat tonight's meal in celebration of life, science, and progress. We dedicate tomorrow to aiding our fellow man and supporting him in the quest for higher knowledge. We reject superstition, divinity, and mumbo-jumbo. Long live the Anti-Delugists!”

“Hear, hear!” they all chanted and sat down.

Ida was a bit flummoxed. What was that all about?

Mrs. Gauge spooned a disappointingly small amount of fish stew into Ida's bowl. She smiled. “So, tell us all about yourself.”

Yeah. That's likely, Ida thought. This group had just renounced any belief in mumbo-jumbo, which Ida took to mean anything not easily rationalized. Science certainly could not explain her predicament, so she would be keeping her history to her darn self.

She was confident she could make up a captivating story of her life that would keep this crowd entertained. In fact, she was looking forward to it.

8

"... And then my father told the man, 'If I ever see you around these parts again, I'll hit you in the mouth *so hard,* you'll taste my armpit!'"

There was laughter around the table, especially from the twins. Ida had just finished a tall tale about her father being the sheriff of a small town in the east. She'd explained that he was chasing a criminal across Venn, which was what had brought her to the Unfinished City.

She decided to tug on her hosts' heartstrings a bit. "I sure hope that criminal didn't get hold of my daddy. I might never see him again." She wiped her eyes with her napkin.

The women at the table, Mrs. Brown and Mrs. Gauge, cooed their encouragement. "I'm sure he's fine, dear. You'll find him in no time."

Ida peeked under her wet eyelashes at Mr. Loor, hoping that he, too, had fallen for her lie, but to her dismay, he was smiling like he'd caught her dealing cards from the bottom.

Dessert was served, some sort of rose-flavored pie that Ida found disgusting. Luckily, the servings were small. The twins gobbled it down and licked their plates. “Is there any more, Mommy?” they whined.

“No, dears,” Mrs. Brown answered. She looked at Ida. “They have insatiable appetites.”

“They're growing boys!” added Mr. Brown. “Isn’t that right, Dag?” He leaned over and ruffled the hair of one of the twins, who still had bits of pie on his face. Ida wished he'd leave it there so she'd be able to tell the two boys apart.

"That was a wonderful dinner, Mrs. Gauge!" Mr. Loor said. "Your ability to stretch a day's catch into a week's worth of meals astounds me."

Mrs. Gauge shone with pride.

The men discussed their work at a mill while the children listened attentively, even the twins. Meanwhile, Punch gathered the dirty dishes from the table. These well-behaved children seemed a real contrast to the laughing guttersnipes who'd helped tip Ms. Neely into a cake. Ida preferred the pranksters to these obedient bores.

Mr. Loor stood. “I'll do the dishes, tonight, son."

"But it's my turn," Punch said.

"I'd like to do them, and I'd like Ida to help me," Loor said.

Uh oh. Here we go. Ida hated doing dishes, and she hated being confronted even more. She struggled to think of an excuse. “I'd love to, but I really should go look for my father—”

“Nonsense!" Loor said with a smile. "It's after dark—no time for a young girl to be wandering the city alone. You'll stay here tonight and we'll help you find your father tomorrow.”

“But—”

“But nothing. It's decided.” Picking up several dinner plates, he walked out of the room. Everyone stared at her, expecting her to follow. *Stinkin' ale.*

Smiling tightly, she walked into the kitchen, where she found Mr. Loor standing over a big bucket of soapy water.

She'd noticed that Mr. Loor was the only person here who didn't wear patchwork clothing.

"How about I wash and you dry?" he asked in a jolly voice.

She took the towel he offered.

"I like doing dishes," he said. "It gives me time to collect my thoughts after a big meal."

"Uh-huh." She dried the first two plates. She felt like a squirrel near a dog, not wanting to make any sudden moves that might shift Mr. Loor's focus from the dishes to her.

Alas, he was determined to have the conversation she dreaded. "I saw you in the market today, didn't I?"

"I don't think so. I was—"

"Don't bother lying to me, Ida. I know it was you. I also know you stole from Mrs. Fran."

Rotten cow patty.

"Don't stop drying."

She glanced down to see that her hands had frozen.

"I'm not going to turn you in."

"Why not?" she asked.

"Because I like you. I like your gumption, and I think you could be of great help to our little family."

"But my father—"

"We both know that you have no father."

She was dumbfounded. Had she lost her fine-tuned skills of fabrication?

"I think you're on your own and that you could use some friends. Am I right?"

She glared at him. "Why do you think that?"

He smiled. "I've had experience helping orphans who are living on the streets, and let's just say there is a certain . . . grace and skill involved with their scams, but if one pays close attention, there's also a desperation that hardens the eyes."

Ida felt like punching him in his Adam's apple. "You don't know anything about me."

"I know you're here for the Treatment."

She spoke softly. "What are you talking about?"

"I heard you talking to that sponge shop owner, and you asked about a cure found in the Unfinished City. He was too cowardly to tell you about it, but I'm not. It's called the Treatment, and it's been curing people for centuries."

Ida's heart became a frog about to leap out of her throat and dance on the kitchen floor. "What is it? How do I find it? How much does it cost?"

"Easy. There's no rush."

Is he kidding? Four years of searching and the man tries to tell me there's no rush!

Taking a dry glass out of Ida's hands, he placed it in a wooden cupboard. He then looked her straight in the eyes. "I have a proposition for you."

She told herself to remain calm. "I'm listening."

"If you work for me and the Anti-Delugists for three weeks, I'll tell you everything you need to know about the Treatment."

"Three weeks! I can't wait that long."

"The Treatment is a time-specific cure. I give you my word that I will not be delaying you by even a day."

"Time specific? What does that mean?"

"It means that it only works during a certain time of year."

"Then *when* is it?" she demanded, getting more and more annoyed with his cryptic answers.

"I'll tell you everything when you are ready to hear it."

"I'm ready now!"

"You're ready when I say you are. Believe me, at this moment you are far from ready. Working for me and the Anti-Delugists is the quickest way to prepare yourself."

She scoffed. "I'll go back to town and ask someone else. If you know about it, and that sponge man knew, then lots of people must know!"

"No citizen of this city will talk to you about it, I promise you that. You're free to try, but if you do, our deal is off. Once you've made a spectacle of yourself you'll be of no use to me."

Ida crossed her arms. "What are the Antee Delushists anyway?"

A dreamy smile came across his face. "We are simply a group of families that believe that the time of the flood has past. We want to modernize the Unfinished City and improve people's lives with an industrial society. I don't know how much of the world you've seen, Ida, but the Unfinished City is a hopelessly backwards town, which is why we live in the cliffs. The flood is unable to destroy our homes. Instead of constantly rebuilding our houses, we're able to pursue higher knowledge. We read literature, study science, engineering, and modern farming techniques. My son Punch is studying how to build a steam engine. Isn't that wonderful?"

Ida had to admit that it sounded reasonable. She'd seen a lot, maybe not of *this* world, but of her own, and the Unfinished City was by far the strangest way of living she'd come across.

His face grew sad. "Every year the flood causes incalculable damage. Sometimes people even get swept away, never to be seen again."

"Why do you think *I* can help you?' she asked.

"Because you're new here, and no one knows your face. We're a small community and we could really use an incognito member."

"What about Ms. Neely? She already knows me."

"That woman is small-minded and dim-witted. She has no interest in the big picture and presents no real threat to us. As long as you help us, we'll provide you with food, clothes, and shelter."

Ida didn't really care about any of that. "The Treatment. You will provide me with the Treatment."

"Of course. Should I bother asking why you need the Treatment or are you going to lie about that as well?"

"I'm going to lie," she responded, relieved at telling the truth for once.

"Then I will never ask. I promise."

Much to her surprise, Ida found herself liking this man. He was straightforward and didn't talk down to her. He was educated, and he seemed to genuinely believe Ida had something to offer their group, which was flattering. It was a rare person who saw potential in a thieving girl.

She crossed her arms. "You'll tell me about the Treatment in two weeks, not three, and I won't do the dishes ever again."

Smiling, Mr. Loor offered his hand in agreement. She wondered whether she should spit in her palm, but decided that was probably just a kid's thing. She shook Mr. Loor's hand, while a little voice in the back of her head wondered what she was getting herself into.

9

The next morning, Ida was sleeping soundly when the twins ran into her room laughing maniacally and jumped on her bed. Before she knew what was happening, they yanked her blankets off, leaving her exposed and cold. "You overslept!" they cried out in unison, and then they skipped out of the room.

Ida was about to scream at them when she saw Punch come through her doorway. She was suddenly self-conscious in the nightgown that Mrs. Brown had lent her. It was many sizes too big and had a big bow at the neck. Unless she was in disguise, Ida hated bows.

Punch didn't seem to notice. "Get dressed. It's a flyering day." And he was gone.

Ida had no idea what he was talking about, but she put her feet down on the cold stone floor. Her room was carved from rock like all the others, but it had a beautiful mahogany bed with the most delicious down mattress and pillows. You could fall asleep just looking at it.

Mrs. Brown and Mrs. Gauge had filled the wardrobe in the corner with clothes they thought would fit Ida, but they'd only chosen from Hilda's patchwork dresses and skirts. Ida would've much rather had a pair of the twins' coveralls. Frowning at the contents of the closet, she put on her own dirty clothes from the day before.

She glanced at the mirror on the wardrobe. Grabbing a comb from her bag, she ran it through her dark bob until she felt she was mildly presentable. She made her way to the kitchen where the other children were bathed and dressed, waiting at the breakfast table. The men were nowhere to be seen. Hilda gave Ida a small wave.

"Uh, you could've started without me," Ida offered.

Mrs. Brown smiled in condescension. "We never start until all children are present."

When Ida sat down everyone dove into the food. Still hungry after the meager dinner the night before, she devoured a sweet bun. She reached for a second one but saw Mrs. Brown raise an eyebrow. Smiling, she put her hand back in her lap. She shouldn't appear ungrateful.

"What does 'flyering' mean?" she asked Punch.

He reached into a bag hanging off the back of his chair. "Handing these out." He showed her a piece of paper covered in elegant handwriting.

Citizens of the Unfinished City,

We cordially invite you to a meeting at the town hall to discuss our proposed dam. Refreshments will be served and we look forward to a friendly discussion and lively debate. Saturday night. 8pm sharp.

Sincerely,

The Anti-Delugists

"Will anyone come?" she asked.

Punch smiled. "They'll all come. There's nothing they like better than yelling at Mr. Loor."

Trak stuck out his bottom lip while Dag frowned. Together they whined, "We hate flyering!"

Punch silenced them with a look.

“Where do we hand these out?” Ida asked.

“Everywhere," Punch said. "We need the whole city to know about the meeting."

"That sounds like a big job," she said.

Puffing up his chest, Punch said, "It is. It'll take all week." He pushed away from the table. "We should get started."

The twins protested. "We're still hungry!"

"Do what you're told," Mrs. Brown said. "And be back by sundown."

As Ida stood, Punch told her, "Mr. Loor says you need to dress like us when we go out. And put on the hat you had on before, the one that hides your hair."

Mr. Loor wanted to make sure that no one learned what Ida looked like. What in the world did he have in mind for her?

"Fine," she said. "But I want pants and they'd better have pockets."

Once she'd changed into a pair of Punch's old trousers and a blouse of Hilda's, Ida was ready to go. Punch insisted she didn't need her satchel, but she never went anywhere without it. Who knew when she might have to make a quick getaway?

"What's the deal with you all dressing alike?" Ida asked Punch, as he led her through the cavelike halls.

"We don't have a lot of money for clothes, and this way when we get new fabric everyone gets a few pieces instead of one person getting a new outfit. It was Mr. Loor's idea."

"Then why doesn't he dress like the rest of you?"

"He says it's an experiment, to see if his one new outfit will last as long as the ones that we patch up."

Looking down at her baggy quilted pants, Ida knew exactly which side of that experiment she would rather be on.

The rest of the children waited for them in the library, which was odd. She'd thought they'd be gathered by the rope ladder, ready to climb down.

"You're going to love this!" Hilda told her, approaching an opening under a bookshelf that looked like an enormous mouse-hole. Hilda sat down and slid herself into the hole. Then she was gone!

The twins were next. They sat one in back of the other, with legs pointed out front. Dag looked at Ida and cackled. "We go together because it makes you go faster!" Then they disappeared into the hole.

Georgie went next.

Ida looked at Punch in confusion. He grinned. "It's a slide we made to reach the ground as quickly as possible. We call it the 'quick exit,' and it's sure as heck a lot more fun than the rope ladder. Want to go next?"

Ida nodded, wondering how high up they were and how steep the slide would be. She sat as she'd seen the others do. Punch kneeled beside her. "Keep your arms tucked in." He gave her a shove.

She went flying down a stone chute made slick by years of use. Her stomach dropped as she headed straight down into the pitch black. She grew terrified as she realized she had no way to stop. Suddenly, the slide looped to the right and her body almost slammed into the hard walls. She adjusted her weight but she kept turning. The slide had become an enormous spiral! She felt ready to spew when she saw a light. It was the end of the tunnel. She flew out through the air, skidded into soft sand, flipped forward, and landed on her face.

The other children roared with laughter. "She ate it!" Trak guffawed.

Dag added, "A perfect nose-dive!"

Georgie was almost peeing himself, he was laughing so hard.

Ida turned red and scowled. "You could have warned me about the end!"

Dag cackled. "What fun would that have been?"

"Don't worry," Hilda said. "We all landed on our face the first time."

Ida couldn't imagine how it was possible to land any other way, until she saw Punch come gracefully gliding out. He landed on two feet and was standing a second later.

Show-off, Ida thought.

They had a long walk along the sand as they headed into town. Ida kept to herself, grouchy that the children had laughed at her again. She was older than all of them except Punch, yet they were treating her like some dumb younger sister. Under normal circumstances she would've told them all to suck snails. Since this wasn't an option, she told herself to smile and make nice, two things she'd never been good at.

10

They reached the edge of town where a wooden ladder led up to one of the walkways on stilts. They climbed up and the twins ran ahead on the path with Georgie. Hilda and Punch hung back with Ida.

As they walked, Hilda stepped in close and said, "It's so dull around here since we can't go to school and we never meet anybody new. It's always just us and I'm so bored I could wilt, you know?" As she lowered her voice she slowed her walk to allow Punch to pass them. "I'm so jealous you've actually been places and seen things. I would love to go places and see stuff." She chewed her nail. "So sometimes when we go to the city we go by the bakery and there's this boy with dark hair and he always looks at me when I walk by but maybe he's just staring because I'm an Anti-Delugist and he thinks I'm some sort of weirdo, you know? Or maybe he likes me but how can I find out if I can't even talk to him or anything? I'm never allowed out on my own and the twins are tattle-tales and Punch is so, all into rules and everything. I'm not allowed to talk to strange boys but maybe I should just try this once. Do you think?"

Ida wrinkled her nose. She knew she was supposed to say

something, but she wasn't sure what. She'd always been focused on her cure, so she'd never had time to think about boys, girls, or anything else. "Ummm. I think you should, uh, talk to him?" This seemed to be the answer Hilda wanted to hear.

Hilda smiled. "You really think so?"

Ida nodded with conviction.

Hilda pressed on. "Maybe when we're close to the bakery today, you could maybe distract the twins and Punch and pretend you hurt your elbow or something, and I could go in and maybe check out the baguettes, and see if he talks to me. Do you think?"

Hilda had obviously put a lot of thought into this. *Act nice, normal, and twelve,* Ida reminded herself. "Okay. Sure."

Grinning happily, Hilda stopped whispering. "Does it flood where you come from?"

Ida shook her head. "Sometimes in some places near the sea, but people try to prevent it from happening if they can."

Hilda was excited. "Just like we're trying to do here!"

"What exactly is it that the Anti-Delugists want to do?"

"We want to build a dam that will keep the floodwaters from reaching the city, so we can modernize and indust . . . *industrialize*." She said the last part with difficulty, but it was obviously a sentence that had been repeated over and over again in her presence.

"Why don't you and your family just move to a city that doesn't flood?"

Hilda frowned at this strange idea. "Because it's our *duty* to help the people of the Unfinished City, not to run *away*."

Ida knew Dunkin the sponge-seller really liked the flood. "What if they don't want your help?"

"They're ignorant and don't know what's best for them."

Hilda likes to sound older than she is. "It's not like we can force them to build a dam—"

"That's not what Punch says." Hilda produced an enigmatic smile.

"What do you mean?" Ida couldn't imagine anything short of an army forcing a city to build a dam it didn't want.

Hilda made sure Punch wasn't listening. "Every two weeks, Punch goes on a boat trip to Reek, and he comes back with these big packages. He won't tell us what's in them, but I'm pretty sure it has to do with the dam."

"Huh. And you've never tried to sneak a peek?" Ida asked, knowing that she would have stolen a glance.

Hilda looked at her funny. "That would be like *lying*."

"You're going to talk to a boy you're not allowed to talk to. That isn't lying?"

"That's different. And I thought you were on my side." She stomped ahead.

Ida frowned. That hadn't ended the way she wanted. What did she care what was in the packages? The dam had nothing to do with her Treatment, so she'd keep her nose out of it.

Deciding that walking on her own was best, she kept ahead of Punch and behind Hilda for the next ten minutes. Just when she'd relaxed she heard Punch say, "How was your meeting with Mr. Loor last night?"

Fig. Punch now walked beside her.

"It was, uh, good. What did he say about it?" How much did Punch know?

His face betrayed nothing. "He said that you came clean about not traveling with your father and that you were going to stay with us for a couple of weeks."

She said nothing, waiting to hear if Loor had told him more. When Punch didn't continue, she said, "It's nice of your family to let me stay."

"I was surprised. Mr. Loor is pretty wary of strangers."

He's probably not fond of strangers he can't negotiate with, she thought. "That makes sense. You're doing important work."

"We are." Punch looked impressed that Ida understood the gravity of their mission. "We're saving lives."

His serious tone made Ida think for a moment that maybe he would be sympathetic to her plight, but she was not about to risk Punch announcing to the group that she was loony. Deciding it was best to change the subject, she asked, "Is Punch your real name?"

He scowled. "It's a nickname Mr. Loor gave me."

"Why?"

He sighed. "When I was little I used to hit people a lot."

Ida was surprised. He seemed like someone who liked to please adults, not break rules. "Why do you call him Mr. Loor? Isn't he your father?"

"Sort of. He found me when I was little, living on the streets. He's as much of a father as I've ever known."

Mr. Loor said he had a lot of experience with orphans. He must have meant with Punch. She kind of liked that they had something in common.

"He calls you his son, so why not call him 'father?'" she asked, feeling like Punch had avoided the question.

"I had a real mom and dad once, and it doesn't seem right to pretend I didn't," he said matter-of-factly.

"So you knew your parents?"

He adjusted his glasses. "No. I was too young. They drowned in the flood."

Ida now understood why Punch was so passionate about being an Anti-Delugist. She could also appreciate why he was so serious for someone his age—she'd felt much older than her years even before her time with the Brothers.

"Listen, I know you're an orphan, too," he said. "Mr. Loor told me before breakfast. You don't have to lie about it anymore." He put a hand on Ida's shoulder. "I used to be angry about being an orphan when I was a kid, but at some point, you just have to let it go."

Hot steam brewed in Ida's gut. Now Punch was going to tell her how to be an orphan? All empathy for him melted away as she considered shoving him off the walkway. “I’m lucky I have an adult around to explain the world to me.”

Ignoring the sarcasm in her voice, Punch said, "Yeah, you are."

What a squid nibbler, she thought.

She didn't say another word until they arrived at the market, where Hilda and the boys were waiting. Punch handed them flyers. When Ida had her stack, she asked, "Where do I start?"

"Anywhere you want," he said, "but I should warn you, people won’t be happy to see us.”

“Why not?”

He raised an eyebrow. “I’ll let you find out for yourself.”

11

"You unholy, sacrilegious, backward little twit! I wouldn't use this flyer to line a monkey's cage! Leave my shop or I'll call the police!"

Ida stared at the shop owner, unsure whether to laugh or flee. So this is what Punch had meant. The other kids stood across the walkway, watching her first attempt at flyering. They were busting a gut. She glared at them. Once again they were having a laugh at her expense, and she was sick of it.

She turned back to the rude man. "Maybe you should keep the flyer and make a paper hat to cover that nasty bald spot you have." She walked out of the shop.

"Thanks a lot," she said to Punch, handing him back a pile of flyers.

He quit laughing and signaled for the others to stop as well. "Sorry, but you needed to know what you're up against. Delugists feel very passionately about their flood, and they don't like the fact that we even exist. Talking directly to them is a waste of time."

Taking a single flyer, he wadded it into a ball and walked to the shop Ida had just left. He waited, and when the shopkeeper's back was turned, he launched the paper ball inside. It flew above the man's head, landing on a counter near the back.

Returning to the group, Punch said, "He'll read it when we're out of sight. They all do. They pretend to ignore us, but they hate the idea of missing out on anything."

He handed small stacks to everyone. "Let's split up and get the north side done fast, ok?" He looked at Ida. "You're new, so you go with Hilda."

Ida didn't want help, but she tried not to show her irritation.

"Dag and Trak, take Georgie with you and take the outer walkways. Ida and Hilda will take the bayside, and I'll take the market. Meet back here in two hours."

"Ok," the twins said.

"You just want the market so you can see Preanne!" Hilda accused Punch.

Who's Preanne? Ida wondered.

"Hilda, give it a rest—"

"Ida and I want the market!" Hilda insisted.

"Do as you're told," Punch answered sharply, telling Hilda the conversation was over.

Hilda and Ida walked eastward for a while until Hilda turned, tears in her eyes, "Today was the day, the one chance I had . . ."

"For what?"

Hilda looked at her wide-eyed, shocked that Ida didn't remember. "The boy in the bakery? I was going to talk to him today?"

Ida nodded vigorously. "Oh, yes. Of course." As an afterthought, she put a hand on Hilda's shoulder, because it seemed the thing to do. After a while of patting Hilda awkwardly, Ida asked, "Who's Preanne?"

Hilda rolled her eyes. "Some girl who works at the lumberyard. She has a thing for Punch."

"Your plan isn't completely spoiled," Ida said. "We could run to the market for a couple of minutes, go by your bakery, and hotfoot it back to the bay. We'll get our flyering done in plenty of time."

Hilda's face brightened. "Really? But what if Punch sees us?"

"Don't worry. I'm an expert in not being seen."

Ida turned them around and they headed up a walkway that ran parallel to the one Punch had used. "The secret," she told Hilda, "is to move at the same pace as everyone else. Never hurry or walk too slowly. Blend in with the crowd."

They caught up to a group of ladies walking home with their daily supply of nails and screws. They kept pace with them, blending in easily.

After a few minutes, Hilda whispered, "I knew it! There's Punch talking to Preanne! The bakery is ahead on the right."

Ida took a sidelong glance at Preanne. Almost as tall as Punch, she had a mane of golden locks that shone in the morning sun. Her face was tanned, and she had one of those tiny noses that made Ida think of a button snapped in half. She wore a pair of work overalls cinched tightly with a tool belt, and somehow the boyish clothes only seemed to emphasize her curvaceous non-boyish figure. She was giggling wildly at something Punch had said while she twirled a piece of hair around her index finger. Ida was disgusted. *He's not that funny, dope.*

"Isn't he sophisticated?" Hilda said.

Hardly. Ida then realized Hilda was not talking about Punch. Following Hilda's sight line, she saw a small bakery not far from where Punch and Preanne were chatting. Inside was a middle-aged woman who was large, as bakers tended to be, with forearms like two loaves of sourdough. She took cash from a customer, while on her left, kneading dough, was a boy around thirteen, so skinny that the strings of his apron had to be wrapped around his waist about ten times before they could finally be tied. He wore a little white paper cap, and Ida couldn't say much about his face, since it was covered in flour.

"Him?" she asked, trying to keep the judgment out of her voice.

"Yes, and remember, I saw him first."

"Uh, yeah, you did. That's just my bad luck I guess."

"What now?"

"Well, Punch's back is turned, so I think you're clear to go inside."

Hilda's voice squeaked. "What do I say? Or do?"

"Just buy something," Ida suggested.

"Some bread, do you think? Or is a muffin better?"

"Just be quick."

Hilda ran up the walkway. Approaching the entrance, she smoothed her ponytail and put an aloof look on her face. Once inside, she avoided the help of the owner, waiting for the boy to notice her.

Turning to hand his mother a tray of fresh rolls, the boy spotted Hilda. From the other side of the walkway, Ida could spot his blushing cheeks under the flour. Hilda said something, and he smiled and said something in return. Things seemed to be going smoothly.

Ida turned her attention back to Punch and Preanne, who were still captivated by one another. *Doesn't she have a job to get back to?* Ida decided to get closer so she'd be ready if Hilda needed her to intercept Punch. Approaching them easily, she hid behind a stack of plywood.

"That framing hammer seems a bit heavy for you. I suggest you use a regular claw hammer." Punch's voice sounded deeper than usual, and he spoke with authority.

Preanne giggled and nodded.

Ida rolled her eyes. *Was he kidding?*

"They mostly just ask me to sand the wood, and it's *exhausting*. My hands are a mess," Preanne said, pouting.

"Those heartless beasts," Punch said, taking her hands into his own.

Punch had become a whole new person for this girl. What must it be like to be Preanne—to be someone who derives such admiration that boys would change their whole demeanor in your presence? Ida couldn't imagine. Was it fun or was it annoying? Ida reasoned it would be good for cons, but did everyone always act fake around you? She wouldn't like that.

She heard yelling coming from the bakery. "Your money's no good here, ya little kook!"

"Mom! Leave her alone!"

"My money is as good as anyone else's!" Hilda said, her voice cracking.

Hearing the ruckus, Punch turned and saw Ida trying to conceal herself a few feet away. "What the—?"

Ida jumped out. "C'mon. It's Hilda!"

Confused, Punch quickly joined Ida and ran toward the bakery, leaving behind an annoyed Preanne.

A small crowd had gathered outside the bakery. Punch and Ida shoved their way through. Punch put a protective hand on Hilda's shoulder. "What's happening here? You okay, Hilly?"

"Uh . . . yeah . . . let's go," she muttered, tugging on his sleeve.

But the owner of the bakery wasn't about to be quiet now that she had an audience. "That little girl there is an Anti-Delugist! I've seen her at the meetings, up there by the podium, along with those other fruitcakes!"

The crowd turned to stare at Hilda, but she kept her eyes on the baker's son, whose mouth was agape. He gawked at her as if she were a snake who'd slithered out of the mud. Tears ran down Hilda's face as Punch dragged her out of the crowd and away from the bakery.

When they were a safe distance away, Punch said, "What were you thinking, Hilly? I told you to go to the harbor! What were you doing up here?"

Hilda said nothing, allowing herself to be dragged like a rag-doll between Punch and Ida.

Ida answered, "It's my fault." Her wheels spun. "I, uh, had this craving for a pistachio cherry chocolate flan surprise and—"

"A what?" Punch asked.

"That's exactly what Hilda asked! When I described it she said the only place in town that might have it would be that bakery. We thought it would only take a minute—"

"We don't fraternize with Delugists, and you just found out why."

"What about *Preanne*?" Ida said sharply. "Isn't she a Delugist?"

Punch glared at her.

"Are you going to tell on me, Punch?" Hilda asked, her eyes red from crying.

Punch opened his mouth to answer, but Ida cut him off. "Of course not, Hilda. He's not going to mention the baker and we're not going to mention Preanne. Right, Punch?"

Punch pinched his lips tightly together. "It's my duty to look out for Hilly's well being. If I turn her in, it'll be for her own good." He took a step closer to Ida. "It's also my responsibility to report back to Mr. Loor about your trustworthiness and reliability. So far you've proven that you're incapable of following directions and that you're not above blackmail. Not a good first day, I'd say."

"Wait. I didn't mean—"

"I know exactly what you meant," Punch said.

What a stuck-up bootlicker.

"We'll be doing the rest of the flyering together today," he said, walking toward the bay.

Ida was at a loss for words, which was rare. Would Punch really tell Mr. Loor that she was deceitful? And would Mr. Loor kick her out before he explained the Treatment?

12

Hilda eventually pulled herself together and gave Ida a secret hand-squeeze of thanks. Ida wasn't sure if Hilda would get in trouble, but it felt good to be a decent friend to someone for a change.

The flyering work continued in near silence.

Ida walked onto work sites, leaving flyers under planks of wood. Hilda went into a cheese shop and left some under wedges of brie. In any other city, they might have shoved the flyers under people's doors, but the Unfinished City didn't have many doors. For that matter it didn't even have that many walls. There were enclosed structures for sleeping, but for the most part, the people lived in public, their living rooms open for their neighbors to see. She saw one whole family lounging in their sitting room in their pajamas. They smiled and waved as the neighbors passed their house, as if it were the most natural thing in the world.

Next, the three of them headed to the water. The bay was large with a narrow inlet—a large circle with a small break at the top—which made Ida think of trying to reach her arms all the way around a beach ball but not quite succeeding. The harbor's skinny channel allowed boats to pass through and reach the dock.

Here, Ida saw the most completed buildings she'd seen all day. A lighthouse stood on the end of the cape called Skimmer's Point, while a mill had been constructed on the opposite point called the Greenhorn Peninsula. With pride, Punch explained that the Anti-Delugists had donated the buildings to the city, in the name of progress and business. He sighed, "These people don't appreciate what we do for them."

At the dock, Ida handed flyers to fishermen. They'd grumble or curse, but they'd read them. She was excited to attend Saturday's meeting. Would there be a big confrontation?

Finally, after three brutal hours, all the flyers were gone. By the time they got back to the cliffs, the twins and Georgie were already back. They were happy to rub it in. “We finished over an hour ago! Where have you slowpokes been?” Dag said.

Punch gave him a look that would silence a woodpecker. Dag instantly stopped talking and ran into the other room. “Mom, they’re back!” he yelled.

Punch went to his room without a word. Ida announced she needed to wash up for supper and escaped to her own room. She flopped onto the bed, grateful to be alone with her thoughts. She was happy to have food and shelter and everything, but these people were making her crazy.

Ida was used to being a lone horse, and that’s the way she liked it. When she'd been a child and had looked her real age, she hadn’t minded being around other children. Now, it was exhausting. Hilda was four years younger than her but didn’t know it. How would Hilda behave if she knew the truth? Well, first she would freak out, because she would think Ida was some sort of witch or monster, but if she managed to get past that part, would she still want to be friends? Of course not.

Ida rolled off the bed and went to stand in front of the full-length mirror on the wardrobe. She examined herself from the front and the side. She was still wearing the ridiculous patchwork pants, which made her look like a court jester, and her hair needed a wash, but for the most part, she looked exactly the same as she always did—as she had for four years. Her legs were short, her chest was flat, and her stomach was a little poochy. She was too short to reach the highest shelf of the wardrobe.

When she got the Treatment, would her body grow instantly? Or would a new body emerge from her current one, like an insect out of a cocoon? Or maybe she would shed her current skin like a lizard! Whatever happened, she wondered if it would hurt.

She was curious if she would be able to return to Gulm with the Treatment to give to the children there—or would she have to bring them here? That would be very inconvenient. When she tried to remember how many children had lived with the Master, she could picture at least thirty. They must be as unhappy as she to be stuck as children—yet she'd never run into any of them in her years of searching for a cure.

What would the Anti-Delugists think of her marching into town with a procession of children and then marching out with a procession of adults? They'd have to start believing in mumbo-jumbo, wouldn't they? She giggled at the thought.

This reminded her of Preanne giggling, while all her parts jiggled along with her.

Ida batted her eyes at the mirror. "Oh, Punch, can you show me which end of the hammer I'm supposed to use?" She swayed her non-existent hips back and forth. She took a towel out of the wardrobe, placed it over her head like long hair, and then grabbed two balled up socks and held them to her chest. She giggled in a high, airy voice. "My foot is so rotten and smelly from this old boot. Maybe you'd like to give it a smell, Punch?" She held up a foot in front of her.

Suddenly she caught a reflection in the mirror.

It was Punch.

Ida spun around, ready to spit out an explanation.

"Dinner's ready," he said and then walked away.

Ida sat down on the bed, humiliated beyond words.

That night at dinner the adults chatted normally, completely unaware of the triangle of tension present at their table. Hilda watched Punch like a hawk, wondering if he were going to rat her out. Ida practically bore a hole through her dinner plate avoiding eye contact with Punch, while Punch scrutinized Ida, seemingly trying to figure out if she were a sane person.

After what seemed like an eternity they were finally excused, and Ida was able to retreat to her room. She got in bed and buried her head under a pillow. She needed to last two weeks here and she'd already angered Punch and then mortified herself in front of him. How much would he tell Loor?

If she weren't kicked out tomorrow, she swore there would be no more breaking of rules. Even if someone in the house asked her to.

She needed to become what she despised most: a bum-kissing goody two shoes. She felt ill. *It's just another con. You can do it.*

Thinking of her time there as a two-week hustle allowed her to nod off. However, had she known then what Mr. Loor had in store for her, she wouldn't have been able to fall asleep that night or any other.

13

The next morning, Ida was summoned to Mr. Loor's office. Her entire body was taut with anxiety. She grabbed her satchel, in case he asked her to vacate the premises immediately.

She went up a spiral staircase that led to an open door. Mr. Loor sat at a hand-carved desk with his back to her. She knocked on the wall, but her hand made little sound on the stone, so she cleared her throat loudly. Mr. Loor swung around. She was relieved to see he was grinning.

"I hear yesterday was quite the introduction to our city," he said, not unkindly.

When she said nothing, he gestured for her to take a seat in one of two chairs. Sitting, she examined the room. The walls were covered in blueprints and math equations. A topographical map of the city was framed behind the desk, and a large brown globe rested on a pedestal. Glass jars of what appeared to be dirt lined a cabinet in the corner.

"I see you are interested in my soil collection?" Mr. Loor said, standing and walking to the cabinet.

"Soil?"

Picking a jar, he unscrewed it and inhaled deeply. He sighed with delight. "Perfection." He brought it over to Ida. "Take a whiff."

She held her nose over the jar. "Smells like, uh, dirt."

"No," he said sternly. "It smells like wheat. And corn. And beans. It smells like progress." He took another whiff and placed the jar back on the shelf. "This city has the finest soil I've ever seen, but no one cultivates it because of the flood. They have to import everything. We will change that, among other things."

She smiled, nodding, hoping to please him. "That makes sense."

"Of course it does." He sat back down. "Obtaining radical change takes planning, and it takes discipline. Punch tells me that you have some difficulty in the discipline arena."

"No, sir. I was only trying to help—"

He waved a hand at her. "I hate excuses and I hate disobedience. Luckily for you, I do believe in second chances."

Her shoulders relaxed.

"You'll be allowed to stay, but you'll be under strict supervision. Hilda is no longer allowed to visit the market."

"And Punch?"

"Punch is in charge of the children and you will listen to him."

Did Punch confess to his interaction with Preanne? Ida doubted it, but she was not going to make trouble by bringing it up.

"You may go." Loor spun around in his chair to examine the map on the wall.

She hurried down the stairs before he could change his mind.

❦

THANKS TO THE DAILY FLYERING, Ida gradually learned her way around the city. The market was central, just off the town square which held the Aquacious statue. To the west was the wealthier part of town where people had brick homes, and to the south was a shantytown where the "Non-Constructionists" lived. Hilda explained that these were people who lived in extremely basic structures, happy to spend the majority of their time socializing, lying in the sun, and swimming in the sea. Punch took care of the flyering in the shantytown, but Ida hoped to see it soon.

Her relationship with Punch improved somewhat. They were cordial to one another, but ever since the bakery incident he never smiled at her or joked around with her, like he did with the others. What did she care? She was leaving soon anyway.

Hilda, on the other hand, adored Ida—she obviously loved having another girl around. She would follow Ida into her room, lie on her bed, and talk about the forbidden love between her and the baker boy. Ida would yawn over and over, but Hilda wouldn't take the hint. Ida would finally have to tell her to leave.

The day of the big town meeting finally arrived. The children and the adults were abuzz with energy.

Ida was sitting at the breakfast table, trying to make her porridge last a bit longer, when Punch came down the stairs from Mr. Loor's office looking furious. Mr. Loor was right behind him saying, "You will not cross me on this, Punch. I've made up my mind."

Punch stormed by Ida. Mr. Loor assumed a big smile. "May I speak to you in my office, please?"

She followed him, hoping she hadn't messed up again.

"Ida, I have a special job for you tonight," he told her. "But it's a secret between you and me."

"Why was Punch so—"

"He's angry because I am entrusting this job to you and not him."

Ida was intrigued.

"As I mentioned before, people in the city don't know you. Punch is a recognizable face and this job requires, how shall I put it, a certain delicacy."

She hated it when people refused to get to the point. "Spit it out. What do you need me to do?"

"*Manners*, Ida. Please."

She rolled her eyes. "What can I do for you, Mr. Loor, sir?"

"I want you to bring me the head of Aquacious."

She sat down. "Uh, you mean the goddess on all your money?"

"Yes, the very one."

"I didn't realize she was a real . . . uh . . . person . . . or whatever."

"Don't be a ninny. She's a bit of superstitious nonsense made up by an ignorant people to help explain a force of nature. While the citizens of the Unfinished City are busy screaming at me during the meeting tonight, you will be in the town square quietly climbing to the top of the Aquacious statue, where you will proceed to cut off its head."

Has this man not noticed my size? "With what?" she asked skeptically.

He handed her a heavy burlap bag. "All the tools you require are inside."

Peeking inside, she saw a chisel and hammer. "That's it?"

"Last week, I took the liberty of finding a weak point and starting a crack. You will insert the wedge into the crack and hammer at it until the whole thing gives way, understand?"

Ida nodded, however she didn't really understand at all. Was Mr. Loor a bit deranged, after all? Why in the world would he want to do this? "But Mr. Loor—"

"Ch-ch-ch," he interrupted. "If you want your cure, this is

what you must do for me—but it is absolutely vital that no one sees you nor catches you. No one can associate you with us. "

Sensing this task was very important to Loor, she crossed her arms in front of her. "I want to know about the Treatment *now*, before I remove the head."

He snickered. "Why do you think you are in a position to negotiate? We have a deal."

She leaned forward. "This is important to you, I can tell, and if you or Punch could do it, you never would've let me into your home."

Smiling, he tapped his fingers on his desk. "You're a clever child. It'll get you into trouble one day."

"Definitely."

They stared at each other, each waiting for the other to give in. Finally, Loor said, "You're right. No need to drag out our relationship. If you take care of the head tonight, I'll tell you about the Treatment in the morning."

She couldn't believe it. *Tomorrow?* That was a week early. "I'll do it."

He stood and patted her on the shoulder. "I thought you'd see it my way."

Ida gritted her teeth and smiled, liking this man less and less, but knowing she'd only have to put up with him for one more day.

14

The whole of the Unfinished City must have been at the meeting, because the walkways were empty. The town was quiet and, just as Ida and Loor had planned, growing dark. By the time Ida reached the main square, she had only moonlight to guide her. Narrowing her eyes, she was able to make out the ladder that would lead her down to the statue—the same ladder that had carried a screeching Ms. Neely careening down into a cake. The memory made Ida smile. Strange to think how much had happened since that day.

She climbed carefully down the ladder. She'd worn dark clothes to blend into the night—*no* patchwork.

Punch had told her that the town meeting would last several hours. Mr. Loor would remind the people of the lighthouse and the mill that the Anti-Delugists had donated last year. This reminder was to soften the Delugists up for the next part, when Mr. Loor would propose the building of a dam that would prevent future floods from entering the city. This, according to Punch, was when the mayhem would begin. Many Delugists felt that their lives were prolonged by a yearly flood. Ida was a bit sad to miss the meeting. She was curious to hear what kind of nut-brained argument could be made for wanting a flood, but she'd been given a job to do.

Arriving at the Aquacious statue, she looked up at the goddess' face, whose eyes overlooked the ocean with pride. Backlit by the moon, she seemed much bigger than Ida remembered. *This is ridiculous*, she thought for the twentieth time. *Why the heck does Mr. Loor want this to happen?* But she positioned her bag of tools on her back and began to climb up anyway.

Using the tail as her first foothold, she hoisted herself up so that she could touch the waist. Finding a spot within the chiseled scales to place her foot, she was able to grab an arm. She grunted as she pulled herself up and swung her legs around the neck. For a moment she feared she could go no higher, but she discovered she could hold onto the back fin and shimmy her torso toward her legs. Soon she sat on top of the shoulders with her feet dangling down, so that from a distance one might think that Aquacious now carried a babe on her back.

Her forehead was covered in sweat. She searched for the crack that Mr. Loor had made—he said it would be on the neck. She saw only carved hair that seemed thick and impenetrable. She stretched forward to see around the front of the neck, which seemed to be the thinnest part of the sculpture. Peering closely, she saw that there was indeed a thin crack running across it. She looked around the square once more, checking to see that no one was watching.

Removing the tools from her bag, she placed the chisel into the crack and swung at it with the hammer. A loud *clang* cut through the silent night. She stopped, sure someone would emerge, but there was no one.

Examining the marble, she saw that she hadn't even made a mark. She tried again, but this time she swung harder. There was another loud *clang*, and then another and another as she beat down on the chisel. Finally, after ten minutes, she had made the crack slightly bigger. She wedged the chisel inside deeper and began hammering again. Her arms grew tired and her teeth vibrated along with the rhythm of the hammer.

It took nearly two hours, but suddenly the weight of the head became too much for the remaining connection, and it teetered forward and fell to the ground. Although she'd been anticipating it for hours, Ida was shocked. The sound was like a roof caving in.

She climbed down nimbly and looked at the fallen head. The front of the face had caved in, and bits of marble lay all around. Ida herself was covered in white dust. Looking at the decapitated goddess, Ida couldn't help but feel she'd done something she shouldn't be proud of. Nonetheless, she knew she must finish what she'd started.

She slowly rolled the head across the square and under the walkways. Mr. Loor wanted her to dispose of the head so that the statue couldn't be repaired easily. He'd suggested using a particularly deep mud pit not too far away. Ida searched for it, exhausted with the exertion of the evening.

She heard voices and froze. Someone was walking above her on the walkway.

"I tell you, Mr. Hew, I'm not a violent man, but if I were, I might have struck that Mr. Loor."

"I'm with you one hundred percent," the other voice answered.

Hot rat mold. The meeting must have ended.

She had to hurry. She spotted some mud not far away on her left. She waited for the men to be out of earshot and then rolled the head into the sludge. She stood back, took a deep breath and then . . .

Nothing.

The head sat still in a few inches of mud.

Ida sighed in exasperation. *Mr. Loor is a jack-eyed fool.*

Walking up to the head, she rolled it forward until she could sense the mud was getting deeper. With her remaining strength, she shoved it as far forward as she was able. Once again, the head threatened to not move.

Ida could hear more voices above, but this time it was a whole crowd of people. At any moment one of them might look down and see her and this *infernal head.*

Holding her breath, she saw that the head was slowly but surely sinking. It made a horrible squidgy sound as it descended, and Ida was afraid the sound might draw attention. She didn't dare move until it was completely under.

She heard more conversation above. "That man is a moron! How could anyone not respect the divine intentions of our beloved Aquacious?"

She glanced at the head. *Sink already!* It was like waiting for an icicle to melt. Dozens of people were now milling about. She was about to get caught. She could *feel* it.

The head had almost completely descended. The last thing Ida saw was an eye staring up at her as if in judgment, and then the head slowly sank into oblivion.

Turning to leave, she found herself stuck in mud up to her knees. *Are you stinkin' kidding me?* With all her might, she pulled up her right leg and felt her foot escape her shoe. *So be it*, she thought. She took an enormous step forward with the free foot, almost falling face first into the mud. Once she had her balance, she pulled her left leg free, once again sacrificing her shoe. She was now in the shallower end of the pit and was able to walk out.

She was feeling quite smug when she heard a scream. "AAAAAH! AQUACIOUS! NOOO!"

Someone had discovered her deed. She quickly hid in the shadows, knowing that the mud up to her knees and her lack of shoes looked very suspicious.

She heard other screams—women and men shocked and

horrified as they came upon the headless sculpture. She didn't understand why anyone would care so much about a dumb old statue.

Deciding it was best to travel below the walkways, she skulked through the darkness and the shallowest mud until she was far away from the town square and felt safe enough to climb up to a walkway. Even then, she ran home as quickly as she was able.

When she reached the cliffs, the rope ladder was already down and waiting for her. She climbed up, her arms wobbly and weak. When she finally flopped over the balcony, she didn't see or hear anyone. Was it possible no one was home yet? When she walked inside, every room was dark. She went straight to her bedroom, pulled off her muddy, dusty clothes, and used a rag and a bucket of water to wash herself from head to toe. Shivering, she put on one of Mrs. Brown's ridiculous nightgowns and collapsed into bed. She was asleep instantly.

15

"You had NO RIGHT!!"

"I was protecting our families."

"You were following your own agenda with *no* thought for anyone else and now that child is in DANGER!"

The screaming voices echoed throughout the caves. Ida awoke in such a daze, she almost forgot where she was. She'd just finished dressing when Dag popped his head in the door. "You're under house arrest!"

"Yeah!" Trak said from behind him. "You can never leave!"

"What are you turkeys talking about?" Ida grumbled.

"Mrs. Brown and Mrs. Gauge say so," Dag said.

The yelling match in the next room continued. "You know the rules, Loor. We VOTE on decisions like this."

"As founder, I made an executive decision!"

"Do you hear that, Mr. Gauge!? He's gone MAD with power!!"

This doesn't sound good. Shoving by the boys, Ida marched into the living room ready to insert herself into the argument. Mrs. Gauge and Mrs. Brown stood in the corner of the room, glowering at Mr. Loor, whose red face told Ida that he was none too pleased. Mr. Brown sat in a chair, trying to look diplomatic, while Mr. Gauge stood behind him staring at a side table as if he might smash it over Loor's head. Punch stood quietly by the door, the only one who noticed Ida's entry.

"What's going on?" she demanded.

The heads of the adults snapped to look at her.

Mrs. Brown attempted a smile. "Everything's fine, dear."

Mr. Brown rolled his eyes at this lie.

Instead of answering, Punch handed Ida a newspaper. The headline screamed *Statue of Aquacious Decapitated in Dead of Night!*

Ida looked up at the others. "Yeah. And?"

Mrs. Gauge shrieked, "We had NO IDEA that Mr. Loor had sent you to do such an inflammatory, irresponsible act. We never would have approved it, as he is *well aware*!"

Mr. Loor took a deep breath. "As I've said several times, the mission was kept secret so as not to endanger any of you. You can now, with a clean conscience, tell the police you had nothing to do with it. While the crime was being committed, you were in a meeting where every citizen of the Unfinished City saw you. More importantly, the silly statue was beheaded, but the sun still rose and the city still stands. The statue has been shown to be what it is: a sculpture made of marble, and nothing more. The citizens will begin to understand that their belief in Aquacious is nothing but childish nonsense. We're one step closer to our goal. Now, unless you're going to apologize for your insults and accusations, I believe I've had enough of this conversation. If any of you wishes to have a quiet, rational discussion, I'll be in my office." He left the room.

No one said a word for several moments, until Mrs. Brown offered her opinion. "He's lost his mind."

Mr. Gauge looked more thoughtful. "I'm not so sure. Maybe he has a point."

Mrs. Gauge was aghast. "Oh no, dear. Don't tell me you *agree* with the man!"

"I don't approve of his methods, but maybe it *is* time we shook things up a bit."

"We'll be shaking things up plenty soon enough. Best to not make people angry before then," Mrs. Brown said.

"But what about *the child*?" Mrs. Gauge tipped her head toward Ida, as if Ida didn't know whom she was talking about.

Ida was furious that she couldn't leave the house as Dag and Trak had said, and she was ready to fight. "So I'm not allowed to leave the house because I'm being punished? I was just following orders."

The adults blinked at her in astonishment.

Mrs. Brown was the first to answer. "Punished? No dear. You're being kept here for your own safety. I shudder to think what the townspeople might do if they figured out you were responsible for destroying their beloved statue. It's best that you stay inside for as long as possible."

Ida had observed that the citizens of the Unfinished City were peaceful, friendly people except when it came to one thing: the Anti-Delugists. One sniff of a person being against the flood could turn a sweet mother into a dragon in seconds. Therefore, Ida had to believe Mrs. Brown that people could turn violent if they knew what Ida had done.

Thinking of staying in the cliff house made her feel suffocated. Nothing made her want to leave a place more than being told she had to stay—spending years in the Higgins Institute would make anyone this way. Loor had given her no warning about having to stay hidden after she completed his task. She took a deep breath, reminding herself that none of this statue nonsense mattered to her. She would learn about the Treatment, obtain her cure, and then use the Brokhun's Crack to quickly leave this oddball city behind.

She needed to talk to Loor. As she left the room, Punch whispered, "I told Mr. Loor that I should handle the job. I knew you'd blow it."

Glaring at him, she headed for the stairway that led to Loor's office. She found him sitting at his desk with his fingers templed in front of his chin.

"What do you need?" he asked.

She was thrown by his brusque manner. "I've come to hear about the Treatment."

He smiled as if Ida were a toddler asking to stay up an extra ten minutes. "Do you believe you've earned it?"

"Of course."

"All right then." Reaching into a desk drawer, he withdrew a piece of folded paper. He handed it to her. She snatched it out of his hand, unfolding it as quickly as possible.

"Is this a joke?" she asked.

"Not at all."

"This paper is blank."

"I promised to reveal the Treatment to you and that's what I have done. The famous cure of the Unfinished City is nothing but empty promises and hocus-pocus."

She narrowed her eyes as her hands balled into fists. "You liar!"

"I assure you, I'm not lying. In all my years here I have never known a person to be cured of anything significant. Although I have heard of a few dying in the attempt."

"Attempt at what?" she pleaded. "What must I do?"

"You must leave this house."

"But we had a deal!"

"We had a deal that you BROKE! Punch was right—you are completely unreliable."

"I cut off the head and rolled it into the mud just like you asked! It was no easy task, *I might add.*"

"Someone saw you, you fool!" He shoved a newspaper toward her. She'd already seen the headline, so she read the fine print. Half-way down the article she saw

Local truancy officer Ms. Wilemina Neely witnessed a child running away from the scene around midnight. Ms. Neely warns our citizens that "We should be more vigilant about the urchins in this city, or more calamities will follow!"

Ida threw down the paper. "That's it? It doesn't even say that it was a girl!"

"Nevertheless, our deal was very specific in stating that you would were to remain unseen and anonymous. You failed, and you should get nothing. However, I chose to be generous and inform you that the Treatment is rubbish. Our transaction is now complete." He spun around in his office chair to face the wall.

Ida's face went red as her breath grew short. Fury boiled in her stomach, threatening to explode through the top of her head. "You deceitful, despicable, cockroach of a man. I'm going to tell everyone in town that you're the one who wanted the statue destroyed."

"And confess that you did the destroying? I doubt you'll do that."

"Watch me."

He didn't look at all nervous, which was infuriating. She stormed out of the room, debating whether she should fetch one of her sharp rocks to take that smug look off his face.

Returning to her room, she threw her few possessions into her leather satchel. Last night's clothes were still wet and grimy, and she refused to wear anything patchwork ever again. Her only option was her green ruffled dress, which she usually reserved for cons. She pulled it over her head unhappily. She'd also lost her comfortable shoes to the mud, so she pulled on the patent leather sandals that always gave her blisters.

She made her way through the living room where Hilda and Georgie were studying math. "That's a *pretty* dress," Hilda said, but Ida kept moving, rushing to the library.

Hilda followed and watched Ida sit down at the entrance to the quick exit. "Are you leaving?"

"Yep." Ida positioned her satchel on her back.

"For good?" When Ida nodded, Hilda got teary. "You're not going to say good-bye to anyone?"

After thinking for a second, Ida said, "Tell everyone I said Mr. Loor is a double-dealing, egg-sucking skunk."

Hilda's eyes got very wide.

"Bye, Hilly. You're a good kid." Ida slid into the darkness.

16

Ida hit the sand. She fell forward but managed not to land on her face this time and began to run immediately. She heard voices calling from the balcony. It was Mrs. Gauge and Mrs. Brown yelling, "Come back, Ida! You're not safe! Come back!"

She kept running at top speed, glad for the excuse to punish her body, to feel the pain in her lungs. *How could I have been so stupid? Why did I trust that charlatan?*

Maybe they'd *all* been in on it—the Gauges, the Browns—maybe they'd all been using her from the start. Even Hilda. Her heart sank. For a brief period, she'd been part of their big family, and, although she was loath to admit it, it had been nice in a way. Admitting that she'd liked living in the cliffs with the Anti-Delugists made her twice as mad at herself.

When she reached the ladder that led to the city, she stopped running. She climbed up and walked at a normal pace, catching her breath. What should she do now? The smart thing would be to leave at once—she was guilty of a serious crime and people were searching for the perpetrator—but the daylight was a problem. She couldn't use the Brokhun's Crack while half the city was awake to witness her. She'd have to wait until dark. Until then, she wasn't overly worried that anyone would recognize her. Even if, as the paper had said, a child had been seen near the scene last night, who would believe a young girl had pulled off the feat? It was a darn big head! Occasionally there were advantages to being underestimated because of one's size and gender.

Arriving at the market, she was surprised to find that most of the shops were boarded up with signs that said "closed." The walkways were crowded with people all walking in the same direction. A stir was in the air. People stepped so quickly and with such determination that Ida found herself being nudged aside. She was dangling precariously off the edge of the walkway when she felt a hand yank her back.

"By Aquacious, child, only an *imbecile* walks so close to the edge!" It was Dunkin, the little man from the sponge shop.

"Thank you," she said, although she wasn't pleased with being called an imbecile.

"You look very nice," Dunkin said. "Are you dressed up to go see the Mayor?"

"Uh, is that where everyone else is going?"

"Oh, yes! He is back and we want to hear what he has to say about the Aquacious statue."

"Back from where?" she asked.

"He has been away learning to weave from the people of Gillent, and before that he was taking part in a yelling competition in the East, and before that . . . well, I cannot really remember."

"Sounds like an odd way to run a city."

"It works well. No one really likes him. He is an *imbecile.*"

"Why did you elect him?"

"We did not. He inherited the position from his father."

Ida was pleased to have run into Dunkin. He had seemed to know about the Treatment. Maybe if she played her cards just right, she could get him to talk about it this time. She walked with him toward the western part of the city.

"Where is your father?" Dunkin asked. "He is feeling better, I hope?"

She sifted through her brain, trying to remember which lie she'd told him. "Uh, he's fine . . . He's seeing a doctor this afternoon who's supposed to be very good."

"That is very good news." Dunkin seemed relieved.

When they arrived, they found a large crowd gathered expectantly at the grand steps of the Mayor's home. Ida was amused to see that *only* the steps of the Mayor's home were there, as nothing else had been rebuilt yet. She supposed the man's travels had kept him too busy for reconstruction.

A brutish man in a red cape and uniform stood like a statue at the top of the stairs, arms at his side, eyes looking straight ahead. The crowd was becoming pushy, edging forward to get the best positions.

"Over here," Dunkin signaled. Leading Ida to a felled tree, he helped her climb up to its highest point. He nimbly hopped up after her. Being small made one always aware of the best vantage points.

The man in the red cape took out a small instrument that looked to Ida like a doll's tuba. As he blew it three times, the crowd grew silent. A family walked up the stairs—a striking woman, two perfectly-pressed children, and a tall man with an enormous smile. He was wearing some sort of uniform that emphasized his broad shoulders and lean waist, but as he turned to look at the crowd Ida couldn't help but notice that he had an alarmingly small head. The matching trousers and coat did nothing but encourage the image of a pea sitting atop a potato.

"Is *that* the Mayor?" she asked.

"I am afraid to say, yes," Dunkin replied.

"You couldn't even fit half a brain in that noggin."

"He descends from a family known for their broad shoulders, good taste in music, and nonexistent intellect," Dunkin sighed.

The Mayor clapped his hands twice and the man in the red cape turned crisply and went to stand by the Mayor's wife and children.

"People of the Unfinished City . . ." the Mayor began. His voice boomed across the crowd, and Ida felt as though she would've been able to hear him even if she'd stayed in the cliffs. She had no doubt that he'd won that yelling competition. "We are a wounded city, an injured city, a scarred city, a city that has been split wide open . . . "

"We get it," Dunkin muttered.

"And as we lick the wounds that bind us, it is clear that the licking must stop."

There was a giggle from the crowd.

" . . . That is to say . . . that licking is all well and good for a while . . . but soon . . . we shall run out of spit."

Dunkin clapped his hand over his forehead. "I forsake every time I have used the word *imbecile* to describe any individual who is not this man."

The Mayor cleared his throat uncomfortably but plowed forward. "Let's get to the point, shall we?"

There was a small round of applause.

"The head of Aquacious has been removed. I remind you that it was my great-great-grandfather who paid to have it made. It is an insult to the Unfinished City and an insult to my family to have Aquacious standing out there like some kind of . . . some kind of . . . statue without a head."

"He does have a way with words," Ida observed.

"Therefore, I am offering a reward: fifty gold coins to whoever finds the head. And for the perpetrator . . . DEATH!"

Wild cheering rose from the crowd. Ida felt as if she'd been kicked in the stomach.

The Mayor continued. “Now if you’ll excuse me, I am due in Jilooin for the birth of a yak.”

He waved stiffly, returning to his family. All four of them produced the same dull smile and waved in unison to the crowd. The Mayor clapped twice again, and the red-caped soldier stepped forward and led the family down the stairs to a waiting carriage. They flicked inside like wasps returning to the nest, and horses led them away.

“Well, that was that,” Dunkin declared. “We probably will not see him again until next season.” He looked at Ida, who'd gone pale as snow. “Are you alright?”

“Of course,” she managed, but inside, her heart was beating so fast it hurt. *Death. Mr. Loor made me commit a crime that is punishable by* death.

“No, you are not. You look quite ill.”

“No . . . I . . . really. I’m fine.” She needed to get out of there. She couldn't wait for nightfall.

“When was the last time you ate?”

“Hmmm?” She was no longer listening. She was deep in her own thoughts, planning her walk back to the exact spot in the mud where she'd arrived, where she would pull out her timepieces and find the door home.

Putting an arm around her shoulder, Dunkin led her away. “You’ll have lunch with me and my Momma. Do you like boar’s brain?”

This question finally brought Ida out of her fog. “Excuse me?”

“For lunch. You’ll love it!”

17

Ida was happy to have received an invitation to spend more time with Dunkin, but she also knew it was madness to stay in town even an hour extra. She would eat a hasty meal, ask about the Treatment, and then scram.

Dunkin led her back to the market district and behind his sponge shop. His house stood precariously at the end of an old rotting walkway. The walkway's brittle wooden legs were askew, causing the house to look like a wounded grasshopper.

Dunkin stomped up the front steps, making Ida nervous that her extra weight would bring the house and walkway tumbling down. She followed him tentatively as he walked through the front door.

"Momma! I am here, and I have a guest for lunch!" he yelled through the house.

A large woman appeared. She had the same shiny black hair, olive skin, and green eyes as Dunkin, but she was twice as tall and twice as wide as he was. Her face was warm and generous, and she wore an apron splattered with grease and various sauces.

She embraced Dunkin aggressively, kissing him on both

cheeks. He leaned his head toward her, but kept his body back, saving his immaculate suit from any soiling.

"Momma," he said, pulling away. "This is Ida, the lost girl I met last week."

The next thing Ida knew, she was being suffocated by Momma Dunkin's ample bosom. Ida could smell gravy, butter, and some sort of citrus perfume. After the stifling hug was over, Momma Dunkin planted a wet kiss on each of Ida's cheeks.

"Welcome, welcome! Dunkin said you were a young girl, but I had no idea!" Her accent was thicker than Dunkin's. "You are not even old enough to wear a brassiere!"

Turning fuchsia, Ida stood uncomfortably. "What a cozy home you have." She looked around. It was cozy, if one considered plastic to be cozy, for there was thick clear plastic on everything: the sofa, the coffee table, the lamps and even over a fruit bowl. Dunkin saw her staring. "We used to put it on and take it off every year at flood time, but it got to be so tedious! And it's much easier to clean this way."

The living room had only three walls. One would never know from the front of the house that there was no back—it was a building in progress, like all the other homes in the Unfinished City.

Unable to keep still, Ida wandered to the room's edge and looked out. She found herself staring into the living room of the next house, where a family sat eating a meal. They waved at her, smiling. She forced a smile and waved back. *This city was so weird.*

She wanted to move things along. "When do we eat?"

"Ha!" A loud nasal voice surprised Ida. "Rude little thing, isn't she?"

A woman Ida hadn't seen was crouched in a rocker in a dark corner of the room. She was the same size and build of Momma Dunkin, but with blonde hair and brown teeth, and she'd bellowed like she was stuck in the bottom of a well.

Dunkin gave Ida a look of apology. “You will have to excuse my Auntie Gertrude. She is so full of rage that she has rotted her spleen.”

“Don’t talk about me like I am not here,” Gertrude hollered. “And the spleen is a highly overrated organ!” Standing, she hobbled forward on a cane. “What do you think of our humble abode?” She pointed the cane at Dunkin. "That worthless under-grown blueberry built our fourth wall, and it fell last week."

Momma Dunkin chimed in. "Now Gertrude, be fair. It takes Wee twice as long as other men to build such high walls."

"Then you should have had two of him!"

Momma and Dunkin ignored her, but Gertrude would not be held back. She turned her sour face to look Ida up and down. "So this is the little twerp who wants her father to try the Treatment?”

Dunkin’s and Momma’s eyes got huge as they shushed Gertrude and forced her into the dining room.

Ida's heart quickened. She took a seat at the dining room table. "Take your time with the food. I have *all* day."

Momma Dunkin filled the table with a veritable feast of fresh vegetables, homemade bread, and the roasted head of a boar, which Dunkin explained was a delicacy in their homeland. The cooked head was upturned, so Ida could easily use her spoon to scoop out the brains. Momma was so enthusiastic about it (and Ida was now inclined to please her) that Ida did as she was told. Much to her surprise, it was not altogether disgusting—kind of like stewed rabbit, but slimier.

As they conversed, Ida learned Dunkin's family was from a country called Motzia, which was a month's journey to the east. Dunkin’s father had died many years ago.

Auntie Gertrude scoffed. "Worst mistake I ever made was leaving Motzia. Now I have to live in this puddle where you cannot even find a decent Strawberry Stew."

Luckily, as soon as Gertrude finished her glass of milkwine, she fell asleep.

When Dunkin had finished his enormous meal, he wiped his mouth and sat back in contentment. “I swear by Aquacious, Momma, there has never been nor ever will there be a more delectable dish than your roasted boar’s brain.”

Momma’s eyes got misty. “Oh, our poor Aquacious statue. Whatever shall we do?” She dabbed her eyes with the corner of her apron. “I cannot endure—”

“Momma, do not talk about it. You will just upset yourself all over again.”

Momma nodded. “Yes, yes. You are right, Wee.” She blew her nose on the apron. “Ida, is it not the most horrible thing you have ever heard of?”

Ida felt guilty about the whole statue thing, but “the most horrible thing she'd ever heard of?” Hardly. Ida came from a land where children were kidnapped and real monsters existed. She remembered the Mayor’s words today: “punishable by death.” The boar’s brains were not sitting so well in her stomach.

“Why is everyone acting like it is some big mystery who committed the desecration?" Dunkin asked. "It was *obviously* the Anti-Delugists!”

Ida felt prickly. “Why do you say that?” For good measure, she added, “Uh, who are the Anti-Delugists?”

Dunkin scowled. “They are a bunch of fanatics—non-believers who want to end our flood. They want to build a dam or some such nonsense.”

Momma groaned, fanning her napkin in front of her face in horror.

Dunkin continued. “Who else would want to destroy our most beloved symbol besides that heathen, Mr. Loor? He has an alibi, but believe you me he is behind it all!”

Wanting to steer the conversation away from the Aquacious

statue, but not feeling like it was quite time to mention the Treatment yet, Ida said, "I'm confused, Momma. I grew up in a place that didn't have a flood, and people loved their houses. None of us would have wanted to see them get washed away. Why is it so bad that the Anti-Delugists want to save your homes?"

Momma smiled. "Our people see the flood as a gift. It cleanses our souls every year and reminds us of what is truly valuable—and, more importantly, what is not."

This wasn't enough for Ida. "But couldn't you do something every year that was. . . *symbolic*? What if you all moved above the flood line, and then one day a year you could gather to watch the flood and remember what's important?"

Dunkin banged the table. "No. The day is about sacrifice, and there is no sacrifice without participation."

Ida scrunched her nose up, trying to understand his logic.

"You have some sophisticated ideas for a girl your age," Momma said.

Ida made a mental note to remember to sound twelve and no older.

Momma wiped crumbs off the table. "I think you are mature enough for me to ask if you have ever loved someone enough that you felt you would die for them?"

Ida thought of her parents. She nodded, thinking of the many times she'd wished she could have saved them.

"You think nothing of giving your life, but you are not ready to sacrifice a house? A thing of wood and nails?" Momma said. "It cannot feel. It cannot express its love for you. It is a transient place of comfort. It is important because of the people within it, not because of the structure itself."

Ida could understand this idea. Since she'd lost her parents, no place had really felt like home. "So . . ." Ida ventured, "You don't like the Anti-Delugists because they think their home is too important?"

“That is part of it," Dunkin said. "They also want us to modernize, to integrate our businesses with the larger world, which promotes the idea that material wealth is more important than emotional happiness, and this idea is dangerous to everything that the Unfinished City stands for. And I fear they are starting to convince people.”

“And if the flood actually stops, like Mr. Loor wants?”

Momma looked despondent. “I was born in Motzia, remember, and I have seen the lonely, drawn-out faces of people who live in a constant state of desire. They work their fingers to the bone. They never see their families—all for the sake of having a bigger home, a nicer pair of shoes, a finer horse. Without the flood, I suppose we would all slowly become like them.”

Ida had traveled and seen much of her own world, and she had to admit that the majority of the people in the Unfinished City (minus Auntie Gertrude and Ms. Neely, perhaps) seemed to possess a lightness that she'd never seen before, as if the weight of the world had never landed on their shoulders. According to Momma and Dunkin, this was thanks to the flood.

Explained by the two of them, the whole idea of a yearly flood didn't seem nearly as hare-brained as the Anti-Delugists had made it sound.

"You also may have noticed that we have a very large elderly population," Dunkin said. "Our residents tend to live ten to twenty years longer than people in other towns."

"Gertrude loves to talk about returning home, but because she has remained here, she has reached the ripe age of one hundred and four," Momma said.

Ida was shocked. Gertrude looked like an old lady, but she certainly didn't look like someone who'd lived for over a century.

“Let us have some dessert,” Momma suggested.

18

Before long, they were sitting in the living room with thick slices of jam pie placed in their laps. Ida and Dunkin sat on the couch while Momma chose a chintz armchair. Auntie Gertrude, awake from her nap, was back in her dark corner.

Ida watched a frustrated fly buzz around the plastic-sealed fruit bowl on the coffee table. She felt a bit like that fly right now—close to the prize but unable to touch it. Her next move felt exceedingly important.

Trying to sound as casual as possible, Ida said, "Father plans to take the Treatment soon."

Dunkin choked on his pie. Momma slapped him on the back, shrieking, "Good heavens, you cannot be serious!"

Gertrude cackled from the corner. "I told you she was a fool, and her father is obviously a lunatic as well. The acorn does not fall far from the tree!"

"Enough, Gertie!" Momma said sternly.

Catching his breath, Dunkin put down his plate. "Please tell me this is not true. The chances of him surviving are alarmingly slim."

Alarmingly slim? This was close to what Mr. Loor had said, but what kind of cure would kill you instead of heal you?

“He does know the danger, does he not?" Dunkin asked. "Has someone explained it to him?”

“Not really,” Ida answered cautiously, afraid to give herself away. “Perhaps if you explain it to me, I can tell him about it tonight?”

Dunkin shook his head. “No, no. I do not like it. I do not like it at all. I will not spread information about the Treatment. If someone got hurt, I would feel responsible.”

“But if we do not caution him,” Momma interrupted, “then he is *more* likely to get hurt. I think it is our responsibility to warn him properly, dear.”

Dunkin crossed his arms like a petulant child. “I will not do it.”

“I would be more than happy to!” Gertrude barked. “You see—”

“No, Auntie, you must not!” Dunkin tried.

“—if you want to be cured of any ailment or complaint, you must stand in the town square on flood day—”

Dunkin slapped his forehead with his hand. "She is like a hyena who was born from a mule!”

“—and while the rest of the city evacuates to the hill, you must wait for the flood to consume you, and if you should happen to survive the flood without drowning, or being thrashed about so as to break your neck, which of course you probably will not, then the legend has it that you will be healed of your sickness. But since no one has been cured in our time, there is no real proof that it works at all, so good luck to you and your father!!” Gertrude laughed like an old grackle.

Ida blinked in disbelief. This was the Treatment? She would have to *stand in the middle of town and survive the flood*? That was completely *bonkers*. “Are you sure there are no *other* cures in the Unfinished City?”

This made Gertrude laugh even harder.

Momma's eyes filled with pity. "I am afraid not, child. I recommend you tell your father that this one is a fiction, so he will not be tempted to try it."

Ida's mind fought against her words. The Treatment was insane, but Gertrude said it would cure *anything*. This was why the door had brought her here. This was her chance to become an adult, to become normal. Adrenaline surged through her veins. "What if the person . . . my father, I mean, is a really good swimmer and really good at holding his breath? Wouldn't he have a better chance of survival than most?"

Dunkin was aghast. "He will not have *time* to swim! The current is so strong, the waves are so big . . . think of putting water into a teakettle with an ant inside. Do you think it matters if the ant can swim? It is doomed from the start. It will die from exhaustion!"

"What if one had some sort of flotation device?" she ventured.

"Bah!" Dunkin waved the notion away with his hand.

Ida was frustrated with their lack of imagination. "It's worked for someone, or there wouldn't be a legend, would there?"

Hesitating, Momma whispered, "There is a man in town called Vernon Lyon. He supposedly survived the Treatment many years ago."

"Did it cure him?" Ida felt a flutter of hope.

"I'm afraid it is rather a harrowing story," Momma said.

"Why? Was he fixed or not?" It seemed pretty simple to Ida.

"This has been a lovely time, but we have spent enough time talking about the Treatment. I do not want to give the girl nightmares." Dunkin rose from his chair, signaling that lunchtime was over.

Ida didn't stand. She needed one more morsel of information first. “Perhaps if my father could speak to this Mr. Lyon, he could be talked out of trying the Treatment, don’t you think?”

Dunkin peered at his mother nervously.

Momma considered for a moment. “Perhaps Mr. Lyon *could* talk some sense into your father. You will find him in the south, just beyond the shantytown. Ask for him by name—everyone knows him there.”

The shantytown was where the “Non-Constructionists” lived. Ida had been curious about their lifestyle, and now she had an excuse to see it for herself. She peeled herself off the plastic-covered couch, generating the sound of a walrus unsticking itself from a block of ice.

Gertrude sprung awake at the sound and stared in surprise at Dunkin, and then at Ida. "Hey look! Wee went and found someone his own size to play with!" And then she was asleep again. Dunkin smoothed his hair and coughed with dignity.

Ida looked at him through new eyes. She and he weren't so different. People treated Dunkin like a child, too, because of his size, and no amount of fancy suits or facial hair would ever change that. Yet here he was, staying and overseeing his family, even though it entailed relentless teasing and humiliation from his Auntie. Ida respected his choice. At the same time, if the Treatment could make Dunkin taller, wouldn't he risk it? Ida took another look at the obnoxious Auntie Gertie, snoring in her corner, and was sure that he would.

Ida thanked Momma and Dunkin profusely for the food and company. She walked out their front door and, although she knew she should leave town at once, she headed south, determined to find the man called Vernon Lyon.

19

Ida was almost a mile south of Dunkin's house when she gasped, cupping her hands to her mouth. She'd had a revelation that hit her as hard as a bag of bricks: The Treatment required the flood. The Anti-Delugists wanted to *stop* the flood. All this time, Mr. Loor knew that if the Anti-Delugists successfully built their dam, the Treatment would cease to exist. She wouldn't have access to the cure ever again. No one would.

That no-good, two-faced, bottom-dwelling piece of roach excrement. Ida wanted to spit in his eye. In fact, if she hadn't had this new goal of finding Vernon Lyon, she would've gone straight to the cliffs to do just that. The important thing right now was to find someone who could tell her as much about the Treatment as possible. Then she'd figure out what to do about Mr. Loor and the Anti-Delugists.

By the time Ida reached the other end of the city, night had fallen and her feet were killing her. She found the shantytown with no problems—it was a great expanse of lean-tos and the simplest of shacks. Lanterns were lit here and there, and many people slept under tarps held up with string. She stepped carefully through the simple structures, wary of sleeping strangers. Laughter came from ahead. A group of men sat around a fire, passing around a jug of what was probably moonshine. Happy to find some people awake, she approached the jovial threesome.

"Excuse me?" she said.

The three men jumped at the sound. The one on the left was so surprised he fell backwards off his tree stump. This sent the other two into hysterical laughter, slapping their knees and wiping tears from their eyes.

A tired voice called out from the darkness, "Keep it down, you drunkards!"

One of the three, a man with a purple scarf, stood and yelled back, "Stuff it up your butter tray!" Remembering that Ida was standing there, he made a little bow. "Sorry you had to hear that, miss. Care for a slug?" He offered her the jug.

She shook her head. "I'm looking for the house of Vernon Lyon."

The man who had fallen sat back up. He had a face like a spoiled raisin. "Well, you won't find any houses around here. You'd have better luck if you asked where to find the *chair* of Vernon Lyon."

This sent the other men back into hysterics, but Ida couldn't see what was so funny. "Okay. Where do I find the chair of Vernon Lyon?"

When Raisin Face had stopped chuckling, he pointed to his right. "About twenty yards that way, by the old oak. Just don't ask to sit down. He's only got the *one* chair." They all started to laugh again.

"Thank you," Ida said, happy to move on.

After some tricky navigation in the dark, Ida finally spotted an enormous oak. On the other side of the tree was a house in mid-construction—a concrete foundation in a tidy square, wooden studs placed in neat lines, and a high gabled roof framed in pine. She was surprised to see such a well-built structure on this side of town.

In the middle of the construction sat a middle-aged man with big strong hands and a potbelly. He was smoking a pipe and staring at the sky. Ida watched him for a while. Inside the frame of his home he looked like a wild bear who'd been caged, but who'd stopped fighting years ago.

"Mr. Lyon?" Ida asked.

The man looked up in surprise, as if he hadn't known other humans existed in the world.

"I know it's very late, Mr. Lyon, and I'm sorry to disturb you, but I—"

"Who are you, and why aren't you in bed?" he growled.

"I'm Ida, and I'm not in bed because . . . well, because I'm standing here talking to you."

He scoffed. "Don't ask for a seat—"

"Because you've only got one," she said. "I know." Approaching the house, she squeezed through two studs.

Mr. Lyon puffed a few more times on his pipe, scanning the structure. "I'm thinking of adding a skylight this year. What do you think?"

Ida looked up, imagining the roof that Mr. Lyon seemed to be contemplating. "In which room?"

"The bedroom, so I can see the stars at night."

"Terrible idea," Ida said matter-of-factly.

"Why?" he snarled.

"The light will come in every morning and wake you before the roosters, and if you ever want to sleep in, the heat will fry you like an ant. Only a man with feathers in his head puts glass above a bed."

Mr. Lyon raised an eyebrow, puffed a few more times on his pipe, and studied her. "You like to speak your mind, don't you?"

"Yes, sir."

"Why is it you wanted to see me?"

"I have a question."

He crossed his arms. "Let's hear it."

"I heard that you and your wife took the Treatment, and I want to know—"

"Who sent you?" He stood up, sending his chair crashing back. "Do you think this is *funny*? Will your little brat friends give you a penny because you asked me about my wife? Now get out, before I kick you into that tree!"

"No. I—"

"OUT!" he cried. His voice was full of such rage and grief that Ida obeyed him.

Walking to the oak, she turned to face him one more time. "I'm sorry, Mr. Lyon. I didn't mean to be disrespectful."

He was still glaring at her, his face a deep crimson. She fumbled her way back shakily through the darkness, trying not to cry with disappointment.

VERNON SAT BACK in his chair and tried to concentrate on his new skylight, but he couldn't. Damn that child! The snotty stray had interrupted a perfectly fine evening. She'd been brazen and rude, and had asked him about his wife! His wife. Delia. A pain spread through Vernon's belly, and he waited helplessly for it to reach his heart. Even after all of these years, he couldn't think of her without feeling like an anvil had lowered onto his chest.

He thought of her laugh, of the dimple on her right cheek, and the ticklish spot on her belly. He could still summon the smell of lavender that permeated her dark hair.

As he thought of her, his memories raced ahead of him, tumbling beyond his control: Delia the first time he saw her sweeping the floor of her father's store; Delia wading in the sea, ruining a new dress; Delia screaming in agony and then weeping with joy as she held a newborn Theodore.

Theo.

Vernon indulged himself occasionally and allowed himself to think of his Delia. It was painful, but he'd trained himself not to stay within the memory for too long. If he felt himself sinking too deeply, he could reach up out of his thoughts and pull himself out of the pain, back to reality.

He had no such ability when it came to Theo. Theo opened a hole within him that was dark and bottomless, and Vernon knew that if he stumbled into it, he would fall forever. As the image of his son fought its way into Vernon's consciousness, Vernon grabbed his chair and violently smashed it against the frame of the house, sending bits of wood spraying into the night. He smashed it again and again until there was nothing left but a stick in his hand. Sweat poured down his head as he struggled to catch his breath.

He felt dizzy, as if he were swaying, but he then realized that the entire house structure was wobbling. He stared at it in consternation. Was his foundation not solid enough? He began examining his support beams, supremely relieved to have found a diversion for his thoughts.

20

Ida was miserable. She wandered around the shantytown until she found an abandoned lean-to that she could sleep under, but rocks poked into her back, she had no blanket to cover herself, and she felt completely exposed to the elements and anyone who might pass by.

Plus, she was infuriated. *Why did Vernon Lyon get so angry? I asked the man a simple question and he nearly swallowed his tongue!*

She doubted she'd be able to fall asleep. *I've failed. The door brought me here to attempt the Treatment, but everywhere I turn, people are trying to stop me from doing it. Why did the dang door bother?*

To distract herself from her misery, she thought of her favorite memory from childhood—the time her mother had thrown an entire chocolate cake at her father just to make Ida laugh.

If Ida ever had children, she would make sure to make every day precious for them, as her mother had done for her. *If* she ever had children. It was a thought that Ida didn't allow into her mind very often, but she was well aware that if she never grew up, she would never be able to have children to throw cakes at. Ida couldn't understand why, if her parents had to be taken from her so early, she should be cursed and kept from building a new family of her own. It was truly unfair.

Loneliness sat like a stone in her gut, but, as always, she was able to transform it into anger and frustration. Her heart raced. She would go see Vernon Lyon again tomorrow, and the day after that, and the day after that. She'd keep going until he talked to her. She'd come too far and sacrificed too much to be thwarted by a surly old man. She felt better as she resolved to show Vernon that she was a girl who would not be ignored.

THE NEXT MORNING, just as the sun poked its head over the horizon, Ida was awakened by a mighty *whoop* that echoed over the shantytown. The inhabitants were awake and running down to the shore, shrieking with glee at the new day. One by one they leapt into the ocean, each shriek at the shocking cold eliciting more and more laughter from the others.

Ida smiled despite herself, finding it impossible not to get caught up in their joy. She stripped down to her chemise and bloomers and was soon running and howling, too and, as she reached the water's edge, she did an enormous belly flop into the waves.

A half-submerged woman said, "You just bowed to Aquacious!"

Ida laughed as she tasted the salt on her lips. She felt more awake than she'd been in weeks. She swam farther and farther out into the sea, away from the crowd, soaking in the fresh air and the call of the morning gulls. Taking a big breath, she dunked her head under the water. She couldn't see much, but she loved the otherworldliness of being fully submerged. For the first time since she'd arrived in the Unfinished City, she was able to enjoy the moment she was in.

Something slimy grazed her leg. A large orange eel with

purple spikes slithered against her. She was so surprised that she gasped, and salt water shot up her nose. She swam upward quickly. As her head broke through the surface, she coughed and sputtered.

A man called out from shore, "You okay out there?"

Waving, Ida yelled, "I'm fine!" She swam back to shallower waters. She hated the feeling of water up her nose—like sandpaper scraping through her sinus cavities.

She thought of the Treatment. Water up her nose would be only the beginning. The waves would be mountains crashing on top of her, powerful enough to break her bones or pin her under the water for far longer than she could hold her breath. Purposefully entering into a flood was pure folly, and Ida knew it. She was suddenly desperate to get out of the ocean and onto dry land.

Digging into the waves, she swam the last few yards quite hard. She scampered out and collapsed onto the sand, catching her breath.

Surviving the flood might be perilous and improbable, but I know for a fact it's not impossible, she thought. Time to visit Vernon Lyon again and learn how to do it.

Ida's green ruffled dress was wrinkled and damp. She ran her fingers through her hair, wishing she'd thought to fabric roll it before it had dried—she looked sweeter with curls. She pinched her cheeks, hoping to bring out some pink. She was going to need every weapon in her arsenal of adorability to get through to the cantankerous Mr. Lyon. On her way back to his property, she gathered wild flowers which had petals that graduated from orange to lime to red.

When she arrived at Vernon's home, she didn't see him anywhere. She walked around the construction site calling his name, but he was nowhere to be found. She decided to explore a little, hoping she might find clues as to what might make Vernon want to talk to her.

Tentatively entering the half-built house, she wandered in and out of the small, wall-less rooms. Carved into each doorway were patterns of vines and leaves. She had to admire the carpentry and detail of the place. Hard to believe that such an angry man could be capable of such fine work. Why go to all this trouble when he knew it would eventually all be washed away? The people of the Unfinished City were still a mystery to her.

She came to what she assumed would one day be the bedroom. A small mattress rested on the floor, and next to it was an old crate being used as a temporary nightstand. Placed prominently on the crate was a worn silver frame, which Ida picked up. Inside was a picture of a family: a man, a woman, and a young boy with a lopsided grin. At first Ida didn't recognize the man as Vernon. The man in the picture was smiling so wide you could see every one of his teeth, he still had his hair, and he looked like a man who thought life was well worth living. The Vernon that Ida had met did not.

"Put that down," a voice growled.

Hot ferret teeth, Ida thought. *This is not how I wanted this visit to begin.*

She placed the picture frame back on the crate exactly as she'd found it. She slowly faced Vernon.

"I'm sorry. There was no one home—"

"What kind of twit goes walking uninvited through another man's home? Someone needs to teach you some respect, young lady!" As he stormed toward her, Ida thought he would knock her across the room.

He stopped short of her, grabbing her arm instead. "Out!"

"I'm sorry," she pleaded. She'd forgotten how large he was.

One of his hands could cover her whole head. Desperate, she held up the flowers. "I brought you these—"

"I'm allergic to Loddy flowers."

Of course, Ida thought.

Pulling her across the room, Vernon shoved her out of his house. "If I catch you around here again, kid, I'll call the police!"

Ida was lucky Vernon had no front door to slam in her face. He could only stand inside his half-finished home and glare at her like she was the termite ruining his entire foundation.

"Please, I've come for your help," she said.

"No."

"I plan to take the Treatment during the next flood."

His eyes flashed with fear, but he said, "How is that my concern?"

"You survived the Treatment. You beat the flood, and I want to know how to do the same."

He smiled unpleasantly. "What if it was just a fluke that I lived? What if I have no answers for you?"

"Then I will face the flood and hope for the same fluke to save me."

Vernon sighed, sat down on a milk crate, and pulled out a pipe. Ida took the opportunity to throw the Loddy flowers into a rubbish pile.

"You are a very precocious child," he grumbled.

"I've been called worse."

The two of them sat in silence for the next few minutes.

Ida decided to risk a bit of honesty. "I lost my family, too."

"I'm sorry to hear that, but that doesn't mean I'm going to help you join them."

"I already told you, I'm going to try the Treatment no matter what you say. You can either make my chances better, or not. Whatever you can live with . . . "

His voice got louder. "Don't try to guilt-trip me into anything, chippie. I stopped caring about other people a long time ago."

"What do you care about then? Money? I can get you that. As much as you want." Ida could arrange a series of card games if that's what needed to happen.

Vernon raised his eyebrow at her in doubt. "I'm not interested in money."

"Everyone wants something."

Scratching his head, he seemed to be genuinely considering what he'd like. "You wanna tell me why you need the Treatment?"

"Does it matter?" Ida asked.

"I suppose not," Vernon conceded.

"All you need to know is that *nothing* will stop me from attempting it. And I'm only twelve. I have my whole life ahead of me!" Smiling, she fluttered her eyelashes in the sweetest way she knew how.

"You're a nightmare," he snarled.

Ida laughed.

He was startled by her laughter, and for the first time the frown left his face. "What are the chances that you're going to leave me alone to finish my work today?"

"None," Ida said. "And I'll be back tomorrow, and the day after that, and the day after that."

Vernon sighed again, but it was deep and guttural, and Ida knew she had him. He stared at her, rubbed his chin, and said, "I'd better make some coffee."

21

The two of them sat in the kitchen area—Vernon on his crate and Ida on the floor—holding steaming cups of coffee. Ida blew on hers as Vernon began to speak.

"I grew up here on a farm, and life was very simple. I helped tend livestock. I prepared for the flood, and I helped rebuild after it. I was happy to live with my family forever—and then I met Delia. The first time I saw her, I swear my feet started to hover above the ground. She took your breath away, my Delia. She could've had any man in the county, but for some fool reason she chose me. I always questioned her taste." He smiled a bit. "We were only eighteen when we married, children really. I think the whole city turned out for our wedding. She had a huge family, and they really knew how to celebrate. The wedding dinner lasted three days. Delia and I disappeared after the first night." Vernon looked at Ida and flushed as he remembered that he was talking to a child.

Ida was amazed to hear Vernon speaking of love. He seemed such an angry man that it was hard to imagine him as a lovesick boy.

"Anyway, life with Delia was wonderful. Our only sorrow

was that we couldn't have a child. We'd accepted the fact that we would never be parents when Delia got pregnant. We were almost middle-aged." He took a long sip of coffee.

Ida remembered the picture she'd found on his dresser of the sweet little boy with the thin face. "What was his name?" she ventured.

Vernon seemed to steady himself for this part of the story. "Theodore. Theo, Delia called him. It was a hard pregnancy, and then he decided to meet us earlier than planned. When he came out he was a wee thing, practically green. Delia doted on him. He was sickly from the start—he never seemed to recover from his entrance into the world—but he was a happy child, always laughing. He had Delia's eyes. One winter he had a cough that shook him down to his foundations, and the doctor said he wouldn't survive to see the spring. That was when Delia suggested . . . the . . . uh—" Vernon stumbled a bit.

"The Treatment," Ida finished for him.

"My parents' generation talked about it a lot more than folks do now. In the old days, people used to travel from all over Venn to try it. Only about fifty percent survived, but those that did were always cured."

Ida shuddered. "Only fifty percent?"

"That was a better chance than the doctor gave Theo, but I knew he'd never survive the flood. He was too small and frail. He'd be washed away like a twig. I decided to do it with him, so I could hold onto him and protect him. Delia wouldn't have any of it. She said that if her family was going into the water, she was going, too. We fought about it for weeks. I was afraid I wouldn't be able to protect them both. She couldn't face the prospect of losing both Theo and me. I was the one who finally relented. It was the biggest mistake of my life."

His voice caught, and tears formed in the corners of his eyes. She looked away to give him privacy. This mountain of a man was breaking down, and it was her fault that he was reliving the tale.

"On the day of the flood the three of us walked down to the town square. Delia and I reasoned that since the Aquacious statue survived the flood every year, maybe it would help to be near it, to hang onto it even. Delia had tried to explain to Theo what we were doing, but he was only three. He thought we were going for a swim, and he was excited.

"Then came the wait. It was excruciating. I come from a long line of Delugists, but that day as I waited for the water, I thought the flood was the most terrible, unnatural thing on earth. The sky turned black and the wind picked up, but unless you're up on the hill above the town, you can't see the wave coming. You hear it before you see it—like thousands of horses galloping toward you.

"We tried to be organized. I had Theo in my arms, tied to my chest so he couldn't be pulled away. Delia was in back of him, secured with a harness to us both. I was terrified, but when I looked at Delia, she was so calm. She was looking straight at me with her big brown eyes, trying to reassure me even though she was about to be hit, too. She was always the strong one. It's hard to describe what happened after that . . . "

His breath quickening, Vernon's face screwed up as if someone were pinching him. Ida stayed very still, afraid that he might change his mind at any moment and stop talking.

"When the water came, it wasn't like water at all. It was like being crushed by bricks. I knew immediately how foolish we'd been. No ropes or harnesses were going to help against a force like that. We were sucked under. I couldn't see anything. I couldn't breathe. Delia and Theo were still with me, but we were weighing one another down and couldn't rise. Theo was so small—I knew he couldn't hold as much oxygen as Delia and me. That's when Delia . . . she . . . she untied her harness. She was trying to remove the weight, so Theo and I could rise, but I weigh so much more! It should have been me!" He sobbed. "She did it before I had a chance to stop her, and as soon as she was free of the harness, she was gone. The current carried her away like a leaf."

Ida worried about little Theo as if she'd known him. "And did you rise?"

"No. I was stuck, you see. My foot was caught in a felled tree. I couldn't move, and we were going to drown. I did the only thing I thought I could do. I untied Theo and let him go, and he rose up and was carried away after his mother."

Vernon couldn't look at Ida. She wanted to wrap her arms around him, but she was still frightened of him. Instead she asked, "How did you escape?"

"I stopped talking about this a long time ago, but . . . " He looked sharply at her. "It was Aquacious that saved me."

22

Without meaning to, Ida raised an eyebrow in disbelief.

Luckily, Vernon kept talking and didn't notice. "I was at the bottom of the square, water filling my lungs, when I saw her. She was beautiful. Not at all like that gaudy statue. She was like a real woman, with the majesty of a lion, and she swam like a great white shark. She freed me. She touched my shoulder, and suddenly I could breathe, as easy as you and me right now. I swam to the top of the water and let myself be carried away, after Delia and Theo. And that's the last thing I remember. When I woke up, I was on the shore, alone."

"Did you ever find out what happened to them?" she asked quietly.

"No."

They sat in silence for a long while.

"Maybe they're still alive?" she offered, knowing that it was a useless comment.

"I used to think so. I convinced myself that if they were dead, I would know it in my bones." His tone assumed its old resentment. “I was foolish. Death isn’t thoughtful, and it doesn’t give us signs.”

“There was nothing you could've done. You tried to—”

“You’re wrong! Aquacious came to me. She *came*! If I'd had faith in her, if I'd waited just a moment longer, she would have saved Theo too. If Delia had had faith, if she’d waited—”

“But you said that only fifty percent of people survive the Treatment. Aquacious doesn’t save everyone. You don’t *know* that she could've saved them!”

“She would've saved my boy!” he croaked.

“Perhaps she had a purpose, a plan. Maybe she needed to save you and you alone.” Ida didn’t know if she believed this, but it seemed like a nice thing to say.

Vernon went silent.

Ida was incredibly disappointed. Nothing Vernon had told her was going to help her survive the Treatment. He seemed to be saying that she could only live through it if Aquacious decided to help her. Ida had never had much time for religion or gods. Could his story possibly be true? She thought it more likely that Vernon’s lack of oxygen underwater had caused a hallucination.

She was curious about one other thing. “You said you stopped talking about seeing Aquacious. Why?"

"People wouldn't stop bugging me about it—like I was the miracle and not the flood. I had to move out here so they would leave me alone."

"Why did you decide to tell me?”

He considered this. “Since Delia and Theo have been gone, my life has been a waste. I’ve just been waiting to die so I can see them again. Now these Anti-Delugists have come along and started to preach that the flood needs to stop. They say that Aquacious doesn’t exist, that she’s just a superstition for old people. I know better. Then you show up, out of nowhere. I think maybe it's my last duty in this life to make sure that the flood continues to happen."

"But the flood killed your family—"

"The flood took my family. I would give anything to make it not so, but the flood has happened since the dawn of time. It is Aquacious' will, and we cannot go against her. Mr. Loor claims that without the flood the Unfinished City will prosper. I know better. Without the flood, the Unfinished City will perish."

She felt her cheeks go red. "I should probably let you know that, uh, I was staying with Mr. Loor and the Anti-Delugists up until recently, but—"

Vernon's eyes flared as he bolted up. "You're a heathen and a danger, and I should hang you by your earlobes right now!"

She jumped back. "I was trying to tell you that I left because I didn't like their ways, and I think Mr. Loor is a horrible weasel of a man. I swear!"

He hovered, unsure.

"If I was working for Mr. Loor, I wouldn't have mentioned him in a hundred years, right?"

He mulled this over, but his temper was ready for a fight.

"How about I give you some information?" She needed to calm the man down.

"Like what?"

She scanned her brain for something of interest. "Uh . . . well . . . uh . . . " She couldn't tell him about the Aquacious statue without incriminating herself, and she didn't think that she and Vernon were on good enough terms to trust him with that kind of confession.

Instead, she offered him the information that had been gnawing at her. "Every week, Mr. Loor sends someone to Reek to pick up a package, and whatever is in it is supposed to stop the flood, even if the citizens of the Unfinished City don't want it to." There, that sounded meaty.

His eyes bulged. "What's in the packages?"

"Um . . . I don't know."

"How big are they? Could it be weapons? Guns? Knives? We're a peaceful people. It wouldn't take much to overthrow us."

"You think Mr. Loor is planning a war?" Ida knew Loor was devious, but she couldn't imagine him staging an uprising, and she knew that the rest of the Anti-Delugist household would have nothing to do with violence.

"I think Loor is a manipulative man who'll stop at nothing to get what he wants," Vernon said. "Did you know that he's been buying up land? Anything that comes up for sale, that man snatches up quicker than a dog swipes up a steak." Vernon proceeded to tell her exactly how much property Mr. Loor owned.

Ida was astonished. The Anti-Delugists had never shown any signs of having that kind of money to spend.

"You've got to find out what's in those packages," Vernon said.

"Too late," she admitted. "I told Mr. Loor to go suck a beehive."

"No matter. Crawl back, say you're sorry, and find a way to sneak a peak inside those packages."

"But—"

"The future of this city may depend on you. I can't defend it against Loor's scheme if I don't know what it is, but if I had a spy on the inside, I could prepare accordingly." Seeing she wasn't convinced, he added, "Remember, if the Anti-Delugists are successful and there's no flood, there's no Treatment."

She scowled. He was right. Left to his own devices, Loor might succeed in his fiendish plans, and she'd never be able to utilize the Treatment. She was going to have to go back to the cliffs and endear herself again to the Anti-Delugists. It wasn't the endearing herself that she hated so much; it was the *apolo-*

gizing. She'd rather eat a live porcupine than apologize to Mr. Loor. Sadly, that didn't appear to be an option.

"Fine. I'll do it. But Mr. Lyon?"

"Yes?"

"When the time comes, you'd better remember whose side I was on."

23

Ida stared up at the cliffs, wondering how she'd get back up. If she imitated Punch's strange catcall, would anyone lower the ladder for her? Only one way to find out. Cupping her hands in front of her mouth, she made what sounded like an owl hoot mixed with a high-pitched cat whine.

Before too long, Punch's head popped out from a balcony above. "Oh, it's you. I thought it was a drowning coyote."

"Ha ha, very funny," Ida shouted, not in the mood to be teased. "Will you let the ladder down, please?"

"Mr. Loor was very clear that you are no longer welcome here."

Miserable old scumbucket. She smiled sweetly. "I need to see him."

"About what?" Punch asked with a smirk. He was not going to make this easy.

"It's private. Tell him I want to talk to him, and if he doesn't want to let me in, then he can come outside. Unless he's afraid of me, which I understand. I'm exceedingly savage."

He snorted. "I'll be right back."

Ida kicked rocks into the sand while she waited. What

should she say? An apology was not enough for Loor. He would only be interested if she had something to offer him. She heard a noise and turned to see Mr. Loor slithering out of the quick exit. Surprisingly agile, he stood up with grace.

Ida summoned all her patience, pasting a hang-dog expression on her face. "Mr. Loor."

Mr. Loor gave her an oily grin. "I knew you'd be back. Life is tough once you've grown accustomed to three meals a day and a clean place to sleep, eh?"

Ida twitched, knowing the many years she'd survived on her own, but she pressed on, forcing a strained, weary voice. "Yes. Life on the outside was . . . hard."

"You should have thought of that before you threw your little tantrum, but it was for the best. Now I've seen what you're truly made of."

And I you, thought Ida.

He continued. "I no longer have any use for you, so you'd better run back to whatever hole you crawled out of."

"That's where you're wrong," Ida said. Her bluff waited on the tip of her tongue, a mouse ready to dart across the floor, hoping the cat will pounce.

Mr. Loor's eyebrow went up in curiosity.

"Punch is betraying you."

"That's preposterous."

It was Ida's turn to be arrogant. "He's in love with the carpenter girl, Preanne. He's promised to abandon you and become a Delugist so he can marry her."

Mr. Loor stepped back, his face registering disbelief and then rage. He rushed forward and shook Ida. "That's a monstrous lie! Take it back!"

Her teeth clacked up into her head. "Stop!" She shoved away from him.

Mr. Loor growled. "How would you know that?"

Ida took a deep breath, composing herself. "I spent last

night sleeping underneath the lumberyard, and I heard Preanne's father talking about it. He's furious. He doesn't think Punch will renounce you."

Loor smiled. "Of course he won't!" He didn't sound as sure as he looked. "I don't believe any of your rubbish. Do you have proof?"

"No, but I can get it. In return, you let me back into the cliffs and give me a place to live."

Loor stomped away across the sand. He was livid, and Ida knew it, but she felt she'd played her hand well. She'd planted the seed of doubt, and if he didn't let her back in, he'd be haunted by the threat of betrayal by the boy who was a son to him. On the other hand, he despised Ida and had no desire to have her anywhere near him or his followers. He hated her for the most common reason of all: she could see through him, and they both knew it.

He walked back over. "Fine. You're welcome back into the cliffs, but if you have not supplied me with proof within one week, you're back on the streets."

"Yes, sir, Mr. Loor." She smiled but wasn't quite sure why. She'd just schemed her way back into the nest of the enemy.

Ida stood in the living room facing Mr. and Mrs. Brown, Mr. and Mrs. Gauge, and all the children. Mr. Loor was giving them a heart-wrenching account of Ida's struggle outside the warm embrace of the Anti-Delugist community. " . . . And so she went without food or water—none of the citizens of the Unfinished City willing to lend the poor child a crust of bread or sip of milk . . ."

Oh brother, thought Ida. *He's laying it on a little thick.*

"She finally came to her senses and returned to us. Aren't we grateful, to see her safe and in one piece?"

Teary, Mrs. Brown embraced Ida. "We've been so worried, dear. *So worried.*" While she squished Ida into her belly, the others gathered around.

Mrs. Gauge hovered. "Whatever were you thinking, child? Running off like that? And at such a *dangerous* time?" She squeezed Ida's arm with relief.

Muttering their joy at seeing her, Mr. Gauge and Mr. Brown patted her on the shoulder.

Ida play-acted at being enormously happy to see them all, but after a few minutes she found that she was actually enjoying their glowing reception. She hadn't expected them to actually feel anything for her. She'd joined their community for one reason and one reason only: to learn about the Treatment. She'd never intended to make personal connections, so she was shocked to learn that she accidentally had.

When the adults made room, Hilda squeezed through. She acted a bit shy, as if Ida were famous, so Ida took the lead. "Hey, Hilly. Nice to see you."

Hilda smiled. "I'm glad you're back. We were worried about you."

Trak stepped in behind Hilda. "We heard the Delugists caught you, cut off your toes, and starved you until you were so hungry that you ate them."

Hilda elbowed him in the stomach. "Muzzle it, Trak!"

Dag was quick to add, "That's not what I heard. I heard they chopped off your head like you chopped off the head of Aquacious, but your head wouldn't die. The eyes kept looking up and blinking, and the mouth kept screaming *ahhhhhhhh,* so they had to drown it in sewer water!"

Little Georgie's eyes filled with tears. "Really?"

Hilda rolled her eyes. "Ida is standing right here, isn't she Georgie?"

After looking Ida up and down to make sure her head was well-attached, Georgie gave her a solid hug. Ida laughed at the depravity of the twins, but deep down she was queasy, knowing that there was indeed a price on her head.

A voice came from a chair in the corner. "A hero's welcome, it seems."

Punch.

Seeing his face made Ida feel guilty for the lie she'd just told Mr. Loor about him and Preanne.

He pushed his glasses higher up his nose. "Mr. Loor has asked me to welcome you back with an open mind, so I will do so." He hopped up, offering her his hand. "Welcome back."

Surprised, Ida shook it. "Thanks."

He didn't seem to have much else to say. "I need to pack for my trip to Reek tomorrow." He left the room.

Now Hilda was free to berate Ida with questions about her time away.

Ida didn't have time to answer them. "I need to talk to Mr. Loor. He said, I, uh, have extra chores because I ran away."

"Ha!" said Dag. "I hope you have to do all of mine."

"Shut it, Dag," Hilda ordered, and then looked at Ida. "I bet it won't be that bad. Mr. Loor's just happy you're safe."

Ida nodded, once again amazed at how Mr. Loor had managed to fool everyone into thinking he was a sensitive, decent man. She left the living room and made her way upstairs to his office.

She found him hovered over his desk as usual. "You need to send me to Reek with Punch."

Mr. Loor's head jerked up. "That's absurd. Why would I—"

"You want proof, and this is how I can get it. Preanne told her father that Punch was relaying messages to her through one of the ship-hands on the boat to Reek. If I can intercept one of the notes, then you'll have your proof."

Mr. Loor leaned back in his chair and stared at the ceiling, as if the cracks in the stone might give him answers. Ida tried to stand casually, as if Loor's answer wasn't terribly important to her.

Loor cleared his throat. "Fine. You shall go with Punch. Bring me back the note, if it exists, but if you don't succeed in obtaining it, then I'll hear nothing more about Punch or betrayal, and you're no longer welcome in this home."

Ida nodded. She had no intention of returning to the cliffs anyway, but if her lie were discovered, she knew that Mr. Loor would stop at nothing to make her suffer for her deceit.

24

Dunkin lay in bed, a small hairnet covering his beard and a glass of warm milk and wine in his hand. He couldn't sleep. He was thinking about the poor Aquacious statue and whether or not it could ever be repaired. The head was still missing, which was very disturbing.

He heard a scraping sound downstairs. He sat bolt upright and put down his glass. Someone was walking around in the living room. Auntie Gertrude would kill him! He still hadn't fixed the open wall, and she'd been warning them about thieves for weeks. Getting out of bed, he searched for a weapon. All he could find was an old umbrella which was pink and covered in yellow ducks. *Not very intimidating*, he thought regretfully.

Tiptoeing out of his room, he could hear Gertrude and his mother exhaling like pigs in their respective rooms. Snoring was a family affliction. He held the closed umbrella like a saber as he walked quietly down the steps. When he reached the bottom he could see someone standing in the middle of the room, but he could only see a silhouette, no details.

Dunkin dropped his voice to its lowest register and growled, "State your business, stranger!"

"Dunkin?"

Shocked to hear his name, he accidentally opened the umbrella, knocking over a plastic-covered vase.

"Dunkin, it's Ida. Control yourself!"

"Ida? What are you doing sneaking around in the middle of the night?" Angrily closing the umbrella, he picked up the plastic sheath, now full of vase chunks.

"You wield a mighty umbrella there, Dunk," Ida said with a giggle.

He raised his head with dignity. "I thought you were a burglar, and no one calls me 'Dunk.'" Realizing he still wore the hairnet on his beard, he quickly pulled it off and shoved it into his pajama pocket.

"Sorry, Dunkin," Ida offered, "but I needed to talk to you."

"It is the middle of the night!"

"*Please*. I have something to tell you."

Dunkin heard her serious tone. "As you wish."

After he lit two lamps, they sat down on the sofa.

Ida took a deep breath. "I'm not who I appear to be."

"Of course you are not!" Dunkin interrupted. "You look like a nice girl, but you are insolent and prone to burglary!"

"That's not what I mean. Please, just listen. I consider you my friend, Dunkin, and I am going to tell you a secret—the biggest secret of my life."

Face softening, he leaned closer to her.

"First, promise me that you won't tell anyone. Not ever. My safety depends on it."

He didn't hesitate. "I promise."

"My name is Ida, and I do come from far away, but I'm not really a twelve-year-old girl." She inhaled, plowing forward. "Next November, I will be sixteen years old."

IDA'S STOMACH lurched as the information hung in the air. She'd been thinking about visiting Dunkin since she left Vernon Lyon. Her trip to Reek might become a dangerous mission, and if she didn't come back . . . well, she felt it was important that *someone* know her story and why she was taking so many risks.

Dunkin's face contorted in confusion.

"When I was twelve," she said, "I was captured by an evil man called the Master. He buried me next to two horrible creatures—we called them the Brothers—and they fed on me, well, really they fed on my life force. That life force was what I needed to grow up." As Dunkin gaped at her, she began to feel that maybe this had been a mistake. "I will always be in this body. I will always look like a young girl."

He lowered his head, and she felt panic rising in her chest.

Knowing the terror that her condition tended to elicit from people, she asked, "Does that scare you?"

He looked up, tears in his eyes. "No, lovely girl, it does not."

Ida hugged him, relief raining down on her. She'd teared up as well.

"Look at us!" Dunkin laughed. "Crying like widows!"

She laughed, too.

Dunkin looked at her differently than before, as if he now understood the sorrow in her eyes. He blew his nose with a handkerchief.

Ida looked at the floor. "Now you understand why I need the Treatment."

He grabbed her hand. "But it is deadly, Ida. You will be killed!"

"You've never thought of trying it? To become normal-sized?"

He dropped her hand, looking offended. "Careful throwing around the word 'normal,' child. Your standard of what is *customary* may have nothing to do with mine."

She was embarrassed.

"I may not be as tall as other men," he said, "but I like my height and myself."

"I didn't mean—"

"I know what you meant, but you will never be happy with your outside if you don't like yourself on the inside. Perhaps you need to work on that first and then worry about the rest?"

“You won’t change my mind. I just wanted to come by and tell you that I'm taking a trip."

“Where?”

“To Reek, but I can’t say why.”

“You are being so mysterious. Are you in danger?” he said.

“I’m coming back. I’ll be fine.”

“Be very careful. People in other cities are not as nice as they are here.”

“Yes, I know.” She stood and hugged him.

“Ida, you can trust me with your secret. Thank you for sharing it with me.”

She smiled, enjoying the relief that comes from being honest. For a brief moment, she considered telling him about the Aquacious statue as well, but when she opened her mouth she found that the only thing that came out was, “good-bye.” She promised herself she would tell him about it when she returned.

She crept out through the open wall, the same way she'd entered.

Dunkin watched the space where Ida had been as he contemplated everything she'd told him. Could it be true? She had always seemed very smart for her age, but her explanation seemed impossible. He'd like to ask Momma for her opinion, but Ida had sworn him to secrecy.

As he walked up the stairs, he could hear exactly what Momma would say if he could tell her the whole story: "You let that child go alone to *Reek*?"

He sighed, knowing how disappointed his Momma would be in him, but what could he do at this hour?

THE OPEN WALL of the house let in a slight breeze, but the night was still and silent. The truant officer Ms. Neely lay quietly under the planks of the floor. She'd seen the foreign girl with the dark hair sneaking across the walkways in the middle of the night and knew she should be followed. She hadn't trusted her from the moment she'd caught her stealing food at the banquet. She'd known the girl was shady, but nothing could've prepared her for what she'd just overheard.

The girl was from the Dark World! Ms. Neely was afraid her heart might give out. If the child had discovered her hiding there under the house . . . well . . . Aquacious only knows what she might have done. Could the girl summon these "Brothers?" What if they turned her into a permanent child as well? She shuddered at the thought, remembering the spindly, pimply adolescent she'd been.

She must be stopped! Ms. Neely steeled herself, knowing that this was to be her most important deed as a civil servant. The authorities needed to be alerted about this demon as soon as possible!

25

The sun was beginning to rise as Ida and Punch approached the dock. Ida carried her leather bag, which, as usual, contained all of her belongings. She planned to learn what was in the packages that Punch was transporting and then head straight to Vernon Lyon with the information.

When Mr. Loor had told Punch the night before that Ida would be joining him, Punch had gotten irritated, which Ida felt went along nicely with her story that he was hiding something. He still seemed pretty annoyed this morning as he led her to a weatherbeaten two-masted ship. A handful of sailors scurried over the deck, preparing for departure. Punch scampered up a gangway made from a shaky piece of wood, not bothering to check if Ida needed help.

Appearing out of nowhere, a young deck hand offered his hand. "Hello, miss! May I assist you aboard *The Milking Cow*?" While the boy's red hair stuck straight up, his large ears stuck straight out. He couldn't have been more than thirteen.

Ida wasn't terribly experienced with boats, but this boy was much too chipper for dawn. Ignoring his hand, she stomped up the gangway in the boots she'd borrowed from Trak.

"A salty one," the boy exclaimed. "I like it!" He hitched up his saggy pants, followed her onto the deck, and approached a little too close for her taste. "If you need anything, just ask for me. Everyone calls me Two Boots."

"Two Boots?" she asked.

"Yeah. The Capt'n said it was so I'd always know how many shoes I should be wearing."

Ida couldn't help but smile.

Two Boots took it as encouragement. "Would you like to eat breakfast together?"

"No," she stated flatly.

"How about a tip then?"

"How about a kick in the lip?"

He wiggled his eyebrows at her. "Playing hard to get. I like that."

"Two Boots!" a voice hollered. A gray-haired man with bloodshot eyes and a two-day growth of beard approached. *Someone else who hates the early morning.* "Leave the passengers alone and get back to work!"

"Aye, aye Capt'n." Two Boots wiggled his eyebrows at Ida one last time and disappeared.

The man held a hand out to Punch. "Good to see you, Punch."

"Morning, Captain Brady."

"Who's the girl?"

"That's Ida."

"Loor making you babysit or what?"

"Sort of. It's a long story."

Ida stood there, humiliated. *First the obnoxious redhead and now this?*

Mr. Loor had told Punch that he had to take Ida to Reek because it was too dangerous for her to be in the Unfinished

City. Whatever. Punch had bought it. She hadn't known that he felt like he was *babysitting*. At least she was wearing patchwork pants and not her frilly dress.

The Captain smiled. Ida could see that he'd once been a strikingly handsome man. "We'll be setting sail in ten. If you want a cot, I'd grab it now."

Punch explained, "There's a bunk downstairs with a few cots where you can sleep. It's a pretty long trip."

A little more sleep sounded great to Ida—she'd spent most of the night sneaking out to Dunkin's house and back, and climbing silently up and down a rope ladder was no easy task. She found the door to the bunk downstairs, lay down with her shoes still on, and was soon snoozing away.

When Ida awoke, her cot was swaying gently back and forth. Outside, the ocean waves lapped up against the sides of *The Milking Cow*. She stood and stretched her arms, releasing a mighty yawn. When she opened the cabin door, she was blinded by the noonday sun. She had to squint to make out the deck.

Two beefy sailors with tattoos and rough hands stood on the edge of the ship holding fishing rods. A large bucket of dead fish sat next to them. The smell worked quicker on Ida than strong coffee—she was immediately wide-awake. At the stern of the boat, Punch stood at the wheel. Brady stood behind him, guiding him. The wind was blowing in Punch's hair and, behind his glasses, his eyes shone. She didn't think she'd ever seen him look so free and happy. She walked away, knowing she tended to aggravate him, and not wanting to spoil his mood.

She'd only taken a few steps when she tripped over a

kneeling figure. She cried out as she caught her balance. The person huddled on the deck moaned.

Ida realized it was some poor soul who was retching off the side of the boat—probably the other passenger. She was sympathetic, being someone who was not crazy about boats herself.

Then she saw the black hair, the beard, and the bright blue suit. “Dunkin?”

Dunkin looked up, his face a horrible shade of gray. He began to smile but was overcome and had to throw up over the side once more. She kneeled, putting a hand on his shoulder. She kept her voice in a low whisper. “What are you doing here?”

"I thought I should join y . . . you," he gasped.

"How did you find me?"

"There is only one sh . . . ship a day to Reek."

“You are the imbecile to end all imbeciles!” she hissed.

Lifting his head, Dunkin managed to lie down on his back, his hands still clutching his stomach. “You're right. This was a terrible idea.”

“You look like a bucket of spit.”

“Thank you. That helps a lot.”

“You need water.”

“No. Please. I just want to breathe the air for a moment.” He inhaled deeply, trying to catch his breath. “You know, it is not so bad if I look up at the sky.”

“I still don’t understand why you’re here.”

After inhaling slowly through his nostrils, he exhaled little shuddering breaths. He spoke slowly. “To . . . look . . . after . . . you . . . ”

“Oh, I see,” she said dryly. “Because you thought I needed someone to show me how to spurt my lunch.”

“Oh Ida, do not say such words. It makes me . . .” He leaned over and threw up again.

"At least you're feeding the fish," she smiled.

"You are crueler than a cobra with a kitten."

"I don't like being followed, and I don't need your help!" she whispered. "You'll ruin my entire plan if they think I'm friendly with a Delugist!"

Dunkin flopped onto his back, closing his eyes. "Could I have that cup of water now?"

"You'll be lucky if I don't drown you in it."

She walked over to Punch and Captain Brady at the wheel. "Captain Brady, that man over there is ill, and I thought I might fetch him some water."

Brady looked at Dunkin lying on the deck and chuckled. "Looks like someone hasn't found his sea legs yet. The water's in a barrel in the bow."

Punch said, "You looked like you knew him."

"I've, uh, seen him in the market before, that's all. He's sort of hard to miss, with those suits." She walked quickly away.

She found the barrel and filled a metal cup with water.

She'd have to tell Dunkin to buzz off the second they landed in Reek, or he'd blow everything. Why couldn't he have left her alone? She was livid. She doused a handkerchief in water, then returned to Dunkin and helped him take a few sips of water. When he'd finished drinking, she dabbed his forehead with the cool cloth.

"Thank you," he muttered.

"I'm sorry I called you a bucket of spit."

"I am sorry I called you a cobra."

She helped him take another sip of water. Some color seemed to be returning to his face.

"Can you stand?" she asked.

"I think so."

"Let's go to the bunk where you can lie down." She helped him up, putting her arm around him. He smelled awful.

Once inside the cabin, she led him to a cot and told him to

lie down, which he did gratefully. When she saw that he was resting soundly, she returned to the deck. Brady had once again taken the wheel of *The Milking Cow*. Where was Punch?

She walked around the deck until she spotted him sitting quietly on the bow. She went to join him and saw he was enjoying a bowl of fried fish and rice. It smelled fantastic.

The only sound was the boat slicing through the water. She opened her mouth to say hello when Punch spoke. "How's your friend?"

Startled, Ida almost lost her footing.

Punch laughed.

“He's not my friend,” she replied. "He's sleeping."

"Good."

She sat down next to him. "What are you doing up here?”

“Enjoying a quiet moment, I suppose.”

After a few silent minutes, Ida inhaled and said as coolly as possible, “So, what are we going to pick up in Reek anyway?”

26

"We aren't picking up anything," Punch said. "*I* am picking up a package and you happen to be with me, okay?"

"Ok. Sheesh. So what are *you* picking up?"

A squeaky voice cut through the air. "Hey there, miss!"

It was Two Boots. Ida glared at him, wishing a shark would leap across the deck and nip off his head.

Two Boots ignored the look, jiggling his eyebrows. "I brought you some lunch!" He handed her a bowl of fish and sat down uncomfortably close to her.

Punch stood. "Why don't I let the two of you have some time alone?" He grinned like he was doing Ida an enormous favor. *How mortifying.*

"No, really—" It was too late. Punch was gone. Two Boots' face was only two inches from Ida's. She leaned in. "You really don't know how to take a hint, do you, kid?"

"Wha?" Two Boots looked crushed. "But I saved you the biggest bowl of fish . . ." His ridiculous red hair seemed to droop in disappointment.

Ida felt like a jerk. "That was nice of you. Thanks."

He arched his brow. "How about a kiss?"

She shoved him so hard he nearly fell off *The Milking Cow*.

Ida spotted land within the hour and knew they'd reach Reek soon. She didn't have much time to consult with Dunkin. When she went down to the bunks, she found him curled up on the cot, exactly as she'd left him.

"Dunkin," she hissed. "Wake up!"

His eyes gradually peeled open.

"We need to talk."

Wiping some drool from his chin, he managed to sit up. He still looked green.

"Once we're in Reek, you're on your own. If Punch thinks we're working together, I'm toast. Understand?"

"Yes, yes. Of course. I will follow you from a respectable distance. You will not even know I am there."

Ida stared at his cobalt suit. "Great choice of wardrobe, Dunk. You'll blend right in."

"I brought a disguise, and do not call me 'Dunk.'"

"Stay out of our way and out of sight, and everything should be fine."

"What if you need me?"

"I won't."

"But what if you do?"

Ida sighed. "I'll yell."

"What will you yell? We need a strong signal."

"I'll yell, 'Hey, Spongehead!'"

He frowned. "I have a feeling that this is meant as an insult, but I am choosing to ignore it. Fine. 'Spongehead' it is."

"Great. See you up top."

Ida returned to the deck. Shortly after, Dunkin emerged looking slightly more refreshed than before. Before long *The Milking Cow* was docking in Reek.

Captain Brady clapped his hands and signaled for his passengers to gather round. When they were assembled, he said, "I'll be returning to the Unfinished City tomorrow. I expect you to be here by noon. You all have return tickets, but I will wait for no man . . . " He glanced at Ida. "Or child. I remind you that Reek is a popular port town, and as such it attracts all sorts of characters and underlings. You cannot behave here as you would at home. Please watch your purses and wallets. They have a habit of disappearing in Reek. And be wary of strangers. That little old lady wanting a crust of bread might be an expert with a three-bladed gilly knife."

Punch smirked like he'd heard this a million times. Ida was not impressed.

"Now, that having been said, I would like to say that Reek is my hometown, and it also holds many charms and fascinations. We have the best entertainment in the land, and the food is unsurpassable. I recommend you see the Bockerian Circus and try the breakfast at the House of Salt; both are favorites of mine. My men will help you debark, and I shall see you tomorrow."

Pinching Ida's sleeve, Dunkin whispered, "This is actually quite exciting, like something out of one of Momma's novels."

Ida ignored him, taking a step away. *What part of* "we don't know each other" *did he not understand?*

Dunkin, Punch, and Ida picked up their bags, walked down the gangway, and stepped onto the dock. Punch started walking without a word and Ida quickly followed, afraid that Dunkin would be tempted to speak to her again.

When they were a block away from the ship, she looked back over her shoulder. Dunkin removed a large black hat from his satchel. He put it on, pulling the rim down in front of his eyes. Was this his "disguise?" Because it did nothing to camouflage his blue suit or four-foot, ten-inch frame.

Ida thought, *I might as well have a gargantuan butterfly following me.*

Punch led her into the chaos of a fish market, where

hawkers tried to out-sell and out-yell their competitors. Housewives sniffed for the freshest catch of the day, while their barefoot children ran amuck in the mud and fish scales. Ida wrinkled her nose. “It smells dreadful.”

Punch inhaled deeply. ”Smells like a real city!”

Fifty feet behind them, a small, filthy boy ran up to Dunkin. “Nice suit!” he laughed, as he swung an enormous halibut at Dunkin’s rear end. It landed with a smack, and the child and his friends howled with laughter.

Dunkin spun around, eyes flaming, and roared at them, “May Aquacious drown you and the inbred mother that reared you!”

The children ran away giggling, but several people in the market turned to look at Dunkin, including an incredulous Ida.

Whispering spread around him: “Did he say ‘Aquacious?";“How old-fashioned”; and “Must be from a small town.”

Punch even noticed, turning toward the commotion. “What’s that guy doing?”

“Who?”

“The guy from the boat, in the crazy suit."

“How should I know?”

“You were taking care of him. Didn’t you talk to him?”

“No, he was too busy making puke pies. Can we go?”

Punch gawked for a moment, but Dunkin had enough sense to leave and walk in another direction.

Punch and Ida continued through the fish market. Ida was afraid of Mr. Loor and what he would do if he discovered her duplicity, but she now realized she didn’t know what *Punch* would do if he found out. He'd been under Loor’s nasty tutelage almost his whole life. Plus, his name was “Punch,” and it wasn't because he liked to hug people.

27

Ida had never seen anything quite like Reek. The buildings were tall, thin, and multi-storied. They were squished up against one another, as if they were holding their breath until she and Punch had passed. The Unfinished City didn't have such height or density, since the citizens had only a year to build everything. The buildings here had stone or brick walls and durable slate roofs, but nothing looked new. It was all crumbling or rotting. One could see that Reek had once been a fine town, but those days had come and gone.

Ida was so fascinated by the architecture that she barely noticed when Punch turned up a narrow street. Before she followed, she checked for Dunkin behind them, but he was nowhere in sight. Maybe he was a good spy after all?

She caught up to Punch, who was half-way up the block, standing in front of a dull gray door. "Go wait in that tea shop," he told her, pointing to a cafe across the street. "Don't go *anywhere* until I come back. Understand?"

This was it. He was about to pick up the package. She could feel it.

"I won't be long," he said. "Probably twenty or thirty minutes. Do you need money?"

Never one to turn down gold, she said, "Yes."

After he handed her five gold pieces, she obediently walked over to the teashop and sat at one of the tables, all the while watching him like a hawk.

He knocked on the gray door, and it opened halfway. Ida could just make out a face emerging from the darkness—an old woman with the severe expression of a cactus. Punch whispered something, and the scowling woman let him in.

Ida continued to stare, but nothing else happened. The building had dark windows obscured by red velvet curtains. A small sign hung above the doorway that read "Mr. Orange's House of Curiosities?"

She didn't understand why anyone would put a question mark on the name of a business. Surely the owner knew if it was a "House of Curiosities" or not. It seemed very curious to Ida. *Aha*! she thought. *How clever of Mr. Orange to begin the curiosities before one has even entered the shop!* She found herself smiling.

Someone peeked out a curtained window—the old woman with the cactus face.

Ida left the teashop before anyone could ask for her order. She looked up and down the street. Where was Dunkin? He could knock on this door and ask to see the House of Curiosities. Of course he disappeared as soon as she actually needed him.

Impatient, she approached the door. She pulled on the handle, but it wouldn't budge. She pressed a rusted doorbell, but instead of hearing a chime, she heard a cat's meow.

Someone shuffled inside. The harsh old woman stuck her head out the door. "Yes?" Her voice sounded like she'd been sucking on rocks.

Ida smiled sweetly. "Hello. I'm here to see the curiosities."

The woman seemed surprised. "You are?"

"Yes."

"You know there's an entrance fee."

"Of course," Ida lied.

"Okay, then." The lady opened the door so Ida could enter.

It was terrifically dark, and Ida couldn't see a thing until her eyes adjusted. In her brief moment of blindness, she wondered if she were about to be robbed or murdered. When she was able to see, she could make out a little ticket booth. The old woman sat inside of it, only now she wore a little red cap with elastic that ran under her chin.

"Welcome to Mr. Orange's House of Curiosities? That'll be three gold coins."

Ida begrudgingly handed her the coins, and the woman gave her a small blue ticket which was faded and worn.

"I'll need that ticket back when you're finished," the woman grumbled. "We've only got the one."

Agreeing, Ida looked for an entrance but could see none. The walls were covered in the same heavy velvet as the windows. The old lady appeared again, only this time she was wearing a top hat. Ida noted that her sagging chin still held the indentation of the elastic from the last hat.

The woman pulled back a section of velvet fabric, causing dust to dance into the stale air. She grumpily announced to the ceiling, "Our next tour is about to begin. Please step this way. No shoving."

Walking through the pulled-back cloth, Ida found herself in a long hallway. The only light came from a series of display windows that were cut into the sides of the walls. She could hear the faint noise of water dripping, as if she were entering a cave. The velvet swooshed shut behind her.

The first display contained an odd-shaped set of teeth with a set of silver molars. According to the placard, this was supposed to be evidence that a certain species of ape had mastered dentistry. Ida rolled her eyes and moved on.

Next was the stomach of a man who had purportedly eaten an entire fishing boat. The stomach was bigger than the globe in Mr. Loor's office and had strange pointed areas, as if wood pieces or nails were inside.

This place was bonkers. Ida wanted to look closely at every display, but she had no time to spare. Walking on, she found another pitch-black room filled with the same velvet-curtained walls as the foyer. She stirred up mold spores and dust in every room she entered. Here she found a model of a horse cart with square wheels that had crossed Venn, pictures of a child who was born with a rubber spine, and a very unnerving map of the Dark World.

Ida pictured a display of herself. The placard would read, "Eighty-year-old woman stuck in the body of twelve-year-old girl. Do not touch. Will bite."

If she didn't play her cards right, this is exactly where she could end up. She had to figure out what Punch was doing here. So far, nothing she'd seen had given her a clue.

The next room was different in that it had a reasonable amount of lighting. Ida was almost blinded by the change. It was a cheery sort of room with flowered wallpaper and painted portraits hung in fancy gilded frames. Ida would have written the paintings off as the usual aristocratic dullness, except for one thing: the portraits were all of cats. Circling the room, she came upon the explanation.

This room exists as a permanent tribute to the cats of Mr. Orange. Each one of these heroes accompanied Mr. Orange across Venn and into the Dark World and acted as companion, guide, and chef. Many of these trips were perilous, and more than one cat lost his or her life in pursuit of artifacts and sacred knowledge. Mr. Orange's House of Curiosities? would not be possible without these valiant souls.

Ida was amused. Surely this was a theatrical touch created

by Mr. Orange to pull on heartstrings. In the portraits, the cats looked oddly surprised, as if they had been caught with one paw in the birdcage. The artist had put them in dignified clothing, with cravats and blazers and, in one case, a pipe. Ida approached the painting of an orange tabby and was admiring the realistic folds of his silk shirt when she heard murmuring.

Putting her ear against the wallpaper, she strained to hear more. No entrance was in sight, but she was sure that people were behind this wall. She glanced at the painting hanging next to her. The frame was not flat against the wall; it stuck out almost half an inch. She passed her finger along the inside of the frame and felt something. Peering inside the crack, she saw a tiny hook. She brazenly used her pinky to lift the hook. The frame swung open. Ida's breath caught. It was a door!

28

Opening the door more widely, Ida saw a passageway. It begged to be explored. Did she have time?

She double-checked that no one was watching her, rearranged her satchel, and climbed into the crawl space. She shut the painting behind her in case the old woman came looking for her, and crawled through the darkness, worried she might run face-first into a spiderweb (she didn't mind spiders, but no-one likes one in their hair).

She'd crawled about thirty feet when her hands touched something deliciously soft. Deciding she must be behind a velvet curtain, she felt along the folds of the material until she found a seam. She peeked carefully through.

She was shocked at what she saw.

Young girls and their mothers filled a small room. The mothers were chatting with one another, looking quite pleased, while the girls huddled in a corner, looking miserable. Ida could see immediately why they would be unhappy. None of them had any hair. Each one had been shorn like a sheep—their heads covered in nicks and raw spots where the razor had slipped. The girls' eyes were red from crying, and stray hair lay on the floor. The shearing had only just occurred.

Ida was more confused than ever. She'd expected to find a cellar full of weapons, not weeping children! And where was Punch?

One of the mothers turned to her daughter, announcing it was time to leave. The girl rose sulkily. As they stood, the mothers fawned over them. Ida heard, "There, there. It'll grow back," and "You're always beautiful to me," and "Now we can buy Daddy a birthday present."

A tall mother banged on a door in the corner. "We're ready to go, Mr. Orange!" she cried.

The large lock scraped as it was turned. In came an odd-looking man with wild red hair and a nose like a rutabaga. His eyes were shifty, as if he were looking at everyone at once.

"Thank you again, ladies! All the best now. Ta-ta." He ushered everyone out with the broom in his hand.

When he was the only person left, he did a quick sweep of the floor, picking up the few remaining strands of blonde, brunette, and auburn hair.

As the bald girls had been marching out, Ida couldn't help but think of a regiment of young boys. Was that the point? Were Mr. Orange and Mr. Loor conspiring to make girls look like boys? Perhaps they were going to be trained as a secret army, or they were going to smuggle weapons into the Unfinished City.

The dust in the curtains tickled Ida's nose. She needed to sneeze! She grabbed her nose with her thumb and forefinger and tried to force the sneeze back down, but it was no use. The tickle filled her head and was ready to shoot out her nostrils. She held her nose so tightly that when the sneeze did emerge it became a raspy squeak.

Mr. Orange stopped sweeping. He scanned the room and then looked at the curtain that hid Ida. He approached slowly, peering at the velvet cloth, waiting to see if another sound would emerge. He put out his hand, ready to seize the fabric and reveal what lay behind, when the door behind him opened and one of the bald girls reentered.

"I forgot my hat," she said, sniveling.

Mr. Orange spun around, startled by the whiny voice.

Ida knew this was her chance. Turning around as fast as possible in the tiny space, she bolted back through the dark tunnel as quickly as her legs would take her. She was in such a panic that when she reached the painting, she unhooked it and fell *smack* through the hole onto the floor. She stood with a groan and quickly shut the painting behind her.

Barely a second after she'd re-hooked the latch, the old woman appeared. Now she was wearing a silk suit that perfectly matched the ensemble of the tabby cat in the portrait. Sitting atop her gray hair was a headband with a pair of tiny orange ears.

"You are finished with the tour." This was not a question.

"Yes," Ida answered, not knowing if she was busted or not.

"You enjoyed the House of Curiosities?" Again, this was not a question.

"Oh, yes!" Ida answered. "It is quite . . . remarkable. I was gobsmacked, in fact."

"Please make your way to the exit. No shoving."

The old woman ushered Ida into the next room, where she saw a door that led outside to freedom. She headed swiftly for the door, trying not to limp from her fall. She'd just touched the handle when the old woman cried out, "Where do you think you're going, you little trickster?"

Ida froze. The woman had seen her open the painting after all. Possible explanations raced through her head.

"You thought you could just leave with our ticket, didn't you?"

Ticket?

Sighing with relief, Ida found the faded ticket in her pocket. She handed it to the old woman. "Sorry about that."

"Of course you are. Swindler."

Ida opened the door and ran gratefully into the clear, cool afternoon, wondering if she could make it back to the teashop before Punch.

29

When Punch entered the tea house, he found Ida sitting quietly in a corner nibbling ginger biscuits. She pretended not to notice him until he sat down. He carried a package wrapped in brown paper that Ida tried not to stare at. It was long and thin, and seemed heavy.

"That took longer than usual," he said. "Sorry."

Ida shrugged as if she'd forgotten why they were even there.

"Let's go," he said.

Wiping the crumbs from her face, Ida placed two gold coins on the table, and followed him out the door. "Did everything go as planned?"

"Yup."

They walked back the way they'd come.

"You got everything you needed?" she said.

He smirked. "I'm not telling you what I picked up, so you can stop trying to find out."

She scowled. "You're so boring. You listen to adults more than any kid I've ever met."

"What's that supposed to mean?"

"You know exactly what it means. You're a suck-up."

"Better a suck-up than a screw-up. Loor told us that you've never had a stable home and that you're fairly deranged, so don't think you can trick me."

I already have. Loor thinks you're about to betray him. She bit her tongue, desperately wanting to tell him how wrong he was. "You think you're so smart," was all she could say.

He marched along, smiling.

His smugness triggered her temper. "Has it ever occurred to you that the flood is good for some people and that you're hurting them if you stop it?"

His smile disappeared. "How did you know this package had anything to do with the flood?"

"Maybe I'm not as off-my-rocker as Loor thinks."

"No. He's right. You're definitely a freak."

She was used to being called a freak, but people usually said it after they discovered her secret. She wasn't used to someone saying it without a reason. "You *didn't answer* my question. What if you hurt people when you stop the flood?"

"We want to modernize the Unfinished City and improve people's lives with an industrial society."

She rolled her eyes at this quote from Loor. "Do you want the Unfinished City to be like Reek? They have modern industry, and look at this place! It might've been nice once—now it's rotting from the inside out. The people look miserable, and Captain Brady said the city is full of crime. Why is *this* a better way to live?"

"No one said we wanted to be like Reek. We're going to be a unique city—like nowhere ever seen—and we'll have modern schools, and I'll become an engineer. When we stop the flood—well, it will be a glorious day."

He was still giving no hints as to *how* they might stop the flood. "What if Aquacious is real?" she asked.

He raised an eyebrow. "I knew you were weird, but I didn't

think you were dumb. Do you really believe there's a half-woman, half-seahorse with magical powers that lives in the harbor?"

Ida would be lying if she said she did, but she wanted Punch to at least consider some of the people who, like her, needed the flood.

"Maybe I don't believe in her, but a lot of people do, and it'll break their hearts if the flood ends."

"Why do you care so much?"

"Why don't you care?" she said back hotly.

"I don't understand why you came back to us if you've become a Delugist."

"I'm not a Delugist. I just . . . think we should be able to have lively debates about important issues. Don't you?"

He adjusted his glasses. "Why?"

Why, Ida? Think. "Because . . . friends debate about stuff."

"You think we're friends?"

"Don't you?"

"You blackmailed me, you stole my job—*I* was supposed to take care of the Aquacious statue—and just when I thought we were rid of you, you show up and ruin my trip here!"

"I'm in big trouble for destroying that statue. The Mayor wants me hanged! Mr. Loor wanted to protect you, so he—"

He put his hand up. "Save it. I already heard Mr. Loor's explanation. I don't need his protection or anyone else's. I can take care of myself."

"Then why haven't you told him about Preanne?"

He stopped dead and got in her face. "Don't you ever say her name out loud again, or I'll turn you into the Mayor myself, understand?"

She nodded, shocked at how fierce he sounded.

"You must really like her," she said.

His face betrayed a flash of sadness.

She said quietly, "If you're not supposed to spend time with Delugists, it must be really tough—"

"Drop it."

They walked in silence.

She sighed. "She seemed to really like you, when I saw you together."

"Really?" he said before he could stop himself.

"She had a huge smile. I could tell. She likes you a lot."

After a few more blocks, he said, "Sorry I got angry. I, uh, have a temper."

"Yeah. So do I." She was relieved when they arrived at the tavern called the House of Salt, which Captain Brady had recommended.

"Go inside and eat dinner," Punch said. "We have rooms booked upstairs for tonight."

"Where are you going?" she asked.

"None of your business." His tone was more teasing than mean.

"Going to look for a ring for Preanne?"

His face turned crimson. "No! I, uh, promised I'd find her a pair of buckled shoes."

Ida smiled, touched he'd shared the embarrassing information. She thought of Preanne's face and giggle. "I would buy a pink or purple pair—something *really* girly."

"Oh, uh, thanks."

"And I can take the package inside if you'd rather not carry it," she said.

"Nice try," he said, walking away.

❧ 30 ❧

As Ida entered the tavern, her stomach rumbled like an approaching storm. Several people turned to stare, not sure if a young girl should be allowed in a tavern on her own—Ida was, of course, accustomed to these type of looks. Scanning the dining room, she was surprised to see an unattractive woman in a garish yellow dress moping in a corner who looked just like Dunkin.

The woman raised her head to look at Ida, and a look of relief filled her face.

Holy gooseberries. It *was* Dunkin!

Ida rushed to his table. "Are you all right?" she asked.

"Do I look all right?"

"No, although that cut is very slimming on you."

"Oh, ha ha! Let's all laugh at Dunkin, shall we? Who cares that I almost died today, or that I was left to rot in a smelly ditch? Let us forget all of that and just sit right here and have a nice giggle at the little man who was stupid enough to try and help his friend."

Ida's mocking smile disappeared. "What happened?"

"Buy me dinner first—my money was stolen—and pay for my drink while you're up there."

Ida approached the bar, which she barely reached. "Two pork pies, please, and one milkwine."

The bartender squinted at her. "How old are you?"

"It's not for me," Ida said. "It's for him." She nodded toward Dunkin.

"You friends with that banana peel?" the bartender said.

"He's not crazy. He's just annoying his wife."

"Come again?"

"Well, his wife was really getting on him tonight, about money, children, drinking, everything! So finally he said, 'I wish you'd shut your gob,' and she said, 'The day I shut my gob is the day you wear an evening gown.'"

"Say no more," the bartender said, winking. "I have a nag of a wife myself. I'd wear a pink negligee if I thought she'd leave me alone. I'll get you that drink."

The people at the bar, who'd all heard Ida's tale, raised their mugs to Dunkin in respect.

When Ida sat back down, Dunkin eyed her suspiciously. "What did you say to that bartender?"

"I just offered an explanation for your ensemble. We don't need to attract any extra attention." She handed him his drink.

"I do not mind the dress itself so much," he said, touching the fabric, "But I would rather be caught dead than be seen in this yellow."

She smiled. "Are you ready to tell me what happened?"

After a long gulp of milkwine, he wiped his mouth and told his story.

"I followed your instructions and stayed back so Punch would not see me, but I got too far behind and lost sight of you. I started searching random streets, hoping to catch up. I turned onto one small street that turned out to be a foul-smelling alley."

"Uh-oh," Ida said, not liking the sound of this development.

"A bald man was there, smoking." Dunkin picked up a knife and held it like a cigar. "*Can I help you, little man?* he said. His voice was deep and raw, like he had been sucking on fish bones."

Dunkin put down the knife, clasped his hands together, and looked up as if speaking to a giant. "I said, *No, sir. Just took a wrong turn.* I tipped my hat and tried to leave, but two men appeared who looked like boulders with hair. They wore long coats, most likely full of knives and rusted ice picks."

"What did they take?" Ida said, cutting to the chase.

His face sank. "Everything—my suit, my hat, my coins, my watch."

"I'm sorry about your new hat," Ida said, although she wasn't really.

"I do not care about anything except the watch. It was a gift from my Poppa. The only thing left—" He reached for his pocket square, which wasn't there. He picked up a napkin, dabbed his eyes, and blew his nose.

"I'm really sorry." Ida hated to see him so upset.

"Momma will be furious."

"So how did you end up . . . " She pointed at the yellow dress. "Like this?"

"After my delightful encounter with those cutthroats, I woke up in a ditch off the side of the road. I had a throbbing pain on the back of my head, and well . . . I was naked. I lay there bruised and battered, while people turned their faces away as if I were some sort of deviant! Not one hand offered, not one word of concern! As soon as I realized where I was and what had happened, I ran for cover behind a horse, but, unfortunately, it was too tall to provide the necessary coverage. I ran to the back of a row of houses and, luckily, found a clothesline draped with drying clothes. Unluckily, the line belonged to a woman."

Glancing down, Dunkin noticed his black chest hair poofing out from the sweetheart neckline. He tugged up the dress and tried to sit up straight in a dignified manner.

Ida worked very hard not to smile, but Dunkin seemed to sense her amusement. "I have decided that Reek is a dreadful place, and I have resolved never to leave the Unfinished City again."

The bartender arrived with their pork pies.

"You'll feel better after some food." Dizzy at the smell, Ida tucked into hers at once. Dunkin only picked at his, which was concerning to her. "Do you want to hear about my afternoon?" she asked. "It was very strange—"

"I don't, actually. I'm going to finish my dinner and go to bed, and I don't wish to hear about anything else that might disturb my sleep."

She was disappointed. Who else could she tell about the bald girls?

Dunkin gave up on his meal and put down his fork. "I'm glad you are safe, and I bid you good-night." He stood and shuffled toward the stairs, holding up his ruffled skirt.

Ida hoped he wasn't angry with her. Surely tomorrow he would be back to his old self. She had no idea if she should call today a success or a failure. All she knew for certain was that she was going to go to bed with a headful of perplexing questions.

31

Ida awoke in good spirits. She'd come up with a plan, and she always felt better when she had a plan. If she wanted to find out more about the girls with the shaved heads, then who better to ask than a girl with a shaved head? And where does one find a young girl on a Thursday morning? School, of course. Like all masterful plans, it was brilliant in its simplicity.

When she decided the hour was reasonable, she knocked on Dunkin's door. He'd bathed, shaved, and sent out a porter to buy him a new suit. Ida was pleased to see that the suit was a brown tweed—much less likely to draw attention than the blue silk. She invited him down to breakfast.

They were soon sitting at a table covered with warm rolls, gingerberry jam, fresh clotted cream, slabs of ham covered in molasses, and coffee so strong it made Ida's feet twitch. It was an excellent meal, just as Brady had promised.

As she smeared jam onto another roll, she explained to Dunkin everything she'd seen the day before. He was so focused on the ham that she wasn't sure he was listening.

"Dunkin?"

"Umffahs."

"Are you listening to me?"

He swallowed his food. "Of course."

"So what do you think?"

"It's the finest pig I have ever tasted."

"No! I mean about the—"

"I know what you meant. I was just teasing you, my little cabbage." He wiped his beard with his napkin. "Forgive me if I am a bit mischievous today. I was quite close to death yesterday, Ida, and it was . . . " He stared into the distance as he searched for the words to describe the truth of mortality. " . . . Stirring. And now I feel lucky to be holding this steaming cup of coffee, eating sweet ham, and talking to you."

Ida was touched. "Thank you, Dunkin. I'm glad you're feeling more yourself today, because I have a plan. I think we should start by checking the local—"

"Ch ch," Dunkin interrupted. "You can eliminate the 'we' from that sentence. I intend to return to *The Milking Cow* immediately and wait on board until it is time to leave this afternoon."

"But I thought—"

"I know what you thought, but underneath my rugged exterior lurks the bravery of this clotted cream. I know that now, and there is no shame in it. I just have not got your gumption, Ida. I would do nothing but hinder your investigation."

Ida was taken aback. How could he give up so easily? But then, who was she to ask him to put himself in harm's way again? "Okay. It might help you to board early, with the seasickness and all. You can get your sea legs before we leave the dock."

Dunkin smiled. "Thank you for understanding."

"Of course." Only yesterday, Ida had yelled at him for following her on this trip, and now she found herself regretting that he wouldn't be helping her any longer. She grabbed her bag. "I should get going. See you at the boat."

"Now?" Dunkin asked. "You have not finished your breakfast. Look at the chocolate swans they have just brought!"

"I'm full." She walked toward the door, but, changing her mind, she returned, grabbed both chocolate swans, and put them into her bag.

"Hey! I wanted one of those," Dunkin whined.

"I'm footing the bill. You can order twenty of them for all I care."

She left Dunkin with a frustrated expression on his face and jam on his new suit.

She exited the tavern and searched the streets. After a while, she saw what she was looking for: a single woman of a certain age shuffling down the sidewalk. Ida approached her with a warm smile. "Excuse me, ma'am."

The woman peered down her ruffled blouse at Ida. "Yes, dearie, how can I help you?"

Eyes wide, Ida spoke like a simpleton. "Today is suppose' to be my first day of school, 'cept I got lost and can't find the schoolhouse."

"Where is your mother, young lady? She should be escorting you."

Ida looked away sadly. "Ma's real sick. She can't walk nowhere."

"She can't walk *anywhere*. I should say you could do with some schooling. The closest schoolhouse is down Grissel Lane, three blocks south, and then one block west."

Ida curtsied. "Thank you, ma'am." She took off running south.

The lady yelled after her, "I might suggest you comb your hair!"

Ida yelled back, "I might suggest you shave your mustache!"

The woman gasped in indignation.

Luckily, when Ida arrived at the school, class had not yet begun. The children were lolling around a small play yard. Ida spotted two girls with newly-shaved heads. She also saw girls who had a short, downy growth, as if they'd been shorn less than a month before.

A ball lay on the ground. Walking casually over, Ida picked it up and began to toss it in the air. She did this over and over, letting the ball go a little higher each time. She watched the two baldest girls out of the corner of her eye. When she felt the moment was right, she carefully aimed her toss so that it would hit one of them in the head. The ball hit its target with a dull thud.

"Ow!" the girl cried.

"Are you okay?" her friend asked her.

They both glared at Ida, who looked horribly guilty. "I'm *so* sorry. It slipped."

"Now I'm going to have an ugly lump, and I'll look worse than I already do!" The girl was close to tears.

Ida approached her. "Do you want some chocolate?"

"Chocolate?" The girl smiled.

Reaching into her bag, Ida pulled out the two chocolate swans. "Here, and one for your friend. I'm real sorry." The girls looked at one another, and then grabbed the swans from Ida's hands as quickly as toads snapping at flies.

While they stuffed their faces, Ida said, "My name is Mildred. How about you?"

One of the girls said, "Cecilia," revealing smeared chocolate on her front teeth.

The other one said, "Henrietta." She licked her fingers, having already swallowed her swan whole.

It was time for Ida to take a chance. She chirped, "Your hairstyle is really neat. How did you get it?"

The girls looked at her as if she'd said that trees were made of butter.

"Are you crazy?" Cecilia asked.

"Are you making fun of us?" Henrietta added.

"Not at all," said Ida. "I've always wanted short hair, but my mother won't let me cut it."

Henrietta whined, "But ours is even shorter than the boys'! Everyone teases us and calls us Peach-Heads. It's dreadful."

"So why did you cut it off?" Ida ventured.

Cecelia made a sound like an angry pig. "*We* didn't, obviously. It was our mothers."

"But why?" Ida felt excited. She was extremely close to hearing the information she needed.

The school bell rang.

Cecelia and Henrietta walked toward the schoolhouse.

"Wait!" Ida cried.

They turned back to her in perfect sync.

"Did your mothers *want* you to look like boys?" Ida asked.

Henrietta looked at her again as if she were crackers. "No, stupid. They cut off our hair because they wanted the hair. Why else?"

"What did you get in return?"

"Cecelia's mother used the money to buy the whole family shoes. My mother bought herself a new dress. Come on! We're going to be late." Henrietta grabbed Ida's arm, dragging her into the schoolhouse.

Ida had no time to think. She couldn't tell the girls she didn't go to this school, or they would know she was up to something dubious. The next thing Ida knew, she was sitting in the back of a classroom.

The dullard schoolmarm began with basic arithmetic. Ida counted her own split ends. The teacher moved on to spelling and grammar, causing Ida to groan so loud that everyone turned to look at her. The only thing interesting out of the whole morning was a chemistry experiment during which the yawn-inducing teacher mixed caustic soda with water. She poured the mixture into a third beaker containing the skeleton of a mouse, which she'd found behind the bookshelves of the classroom. As soon as the soda and water began to react they created a corrosive liquid that quickly ate its way through the skeleton. The children oohed and ahhed, and a few girls screamed in disgust. When the skeleton was completely gone, Ida stood and gave the teacher a standing ovation.

"Bravo, ma'am. Bravo! I am so impressed with this outstanding demonstration of the miracles of science that I'm convinced you'll not be able to top yourself today. In the name of ending on a high note, I now choose to excuse myself. But again, thank you for your contribution to my education. I hope to catch your act again in the future." She backed out the door and made a run for it.

The teacher stood with her mouth open, unsure whether she should run after the strange child. In the end, she decided she didn't want to encourage any of the other children to speak their minds, so she distracted them as quickly as possible, demanding that Harry Finick hand over his left shoe so she could dissolve it in her remarkable solution.

32

Dunkin sauntered back and forth on the deck of *The Milking Cow*. He felt perfectly calm within the safety of the ship. He'd told himself he was practically back in the comfort of the Unfinished City—their journey home was set to begin in an hour—yet something was bothering him, like a gnat caught in his trousers. He couldn't ignore it, for deep down he knew what it was: his own cowardice. He'd let Ida continue on with her mission, and she could encounter greater danger than the three thugs Dunkin had faced.

This morning, he'd felt solid in his decision not to join her. He'd felt confident from his perfectly coiffed hair down to his newly shined shoes. Now the doubt was starting to weigh him down so much, he felt he might sink *The Milking Cow*.

As he contemplated his lack of valor, he heard someone approaching. Walking to the port side of the ship, he looked down the dock. It was Punch, and he was trying to manage an armful of packages.

Dunkin jumped over the edge of the boat onto the dock. He jogged up to meet Punch. "Can I give you a hand?"

"That would be grand," Punch said.

Dunkin took several shoeboxes from the top of the stack, leaving Punch with the very wide, thin package. They approached the boat slowly.

"My name is Dunkin," Dunkin said amiably.

"I'm Punch," Punch said politely. "Are you feeling better?"

"Indeed, yes." Gesturing toward the shoeboxes, Dunkin said, "Did some shopping, I take it?"

"I couldn't make up my mind," Punch said sheepishly. "So I bought a few things."

"Don't be embarrassed. I love shoes. Must have a dozen pairs at least."

Punch looked indignant. "They're not for me."

Dunkin smiled. "Of course not." When they reached *The Milking Cow*, he said, "Why don't we swing the long one over together?" Perhaps Dunkin could help Ida today after all.

Putting down the shoeboxes, Dunkin took one end of the wide parcel. Punch held onto the other end. They swung it back and forth, and, when it had enough momentum, Dunkin shouted, "Now!"

Dunkin released his grip, but the second before he did, he allowed his fingernail to pierce through the plain brown paper. As the package left his hands, he could hear the paper tear.

Punch gasped at the sound. Suddenly his package was sprawled out on the deck, its innards revealed.

Punch leapt onto the boat and blocked the torn package from Dunkin's view, but it was too late. Dunkin had already seen what was inside, and he was astonished.

"May I help you with that? I am so sorry," Dunkin began.

"STAY AWAY," Punch ordered. He gathered up the spilled contents and stuffed it back into the package, which he tied off with fishing line he found on the deck. He carefully dragged the package toward the cabins below, careful to cause no new tears in the paper. As he disappeared, Dunkin could hear him cursing.

Dunkin smiled. Ida would be so pleased! Dunkin had actually turned out to be a semi-decent detective.

DUNKIN BECAME MORE and more anxious as the minutes ticked by. *Where was Ida?* It was almost noon, and she was about to miss the boat. Two Boots was pulling in the gangway, and Captain Brady was unknotting the mooring lines.

Suddenly Ida appeared, sprinting up the dock. "Wait!" she cried.

The Captain shook his head. "You're pushing your luck, kid."

Two Boots put the ramp of wood back down for her and she ran aboard.

Dunkin rushed to greet her. "Where were you? I was sure you'd been killed!"

"I'm fine," she said, out of breath. "I had an important errand to run."

As *The Milking Cow* set sail, Dunkin mopped his brow with a pocket square. "You cannot frazzle my nerves like that. I've been sweating through my new suit!"

"Don't be mad. It took me time to find this." She held up his watch.

Speechless, he took it. "But how . . . where . . . ?"

"I figured if someone stole it yesterday, someone would be selling it today, and I was right. There's a whole string of pawnbrokers close to the—"

He embraced her. "Thank you, young lady. Your heart is a moon over Motzia—always big and full."

"You're, uh, welcome," she said, seeming embarrassed.

Releasing her, he put on the watch, stroking the leather

strap that would always remind him of Poppa. "I will find you the finest sponge in all of the Unfinished City!"

She grinned. "Perfect."

Excited to tell her his news, Dunkin lowered his voice. "I have to talk to you." He walked her below for privacy, but when he opened the door to the sleeping cabin, he saw Punch inside. Punch glared at Dunkin like a snake taking in a gerbil. Unsettled, Dunkin quickly turned Ida and himself around and went back on deck.

When they found an isolated spot in the stern of the ship, they both opened their mouths at the same time: "IT'S HAIR!"

Each was equally surprised that the other already knew. First, Ida explained her experience at the schoolhouse, and then Dunkin told her about the package incident with Punch. Ida was very impressed with Dunkin. "I can't believe you found out the same information as me but without having to suffer through any math."

"Unfortunately, I do seem to have made an enemy," Dunkin said. "The boy looked at me like he would like to have my head stuffed and mounted."

"He's harmless. Just stay away from him until we land."

"Stay away? We're on a ship the size of a cracker!"

"You know what I mean."

Dunkin was puzzled. "What on earth can the hair be for? Supplying the Unfinished City with wigs is hardly going to stop the flood."

"I don't know yet, but it's driving me crazy."

They sat comparing theories about the hair for another hour, but neither was satisfied with any of the explanations. Finally, Dunkin lifted his nose in the air and said, "Is that food?"

Ida didn't answer. She was too preoccupied with the puzzle to think about eating.

"I am starving!" Dunkin said. "Shall I bring you back something?"

Ida nodded vaguely as Dunkin stood up. All this talk of conspiracy and intrigue had his stomach grumbling. The cook was on deck with a huge vat of hot soup. Dunkin knew the soup wouldn't begin to compare to his Momma's cooking, but it would have to do. He walked to the stern to wash his hands in the water barrel.

He found Punch there, also washing his hands. Punch's forehead was creased with worry but as soon as he saw Dunkin, his expression turned to anger. "You here to 'help' me again?"

"No, no. Just need to wash up." Dunkin wanted to turn around, but it seemed too late, and Punch was only a boy, after all. What harm could he do?

Pulling his hands from the water barrel, Punch advanced and was soon towering over Dunkin.

Dunkin now realized there was probably a great deal of harm the boy could do. He was large.

Dunkin took a step back. "It was an accident. No need to get angry."

"Was it? An accident? Or are you just a nosy Delugist?"

Dunkin took another step back. "Please. Remain calm."

"I'm very calm. You're the one who seems to be nervous."

Dunkin took one more step backward . . .

33

Ida sat alone on the bow, staring at the gray sea, contemplating the mystery of the hair. Over the wind, she heard a sound like a barrel dropping into the water. The noise brought her out of her reverie.

Where's Dunkin? Wasn't he supposed to bring me dinner? He'd been gone a strangely long time. She had a sudden sense of dread.

She jumped up and crossed the deck as swiftly as she could. She called Dunkin's name, but no one answered. When she reached the stern she found Punch staring into the ocean with a look of horror on his face.

"What's going on?" she asked, panicking. "Where's Dunkin?"

"I was talking to him . . . and he . . . he backed right off the ship!"

"He's in the water?" she said, praying she'd misunderstood.

He nodded, face white.

Running to Brady, who was at the wheel, she screamed, "*Stop* the ship! Dunkin's in the water! STOP!"

Captain Brady gave her a confused look, but as soon as her

words sunk in, he bellowed, "MAN OVERBOARD!!" A bell began to ring as he turned the ship around.

Ida scanned the waves. As she leaned forward, water sprayed her face—ice cold and salty—but all she could think of was Dunkin submerged in the violent waves, struggling, sinking, and it was her fault. He would never have been on this horrible journey if it weren't for her.

Two Boots cried out from the crow's nest, "Ahoy! I see somethin', Capt'n! Just ahead, to starboard!"

Ida's knees went weak as she looked to the right of the ship. At first she saw nothing, but soon she could make out a shape floating in the water. Whatever it was, it wasn't moving. Two sailors dove into the water and swam expertly toward the figure. As she waited for them to return, she felt time stop.

I'm so stupid. I'm so selfish! I knew this trip was dangerous. Dunkin has been nothing but kind to me and now . . .

When the men were alongside the boat, Captain Brady threw down a dinghy. Once it was secured around Dunkin, Brady and Two Boots heaved him up onto the deck. With misery, Ida thought that it looked as if they were hauling in a large boiled egg in a tweed suit. As Brady removed the dinghy, Ida could see that Dunkin's eyes were closed.

"Is he . . . ?" She couldn't bring herself to finish the sentence.

"Dead? Not yet," Brady answered. "Fetch me a barrel!" he told Two Boots.

Two Boots quickly returned with a cask of wine. Captain Brady laid Dunkin over the barrel, and then Brady and Two Boots rolled the barrel back and forth.

Ida was baffled. What on earth were they doing?

The crew was silent, and even the waves seemed to grow quiet as they all waited. After a minute of the rolling back and forth, Dunkin suddenly coughed up a bucket of seawater.

Captain Brady patted him on the back. "Well done!" The

Captain lifted Dunkin gently from the barrel and laid him on the deck.

Ida knelt beside Dunkin. “It’s okay. You’re safe. Don’t move.”

"Is he going to be alright?" Punch stood a few feet away.

Ida was seething. She pointed at Punch. “It was him! He tried to murder Dunkin!”

Shocked, Punch said, "It was an accident!"

Captain Brady looked at Punch and then at Ida. He had no idea what was going on.

"Arrest him!" Ida said.

Punch backed up, waving his hands. "You know me, Captain. I wouldn't do that!" Seeing Brady's uncertainty, he added, "Ask Dunkin!"

Dunkin, who'd only just stopped coughing up water, lay on his side, looking ready to pass out again.

Ida leaned in close to his face. "Dunkin. Did Punch throw you overboard?"

Everyone, including the sailors and the cook, leaned in to hear the answer. Dunkin seemed neither to hear nor understand the question. He stared straight ahead.

"He wasn't watching where he was going," Punch said. "He stepped right off the deck!"

Ida walked over to Punch and poked him in the chest. "Your story makes no sense. Even if he did fall, someone made it happen, and I know it was *you*."

Punch looked at everyone but her. "It wasn't! I sw—"

"Tie his hands," Captain Brady told two sailors. "We'll get the whole story when the little fella is ready to talk."

"I won't forget this," Punch said to Ida as his hands were bound.

"Good," she said. She would never forgive him.

After Punch was tied securely to one of masts, Brady said, "All hands to stations! Nothin' more to see!"

The men wandered away, whispering.

"Take this man downstairs so he can lay down," Brady told Ida.

Two Boots helped Ida get Dunkin down the stairs. Once Dunkin was on the cot, he faded in and out of consciousness. He had a horrible fever, and no matter how many blankets Ida piled on him, he seemed to stay chilled.

Even from below deck, she could hear Punch's tirades of complaint and anger—some toward Brady, but mostly toward her. When she left the cabin a few hours later, Captain Brady was back at the helm, and Punch was sleeping in an awkward position with his hands tied behind his back.

Ida approached Captain Brady. "Thank you for your help. If you hadn't turned the ship around, Dunkin would have drowned."

"I acted like a captain, that's all."

"Not everyone believes children, especially girls. Thank you for listening."

He seemed to ponder this. Ida thought he was about to comment on the injustice of it all, when he said, "We're about to dock."

Finally, thought Ida. This had been the longest trip of her life.

Narrowing his eyes, he added, "Law enforcement appear to be waiting on the docks."

"They're here for Punch?" Ida asked. She was furious, but did she really want him arrested?

"I had no way of sendin' a message, so no."

They weren't there for Punch. Ida's heart skipped a beat. *Maybe they've learned about the Aquacious statue. They could be here for me!*

She backed away from Brady. "Thanks, Captain. I'll go prepare Dunkin." Trying to look calm, she hurried back to the cabin. She grabbed her satchel as she looked regretfully at

Dunkin, who was still asleep. She would've liked to have taken him home to his Momma, and now she'd have to trust Captain Brady to get him home. Whispering, "Good-bye," she squeezed his hand.

She took a deep breath, opened the door, and strolled out nonchalantly. Smiling at one of the sailors, she casually strolled to the back of the ship. Why should they suspect that the police might be waiting for her, an adorable child? The same bias that led people to not listen to her should work to her advantage now.

She swung her bag to her back. Surely the ship was close enough to shore for her to swim to safety. Then she would flee into the mountains and hide out until the day of the flood. Once she'd done the Treatment, she'd be years older and would be unrecognizable. She smiled imagining her taller, longer-limbed self asking Ms. Neely for directions. The old bat would have no clue who Ida was.

Reaching the edge of the deck, Ida leaned forward, bent her knees, and jumped, but a large hand grabbed her bag, causing her to dangle off the edge of the boat, her feet hovering above the water. She peered up to see a sailor who outweighed her by at least a hundred pounds.

“Going somewhere?” asked Captain Brady. He stood next to the sailor who continued to dangle Ida above the water, enjoying her predicament.

“Hold onto her,” ordered Brady. “No one leaves my ship until I say so, got it?”

As Brady walked away, the sailor reeled Ida in like a hooked fish.

“You was in such a hurry to leave!" the beefy man said. "Maybe you the one who tried to kill that little guy?”

Ida was enraged. “Put me down.”

“Nah. Ya heard the Capt'n. I’m hanging onto ya ’til we're ashore.”

Much too soon, Ida felt the slowing of the ship and the mooring of the lines. Then she heard the police boarding the ship. Anxiety vibrated through every nerve-ending as she tried to figure out a way to escape.

A young policeman in a brand-new uniform peeked his head around a mast and saw Ida in the clutches of the deckhand. Eyes widening, the man yelled, "I found her, Sergeant Punctal! She's back here."

Ida's fear was confirmed. They were here for her.

The sailor lifted Ida higher. "Sounds like you been up to no good, little girlie." She gave him her best death-glare.

Sergeant Punctal arrived. Older than the first policeman, he had bulging eyes, ruddy cheeks, and a belly that suggested he enjoyed more than the occasional ale. The sergeant approached Ida and the sailor slowly. "We'll take her now."

The sailor dropped Ida roughly onto the deck, and Sergeant Punctal grabbed her by the wrist. The crew, including Captain Brady, gathered around to watch. A sickly-looking Dunkin appeared, wrapped in blankets and blinking against the daylight. "What is going on? Ida?"

"Dunkin, help!" she cried.

"This girl is under arrest," Sergeant Punctal announced.

"There has been some kind of mistake," Dunkin said. "Ida is not a criminal!"

Sergeant Punctal tied Ida's hands behind her. "This person is not really a child. We don't know how old she really is, but she's using dark magic to pretend to be a girl. The whole city knows about it."

Brady and the crew looked at Ida in shock. The deckhand who'd been holding her jumped away as if she were a cockroach.

Ida couldn't believe it. How had they found out? Had Dunkin betrayed her? She looked at him, the question clear in her eyes.

"Ida, I swear I told no one!" Dunkin turned to Sergeant Punctal. "Please, this is a misunderstanding. She is an innocent girl . . . young lady, whatever. You must not treat her like an outlaw!"

"Really?" Sergeant Punctal asked dryly. "If she's so innocent, then why did she cut off the head of Aquacious?"

There was a gasp from Dunkin, while the others were too surprised to speak.

"I wanted to tell you, Dunkin," Ida said as she was led away. "But I couldn't. I had no idea what I was doing. It was a mistake, and I'm so sorry—"

Sergeant Punctal sneered. "See? A confession."

Dunkin was so dismayed that he couldn't look at Ida. After an excruciating silence, he muttered, "Good-bye, Ida."

"Dunkin, please!"

Sergeant Punctal dragged Ida off the boat and down the dock. When they reached shore, she was hurled into a carriage and driven away. She banged on the doors, knowing that she was in an inescapable mess, and the worst part was, she was guilty. She'd committed the crime. Like every con artist, she'd frequently imagined being caught, but she'd never considered that her misdeeds might hurt other people, especially people that she cared about.

She continued to try to find a way out of the carriage, but to no avail. The carriage stopped fifteen minutes later, and Sergeant Punctal opened the door and told her to exit. She had no choice but to obey. He marched her into the police station.

Once inside, she was asked no questions, not even her name. The men in the station seemed spooked by her presence. A policeman with squeaky shoes escorted her through the front rooms and led her to the back, where, to her dismay, she saw a jailhouse, and it was *not* under construction—it had stone walls and floors, and cells with metal bars.

She tried to get the policeman to talk to her, because

talking was what she was good at—talking had gotten her out of every sticky situation so far. But as she opened her mouth, the officer threw her in a cell and slammed the door, causing the bars to clang ominously. He locked the door and left. She listened as the squeak of his shoes grew fainter and fainter.

She was surrounded by five other cells, each one filled with a gruff-looking man. None of them would meet her eye. Her villainy was so appalling that even thugs were terrified of her.

Surveying her new predicament, she tried to form a plan or find a reason for hope, but after she'd kicked the bars and pulled at the fat lock that sealed her cell door, she had to admit that she was stuck. She had no idea what to do next.

34

The next few days were worse than a bad dream. Ida was unable to sleep, and she spent most of her hours pacing back and forth across the hard stone floor, trying to figure out how the police had discovered both her crime and her age. She'd believed Dunkin when he'd said he'd told no one. She knew that knowing the police's sources wouldn't change anything, and that her time was better spent on planning for the future, but she couldn't help herself. She needed to know.

And where was Vernon? Ida wanted to tell him about the hair, but she'd seen no sign of him. He must be avoiding her so that no one would think he was involved with her crime, which was fair enough, but didn't he realize that she must have learned something in Reek? His absence was driving her crazy. Every day that she was in this prison was another day for Loor to continue hatching his plan, and they only had a few weeks left! She wanted to tell the police about Loor and his packages, but they avoided talking to her as much as possible, convinced she was wicked.

On what she guessed was Sunday, she asked the guard for his old newspaper, and he seemed so frightened of her that he handed it over obediently (if only he would do the same with the key to her cell.) The paper still featured headlines about Ida. People seemed incapable of talking about anything else. She finally learned the sequence of events:

Ms. Neely had come to the police with the wild story of Ida's true age, and the police had been inclined to ignore her, until Ms. Neely reminded them that she had witnessed a child leaving the scene of the Aquacious vandalization. Ms. Neely said at the time of the crime she'd thought she'd seen a boy with long black hair, but she now believed it was a girl with short black hair. The police searched the area around the town square again and found the statue's head, as well as a pair of girls' shoes. Ida being "from the Dark World" was the perfect explanation for why she would have committed such a heartless crime. The police were thrilled with the neat solution. The article ended with the announcement that Ida was sentenced to death, just as the mayor had promised. On the day of the flood, she would be left in her cell to drown.

Ida turned toward the wall so the other prisoners couldn't see her face. She didn't want them to see her cold, hard fear. Everything she'd feared about experiencing the Treatment was going to happen to her—but she would have not one chance of survival.

She wasn't ready to give up. Using the tin cup she'd been given for water, she banged on the bars of her cell. She didn't stop, even when the other prisoners complained. She didn't give a grain of soggy rice about them. She'd heard them whispering in the middle of the night about how she was a witch who was actually sixty years old. Sometimes she bugged her eyes out at them and wriggled her fingers, just for fun.

A guard finally came into the room. "Stop that, or no food tomorrow!"

"I just wondered if I could send some letters," she said sweetly.

He frowned.

"Don't I get to say good-bye to my loved ones?" she asked, twirling her hair.

He clearly was not sure what to say. "Hold on."

Hold on? Where did he imagine she was going to go?

He was gone for ten minutes, probably debating with the other policemen. He returned with paper and pen. "I'll be reading that before you send it, so don't try to write any crazy spells or anything."

Smiling, she nodded. "Yes, sir."

She was happy to have the supplies, but it was only one piece of paper. *One* letter. To whom would she write? Dunkin despised her now. That left Vernon Lyon or the Anti-Delugists. She decided one letter to the Anti-Delugists would reach more people. Surely one person in that large group would take pity on her and supply her with an alibi, or act as a character witness to help her plight?

Whom should she address it to? She knew Loor would never help. Hilda liked her the most, but would she understand the severity of the situation? Maybe one of the women might take pity on her. Mothers tended to be more tender-hearted.

Dear Mrs. Gauge and Mrs. Brown,

I'm in awful trouble and you know that I am only here because I was following the instructions of Mr. Loor. He asked me to cut off the head of Aquacious before I even knew who Aquacious was. He used me and now I am about to lose my life unless one of you comes forward. Please help me. Tell the truth! I know you are good people who will do the right thing.

What else was there to say? She signed her name.

Yours in need,
Ida

After she gave it to the guard, she had nothing to do but wait.

35

After an excruciating forty-eight hours, Ida received a response to her letter. Her pulse quickened as she ripped open the envelope. She was crushed to discover the letter was from Mr. Loor and not one of the women.

Dearest Ida,

So sorry to hear about your latest predicament. I regret to say that none of us will be able to act as a character witness on your behalf. We were shocked to hear that you had been apprehended by the authorities and even more shocked to learn that you are an oddity of the Dark World.

We don't appreciate being lied to. When we open the doors to our homes we do so with honest hearts and expect the same from our guests.

What? Mr. Loor's heart was about as honest as stolen coal. Ida's fingers trembled with anger.

I told the police that at the time the Aquacious statue was destroyed, I and the rest of the Anti-Delugists were in a town hall meeting. Every member of this city was a witness to our whereabouts. Why would you claim I had anything to do with your unspeakable crime? I have heard creatures from the Dark World are vindictive and mean, and this incident leads me to believe those rumors are true.

What? Mr. Loor believed in science, not the Dark World. He hadn't written this letter for Ida—it was written for the police, in case they opened it. He and his precious Anti-Delugists could suck turkey bones.

Punch told me about your trip to Reek. Despite your best efforts to thwart him, our families will thrive.

Loor was telling Ida, "I know what you saw, but it won't matter. I will stop the flood anyway."

May you find peace in the next life,
Ancel Loor

She crumpled the letter, throwing it to the ground. She wasn't surprised that Mr. Loor wasn't going to save her, but she couldn't believe that the others would leave her in this cell and do nothing to stop her execution. Sweet Hilda? The twins and Georgie? Even Punch! She knew he was furious with her, but would he really leave her here to die?

This is why you couldn't make friends—they would betray you sooner or later.

People couldn't handle seeing the whole truth. They only wanted what was safe and familiar, and Ida was neither of those things. Even if she managed to grow up, she would never be those things.

She put her head in her hands. She'd never felt more wretched or defeated. Maybe this was it. She'd never see Fargus or Josephine again, and her quest was an utter failure.

She didn't care anymore if the other prisoners could see her or not. She began to sob.

DUNKIN BLINKED, looking around the room. *Where am I?* he wondered. He thought at first that he was at home in his own bed, but the possibility seemed too good to be true. Surely he was still on that horrendous ship, or lying in some ditch in Reek. He studied the room for a few moments longer and finally accepted that he was truly awake and truly home. He sank back into his bed in gratitude. "Thank Aquacious and all that she made."

Throwing off his feather duvet, he placed his feet on the ground just as his Momma came through the door holding a large breakfast tray. He could smell fried eggs with sardine, his favorite. Momma gasped when she saw him.

"Wee, get back in bed this instant!"

"Momma, what has happened? How did I get here?"

Resting the tray of food on his bedside table, Momma physically forced Dunkin back into the bed. "You have been down with fever for days. I will not have you making yourself ill again by dashing around the house." She tucked him in tightly.

"MOMMA!" he bellowed. She stood back, alarmed. "Stop treating me like a child! I need to know how I got here!"

She sat on the edge of his bed. "You have been ill, so I will overlook your tone of voice." She smoothed her apron. "A nice man named Captain Brady brought you home. He was with some frightful-looking sailors and an odd, chatty boy."

Images came rushing back to Dunkin: a bald man in Reek, a yellow dress, Punch walking toward him with anger . . .

"I almost drowned!" Dunkin cried. He put his hands on his

chest, remembering the burning saltwater filling his lungs. He'd been sure his life was over.

"You told Captain Brady that you slipped, and that the boy did not push you. Is that true?" she asked, worried.

He was embarrassed. "Yes." A new image hit him with a wallop: Ida being led away by the police. "Momma, is it true? Did Ida really cut off the head of Aquacious?"

Momma patted his shoulder. "I am afraid it is. It has been all over the papers."

"That traitor!" he growled. Momma said nothing. "To think we welcomed her into our home! From this day forward she is dead to this family."

"That will not be necessary. She has already been sentenced to death."

Dunkin's eyes betrayed concern. "She has? When?"

"The police intend to leave her in jail on flood day."

Dunkin shook his head. "That is monstrous."

"Yes."

"How many days until the flood?"

"Ten days."

Dunkin contemplated this cruel punishment, trying to reconcile his affection for Ida with the heinous crime she had committed.

"There is something else you should know," Momma said. "Captain Brady said that it was Ida who discovered you had gone overboard. He said that without her help you would surely have drowned. So regardless of your feelings toward her, I shall forever be in her debt."

Dunkin inhaled deeply, sinking into his pillow. This was all very complicated. Ida had been his friend, and it seemed she had saved his life, but her crime was unforgivable.

Momma seemed to read his thoughts. "We all make mistakes, Wee. Look into your heart and picture Ida. Do you see wickedness or hatred there? Or do you see kindness and desperation? We should be careful if we judge people when they are hopeless or needy. They can hardly see straight."

He thought back to his last conversation on the boat with Ida. He shot upright. "Momma, there is something very important that I have to tell you. It is about hair."

"Auntie Gertrude has clogged the tub again. I know. That woman sheds like a St. Bernard."

"No, Momma! This is deadly serious. Mr. Loor is importing hair into our city. Pounds and pounds of it every week. He's been doing it for months, maybe even years. It has something to do with stopping the flood. It is why Ida went to Reek, and it is why Punch tried to kill me."

Momma's eyes got big. "You just told me he *did not* try to kill you!"

"Well, I mean, he did not strangle me or anything, but he gave me a very nasty look that caused me to lose my footing and fall overboard. We have to tell the police!"

"About the nasty look?"

"About the hair!"

"Lie back down. The police are not going to listen to any gibberish about hair."

"Ida knows about it, too. She was supposed to report back to Vernon Lyon." Ida had told Dunkin about her alliance with Mr. Lyon shortly before Dunkin's plunge into the sea. "We have to get her out of that jail, Momma."

"I am glad you have come to your senses about her."

"What can we do?"

Momma pondered for a moment. "First, I will visit Mr. Lyon and get his opinion on the matter."

Dunkin worried about his momma getting involved. "You must be cautious. The Anti-Delugists are very serious about their cause."

"Momma may be old but she still has a few tricks up her sleeve," she said with a cunning smile. "And if that Mr. Loor tries to mess with me, I will show him some old-fashioned Motzia wrestling techniques!"

Dunkin laid back upon his pillow, relieved to have shared his information. Now he needed to get well enough to take care of his household duties—like unclogging bathtub drains.

He sat bold upright. "*Blessed fin of Aquacious*, I think I know what the hair is for!"

36

Several days later, when Ida's guard said someone was there to see her, Ida thought perhaps Mr. Loor had come to torment her in person. She was relieved to hear that it was Momma Dunkin.

Momma entered the prison, and upon seeing Ida, she hollered at Ida's guard. "Are you not feeding her? She will be able to slip between those bars in no time!"

The guard, Officer Smitty, jumped. Smitty was a nervous young man who'd become a policeman when he should've become a gardener. The thorn of a rose was the scariest villain he was capable of facing.

Momma carried a heavy basket, and she asked Smitty for a chair. He fetched her one, and once she'd settled her large rear end into the seat, she dug into her basket. Pulling out a small cake with an almond on top, she handed it to Smitty. "For you, dear. It is hard to be on your feet all day." Surprised but very grateful, Smitty took the cake to his position by the door and began to wolf it down.

Momma pulled out a loaf of hot cherry bread wrapped in

cloth and a tin of creamy butter. She offered them to Ida. "Eat up. You look like an ant's toothpick." Ida hesitated. "Well, go on. I am not trying to poison you."

Ida wasn't worried about poison—she just felt too ashamed to accept anything from Momma—but the bread smelled heavenly, and soon her hunger won out. Taking the bread, she began to gobble it down in large chunks, hardly stopping to taste it. It was warm, and soft, and the sour cherries burst and trickled down her throat.

"Now there is no need to be uncivilized." Momma handed her a napkin, the butter tin, and a small knife. Ida happily took all three. While she ate, Momma talked.

"I always knew there was something special about you, Ida, but by Aquacious' gills I never could have guessed how special!" She chuckled.

Ida was glad someone thought her situation was funny. She most certainly did not. "Aren't you afraid of me?" Ida mumbled, breadcrumbs flying.

"Do not be silly. I have broken bread with you in my home. I think I know a good soul when I see it." Her eyes crinkled as she smiled. "People are not afraid of you, Ida. They are afraid of deception, and you lied about who you were."

"So if I'd walked into town and announced that I was a girl who would never grow up, no one would have been afraid?" Ida scoffed. "Sure. They probably would have thrown me a parade."

"How do you know what they would have done? You were so afraid of them judging you, that you judged them."

Ida had had enough of this visit. She was stuck in prison with an execution date in two days. The last thing she needed was a lecture.

"How's Dunkin?" she said, attempting to change the subject.

"He is better. He finally got out of bed this morning."

Ida smiled. "I'm glad."

Momma sighed. "That Captain Brady told me how you sounded the alarm when Wee fell overboard."

"Fell?" Ida was taken aback.

"Yes. Wee is quite embarrassed about it."

Ida needed to apologize to Punch. *Slug nuts*. She hated apologizing. On the bright side, she thought, I will probably drown before I have a chance to see him again.

"Wee is not proud of the way he acted toward you with the police," Momma said. "He is not well enough to visit you, but he wanted me to say 'thank you,' and, as his mother, I also wanted to say one hundred times, 'thank you.' I do not know what I would do if I lost him."

Dunkin had forgiven Ida. The fist around her heart lessened its grip. She put down the bread. "Thank you. And . . . I need to apologize to you for what I did to Aquacious."

"This brings me to the next topic of conversation. You could not have destroyed Aquacious just out of malice. Why did you do it?"

"Let's just say I made the wrong friends when I arrived."

Momma arched an eyebrow. "Surely you can tell the police about these 'friends.'"

Thinking of the crumpled letter, Ida shrugged. "They won't listen to me. It's no use."

After clucking her tongue, Momma turned to Smitty and said in her warmest voice, "Dear, I am feeling very parched from my journey. Could you possibly fetch us some tea?'

Smitty hesitated, but seeing Momma's gentle smile, he nodded. "Coming right up, Ma'am." He left the prison room.

When Momma turned back to Ida, her smile had disappeared. "In a toddler this behavior would be called stubborn, but in you, I am sorry, it is just plain dumb."

Ida blinked in surprise.

"This is your life! You do not get another one. This is hardly the time to stop fighting."

"What do you want me to do? Dig a hole in my cell with your butter knife?"

"At least that would be something. You are in here moping like your fate is already decided!"

"Isn't it?"

"Back in Motzia, it was traditional for parents to arrange marriages. My father promised me to a wretch of a man. He was a butcher with bad teeth, and every time I was alone with him he would tell me why women should be treated like cattle. I sat in my room for weeks crying and feeling sorry for myself, and then one night I stood up and thought, 'Right. Enough of this.' I packed a suitcase and left. I sold all the jewelry I owned and booked passage on the next ship leaving Motzia. It happened to be sailing for the Unfinished City. Dunkin's father, Shelton, was a first mate on that boat. He was the nicest man I have ever known and a wonderful father."

"That's a romantic story, Momma, but it hardly applies here. I'm in a prison cell, not my parents' house."

'Actually my father locked me into my room every night before I went to sleep. I had to fashion a key to escape."

Ida's ears perked up. "What did you use?"

Momma leaned in close to whisper. Her eyes gleamed. "A butter knife, as a matter of fact."

Ida had to stop herself from laughing. Momma was trying to help her escape! Life never stopped surprising Ida. "How did you know that Officer Smitty would leave us alone?"

"Honey, that almond cake was as dry as an old tumbleweed. He is probably still gulping down water as we speak."

Smiling, Ida placed the butter knife up her sleeve and handed Momma back the napkin and tin of butter. Momma carefully repacked the basket, picked it up, and walked toward the door.

Smitty reentered, holding a tray of tea. He looked dismayed when he saw that Momma was ready to leave. “You’re going, ma’am?”

“Why don’t we have our tea in the station? My neighbor Maude tells me you have a lovely new wife, and I want to hear *all* about her.”

Smitty grinned. “All right.”

“You can have more almond cake if you want.”

“Uh . . . no, thank you, ma’am.” The door swung shut behind them.

Ida didn’t waste a moment. The lock on the cell was an old-fashioned bolt, and the key was enormous—Ida had seen it hanging from the guard’s belt. She slid the knife out from her sleeve and carefully inserted it into the lock. She wasn’t a terrible lock-picker, but this one was complicated. She hoped Momma could distract Smitty long enough. She turned the knife to the left and then a fraction to the right, trying not to snap off the thin blade. Her hands were clammy with nerves.

The brutish man in the cell next to her, Mel, said, "Hey! The witch is trying to escape!"

"We gotta stop her!" another prisoner said.

"If you say one more word," Ida told them, "I will cast a terrible spell, and I will turn all of you back into children."

Mel ignored her. "Officer Smitty—!"

Closing her eyes, Ida began to chant. “Tuenray bentuo mendicky dicky!" It was a nonsense language she'd made up with Fargus. She repeated the words, getting louder. “Tuenray bentuo mendicky dicky!"

"Shut your gob, Mel!" the second prisoner begged. "I don't wanna be no pipsqueak again!"

The men went silent, so Ida stopped chanting. She put her ear right next to the lock and began turning the knife again.

She listened carefully, waiting for the series of clicks that would signal she'd triggered the mechanism. She turned it to the left, this time a bit further, then slightly to the right, and then, like a new egg on a spring day, it cracked open. Ida released her breath.

37

Ida opened the cell door slowly, trying to keep the metal from squeaking. What had Momma meant for her to do once she was out of her cell? If she went through the door, she'd find herself in the station surrounded by police. Not a good escape route.

The prison only had a few windows. Most were in the cells of the other prisoners, but she spotted a tiny one near the top of the wall at the end of the room. Running to it, she was discouraged to find it was more than six feet above the ground—too high for her to jump to. The wall was made of stone, so she searched for a foothold. Her tiny foot just fit on top of a small rock that jutted out.

Mel said, "You'll never fit through that window, toots."

Ida began chanting again, and Mel quickly stopped his commentary.

With everyone quiet, she placed her left foot onto a higher rock and then found a new one for her right. Soon, she was high enough to reach the window ledge with her hands. She was grateful that Momma had just fed her, because Ida was going to need all of her strength. Taking a deep breath, she heaved herself up. She kicked her legs as if she were swimming. Her body weight threatened to drag her back down until her foot caught the edge of a higher stone and she was able to pull herself up the rest of the way.

She hunched in the small window opening. No one but a prisoner as small as she could have used those footholds or fit into this window opening. Every so often, her size was a blessing.

Now she had to figure out how to break this glass.

She looked through the window outside. A man stood by the road. She thought it was a policeman, but as she focused she realized, much to her surprise, that it was Vernon Lyon!

He spied her and gave a slight nod, as if he'd been expecting her. Next to him stood a bored-looking mule with a rope attached to its saddle. Vernon sauntered casually toward Ida, carrying the other end of the rope. He arrived outside the police station wall and reached up to Ida's windowpane. Attached to the end of Vernon's rope was a suction cup, which he stuck to the pane with a *squish.* He walked back over to the mule and smacked it on the rump. Braying in anger, the mule jumped and sprinted away. The rope went taut, and the glass from the window popped out in one piece, shattering as it hit the ground. The mule ran away, trailing the rope and suction cup behind it.

Vernon signaled to Ida to jump out of the hole he'd created. Before she did, she said to her cellmates, "I've cast a spell on you that will last for twelve hours. If any of you opens your mouth before then, you'll become a foul little bedbug!"

She wanted to laugh at their frightened faces.

She hopped out of the window, landing gracefully on the grass below. She was amazed that she was leaving the prison alive. She opened her mouth to ask Vernon the million questions she had, but he signaled for her to follow him and remain silent. A block away, Vernon had a cart and horse waiting. He buried Ida under a pile of blankets and building supplies. She heard him climb into the seat of the cart and signal the horse to lead them away.

She was in an uncomfortable position with pieces of wood sticking into her side, but she didn't care. She was free! Her friends, people who now knew all of her secrets, had helped her escape. She couldn't remember the last time she'd felt such happiness.

THEY MUST HAVE TRAVELED for an hour before Vernon stopped and pulled the supplies out of the cart. It was nighttime by the time Ida stood and stretched her aching body. She was disoriented. "Where are we?"

"Just outside of town, to the south." He handed her her leather satchel.

Delighted, she asked, "How did you get this?" She checked the contents, making sure nothing was missing.

"Momma Dunkin brought it to me. I believe the captain of the ship gave it to her."

That Captain Brady was a good egg, even if he *had* stopped her from escaping the police.

"You okay?" Vernon asked. He looked haggard, as if he hadn't been sleeping.

"I'm terrific now that you've sprung me from that death box. How are you?"

"Worried about the flood . . . and you."

"I thought you were going to let me drown—since I'm a demon who can't age."

Vernon thought for a moment and said delicately, "I did think it was a very strange thing when I read about it. It certainly explained why you wanted the Treatment. After a while I figured, heck, if a higher power can save me from drowning, than why couldn't a lower power keep you from growing?"

"I appreciate that, Vernon, but why didn't you come to visit me?" She'd spent some dark days thinking she was alone in the world.

"I knew if I had any chance of helping you, it was imperative that the authorities didn't know that you and I were connected in any way. Otherwise, they might've had men on the lookout for me."

Ida nodded, unable to berate him since he'd helped her to escape. She now wanted to move on to the topic she'd been dying to talk to him about. "I have to tell you what I learned in Reek! I—"

He interrupted. "Momma Dunkin told me about the hair."

"Oh," Ida said, disappointed not to be the one to break the news. "So what do you think it's for?"

"Momma Dunkin's son had a theory he came up with before unclogging a sink, and it's not a bad notion."

Ida's pulse raced with anticipation.

"Dunkin believes the Anti-Delugists are using the hair to make a dam—a clog in the bay if you will."

Ida laughed. "That would be . . . How much hair would they need? Surely that's impossible."

"I'm not sure I agree with Dunkin. I'm not convinced that hair alone could create the blockage that Mr. Loor needs, and why haven't I seen anything?" Vernon scratched his stubbly chin. "I should be able to make out a dam from the shore. Maybe the Anti-Delugists are planning to build a dam next year?"

"Are you willing to sit around and find out?" Ida asked.

"It's not your concern anymore." He began to repack his cart. "If you leave the city now, you'll have a good head-start on the police."

Ida knew he was right—running was the smartest thing she

could do—but there was no question about where she was going. "I've been searching for a cure for four years. If there's a dam, find me a pick-axe, and I will personally rip it down."

"The flood and the Treatment aren't worth your life, kid. It's madness to risk getting caught by the police again."

"It's my madness and my choice. If you're going to search for a dam, then I'm coming with you."

Vernon frowned, but she could see he wasn't truly surprised by her words. "We'd have to wait until morning so we could see clearly—that would leave us with less than five hours until the flood—and it would only be you and me. Momma Dunkin has to look after her son."

"Surely there are other people in town who feel as strongly about the flood as you?"

"Most of them do." His brow furrowed. "But you aren't very popular right now, and people have never liked me much. We need proof if we want them to believe us."

Hot mackerel spit. Why did everything always have to be so hard? "Then let's get some sleep," she said, "and go find us a stinkin' dam."

38

Very early the next morning, Vernon and Ida made their way through the city in near-blackness. They'd left the horse and cart behind, knowing they'd be quieter on foot.

Vernon still wasn't overjoyed that the girl had decided to stick around. Whether she was twelve or sixteen, she was Vernon's responsibility as long as she accompanied him, and he didn't like the feeling. That said, he didn't move as quickly as he used to, and his eyesight was not as sharp as it once was, and the girl could prove to be useful in spotting a dam, if one existed.

If they didn't find a dam, he knew the foolhardy girl would want to do the Treatment, and he wasn't sure he'd be able to talk her out of it. He probably should have carted her to the next county and tied her to a tree.

They reached the walkway that overlooked the harbor. The darkness of the night was turning into a soft charcoal—it was close to dawn. Vernon studied the water and pointed. "If I were going to construct a dam, I would do it in that area, between Skimmer's Point and the Greenhorn Peninsula." Once upon a time there'd been an isthmus there—land connecting the two points—so if you built a dam thereabouts it would have a foundation to rest on.

"I don't see anything," Ida said, as she looked at the sea.

"Let's get closer," he said.

They walked along the north side of the bay toward Skimmer's Point. As the morning grew lighter, and they could see the pebbles and clam shells at their feet, they were able to pick up speed. Vernon couldn't remember the last time he'd moved so fast. It felt good.

The journey to the end of the Point took over twenty minutes. The sky blazed orange as the sun came into full view.

"Shouldn't we be able to see something by now?" Ida said.

Vernon grunted. Could they be wrong? They stood in silence, staring at the water.

"Only one way to know for sure." Vernon unlaced his shoes.

"What are you doing?" Ida asked, alarmed.

"Going in." Throwing the shoes aside, he peeled off his socks. He needed to see with his own eyes if there was something under that water or not.

"What does it matter?" the girl said. "Even if Loor has put something on top of the ith . . . ith . . ."

"Isthmus."

"Whatever. Even if Loor put something on top of it, his dam isn't big enough to do anything. It's covered in water!"

"Either way." Vernon took off his sweater.

Mr. Loor worked quickly in the dark. He unspooled a long fuse around and around the bottom of the building, and when he had enough, he clipped it off. He produced matches from his coat pocket and, with great ceremony, he struck one and lit the end of the fuse. It flickered for a moment before it caught, but then it was off and running. The flame sped down the line. Loor looked at his watch and giggled with happiness. He figured he had a good thirty minutes to reach safety. He opened the door to leave but turned one last time to look at his little babies lying on the floor: twenty long sticks of dynamite.

Hairy tick bottoms. Ida was very irritated.

Was Vernon really going to force her to do this? She threw her satchel onto the sand. Taking off her shoes and socks quickly, Ida stripped down to the grotty long underwear that had once belonged to one of the twins. Avoiding the sharp clams, she ran and leapt into the harbor before Vernon could stop her.

The second her body hit the water she knew she'd made a mistake. The water was freeeeeeeeeezing—nothing like the day she'd swum with the Non-Constructionists. As her head emerged from the water, she screeched like an injured gull.

"Serves you right," Vernon said from the shore, arms crossed. "I don't like being undermined."

Ida did not say what she was thinking: *you're too old to be exploring dark waters*. Instead she said, "I'm a great swimmer. I'll be quicker than you!" Without waiting for a response, she swam toward the area where Vernon said the isthmus used to be.

She reached a place that felt like it was directly between the tips of the bay. She still saw nothing. She dove under the water, swimming as deep as she dared. She opened her eyes, although the salt water burned like mad, but saw only fish. When she ran out of air, she surfaced. She was determined to see the bottom of this land mass, to feel it and convince herself that nothing had been constructed on it. Taking a larger breath, she dove again.

She swam deeper this time. Her lungs felt like bursting, but she was determined. When she finally saw seaweed swaying, she knew she'd found the bottom. Sand, coral, and rocks made up the sea floor. Nothing else. She hurried to the top.

Minutes later, she stepped back onto the shore with her teeth chattering. She told Vernon, "We were wrong."

Vernon grunted and frowned as he threw her her clothes.

"That's good, right?" She wanted to put on her dry clothes right away, but then everything would be soaked.

"I can't believe Loor isn't up to something," he grumbled.

She jumped up and down, trying to warm herself. "I agree, but where else should we look? How much time do we have left?"

Vernon looked at the sky. "Three, maybe four hours." He sighed. "We'd better get you out of town. The police will have realized you're missing by now."

Was he nuts? "I'm not leaving."

"Don't be foolish, kid."

She stopped jumping. "There is no dam. The flood is going to happen. And I'm going to do the Treatment."

He pulled on his sweater so hard that Ida could hear a seam tear. "I've told you that the only chance you would've had was to tie yourself to the Aquacious statue, and you destroyed that statue. Even if you could use it, you'd never make it to the town square without being arrested again." He ran his hands through his hair in aggravation. "And even if, by some miracle, you managed to slip by all those people and get to the square, the flood would kill you. Why would Aquacious save you after you desecrated her image? Every single part of your plan is idiotic."

He had called Ida an idiot, and she wanted to call him every bad word she'd heard in every tavern she'd ever entered.

As she fumed, she put her clothes on over her soggy long underwear, which made her mood even worse. She put her socks on, tempted to throw her shoes at Vernon's head. Prepared to yell out a stream of obscenities, she opened her mouth and shrieked, "You don't understand! I don't belong in this body! I was born to be something else—the person you see is not who I am!" Tears swelled in her eyes. This was not what she'd meant to say, and Vernon was not supposed to see her cry. She turned away, embarrassed.

To her shock, his voice became even louder and angrier. "What is this obsession, Ida? You have *life*. You are healthy and smart and you seem capable of making friends when you try. But you're ignoring the life that's happening right in front of you because you are obsessed with the life that you *think* you should have! No one gets the life they think they should have! That doesn't mean you *throw away* the one you've got like it's some . . . some hat that doesn't fit! You can't get a replacement. You get ONE. If you throw it away this easily, then you are just selfish, and wasteful, and have no feeling whatsoever for the people that care for you, and that includes me!"

Ida was stunned by his outburst. This bear of a man—who usually communicated by grunting—had expressed not only anger and frustration with her, but affection. She wiped her eyes on her sleeve, wishing she didn't have to disappoint him. "I'm sorry, Vernon. I can't change what I want."

He looked to the sky. "It's taken me over a decade to learn this, but the secret to life is realizing that you *always* have the power to change what you want." He walked away, leaving her to shiver alone by the water.

As she watched his figure grow smaller and smaller, she convinced herself that he was wrong. She wasn't asking for something outrageous, something that wasn't rightfully hers. She had been robbed of her adolescence, of her adulthood, and it was only natural that she should want them back. When

Dunkin was sad about losing his favorite watch, Ida didn't shame him for feeling despondent. Instead, she searched for and found the watch. *That* is what real friendship was: helping people get what they wanted. She sniffed. Vernon could go jump in mud.

She hopped around more, trying to distract herself from the cold. The sky was turning a lovely brilliant blue; how could a flood possibly happen today? As she thought about the flood, her hopping became dancing. It was going to happen today! She would do the Treatment and finally age! She would be a normal girl! She felt a curious new sensation—could this be joy? She raised her arms and waved them at the sun as her feet continued to hop around the pebbled sand.

After a few minutes of this, she became self-conscious of her oddball jig, and she double-checked to make sure no one was watching. The only building on Skimmer's Point was the lighthouse donated by the Anti-Delugists. As she glanced at the lofty tower, she saw someone coming out of the door.

She was embarrassed, but more importantly, she needed to scram before she was recognized. She kept an eye on the figure as she walked away from the Point. It didn't come toward her; instead, it circled the building. As she narrowed her eyes, the shaded person came into slight relief. She drew in a breath. It was Punch! That no-good backstabber. He was up to something, and whatever it was, Vernon was too far away to help Ida stop it.

Curiosity overwhelming her, she set out for the lighthouse.

39

The lighthouse looked like every other lighthouse Ida had ever seen. It was tall and made of stone and had a cupola on top for the lens and lantern. Her friend Fargus had grown up in a lighthouse, but he never told her much about it. She had always thought it sounded neat.

Punch knelt at the bottom of the building, and he was concentrating so hard on his task that he'd neglected to notice Ida approaching.

Ida stood as tall as she could, hands on hips, hoping she looked intimidating. "What are you doing?" she said loudly.

Punch jumped nearly a foot, swinging around with a look of terror. "Holy Aquacious!"

She almost laughed at his use of the deity's name.

"You scared me to death!" he said.

"*What* are you doing?" she repeated.

He looked up at the lighthouse and then at her. "Let's talk over there." He grabbed her by the elbow and pulled her away from the building.

"Hey!" She wrested herself away. "I'm not going anywhere until you tell me what you're up to!"

He looked nervous. "We'll talk on the walkway."

"Why? What's going on in there?" She walked back toward the entrance.

"STOP!" he yelled.

She froze. "Punch. Tell me what's happening."

"Walk this way, and I'll tell you."

She bit her lip. She didn't trust him. "I think there's something in there you don't want me to see, and if I go with you, you'll have me arrested."

"I won't! Just come here!" He looked at his watch and scowled. "*Please*!"

He seemed genuinely desperate. Ida hadn't known him long, but he'd never seemed as sincere as he did right now. Maybe she could get something out of his distress? "Fine. I'll come with you, but only if—"

Before she could finish the sentence, he stomped over, picked her up, and threw her over his shoulder. He began running toward the city, jostling Ida up and down like a netful of fish.

"Put me down!" she cried.

"You're as stubborn as a stain!" he said, continuing to run.

"Put me down you arrogant, suck-up, mold-eating—"

Suddenly, a deafening *boom* came from the end of Skimmer's Point, and the sound echoed across the water like an army sounding the drum for war. Ida covered her head, sure that the flood had come early and was about to swallow them. When they were not immediately consumed, she lifted her head to see the lighthouse was on fire, a towering blaze spitting debris in every direction. They were close enough that she could feel the heat on her skin.

Punch ran until they were at a safe distance and then put her down on the ground.

"That was you?" Ida said, panting, although she didn't really need to ask. "Why?"

He glowered at her. "How did you get out of jail?" Before she could speak he said, "Actually, I'm no longer surprised by anything you do. You're the biggest hoodwinker I've ever known."

Ida couldn't wait to be in her real body so that she could sock him the mouth. "Why would you blow up your own lighthouse, Punch?"

"Wait a minute, and you'll see," he said, sounding proud.

She looked around, knowing she couldn't stay put. The fire would bring the townspeople running, and she couldn't be seen by any of them. She put her satchel on the ground, double-checking that nothing had fallen out when she'd been upside-down on Punch's shoulder. When she was satisfied, she said, "You gave the people a gift, and now you've destroyed the gift. Big whoop." She was about to leave, when she noticed the lighthouse swaying. "Isn't the lighthouse built of stone?" Ida asked.

He smirked. "It has a thin stone facade. It's mostly wood."

She considered what this meant and felt sick. "It's going to fall."

"Yep." As he said this, the burning tower crumbled, and Ida watched in horror as the debris landed across the underwater isthmus she'd just searched.

"What was inside the lighthouse?" she asked, already knowing the answer.

"Stone, wood, cement, and hair. Lots and lots of hair."

But was it enough to cause the blockage the Anti-Delugists needed? "That's not enough for a dam," she said triumphantly. "Look, the wreckage didn't even reach the surface!"

Punch raised an eyebrow.

What was she missing?

With horror, she remembered the mill, which was positioned in the same place as the lighthouse but on the opposite side of the bay. She sprinted south.

"You're too late!" Punch shouted with glee.

She didn't care. She had to try.

She'd barely begun running when the second blast occurred. After she heard it, she felt it—a huge vibration that ran through the earth and up her legs. She saw the bottom of the mill blow out, and she watched helplessly as it burned and then crashed on top of the remains of the lighthouse, adding more debris and spreading freshly milled flour across the hair. Soon the water, flour, and hair merged to form a dense pasty mass big enough to stop any water from penetrating the harbor.

She collapsed onto the beach. Tears burned her eyes. What fools she and Vernon had been. Loor had won. There would be no flood this year. No Treatment. No becoming who she was meant to be—no new body to rejoice in. She would be stuck as this wretched, lonely girl forever.

40

Mr. Loor danced a little jig as he approached Punch on the beach. He'd never looked so happy. Rain beat down while he jumped in a puddle, splashing around like a child.

When Loor reached Punch, he embraced him. "We've done it! We've finally done it!"

Punch embraced him back awkwardly, as if Loor had never hugged him before.

"Imagine the people's faces right now!" Loor laughed, as he gazed up at the town. "I wish I could see them, but we must get home quickly. The Delugists will arrive soon, and they'll be *furious.*"

Loor noticed Ida crumpled on the shore. "Good gosh. What is that monstrosity doing here?"

"She was trying to stop us," Punch said.

Loor's lip curled. "And not even her dark powers could help her?" he said with sarcasm.

Lifting her head, Ida wiped her eyes. "You can stop pretending now, Loor. It's over." She was wet and covered in mud. She knew she looked like a wild thing raised in the woods.

Loor approached her slowly, looking as if he might kick sand in her face. "Oh, I know it's over. For you. If we weren't in such a hurry, I'd really enjoy turning you back over to the police."

"You can stop pretending that you want to improve this town or care anything about the other Anti-Delugists."

A fleeting look of pure hatred passed across Mr. Loor's face.

"Mr. Lyon told me that for years you've been buying up every last bit of cheap property in the Unfinished City. You own nearly half of the homes in town, plus the entire shantytown. If this city industrializes, you'll become a very wealthy man."

Punch looked astounded. "What's she talking about?"

"You can't believe this urchin," Loor said, waving Ida away. "She's the most manipulative little brat I've ever encountered."

"So it's not true?" Punch said. "You own no land?"

Loor looked away from him. "I may have made a small investment here and there."

"Where did you get the money?" Punch's face grew red with anger.

"Outside investors, boy. It's common practice to get businessmen to invest in real estate that will soon go up in value. Many wise men in Reek were interested in—"

"All these years of wearing rags and half-starving, and you were buying houses?"

"Let's discuss this on the way to the cliffs," Loor said. "The townspeople will be here any moment."

"Let's discuss it *now*." Punch took a step toward Loor, who stumbled back. They both looked surprised to learn that Punch had grown as tall as Loor. "What about giving people the gift of higher knowledge and helping our fellow man because it's the right thing to do? What about science? And progress? And the altruism of helping people who can't help themselves? All the things you've preached my entire life?"

"They're still true of course—"

"Why did you lie to us?"

"I never lied. I just . . . " Loor smiled. " . . . didn't want to get everyone's hopes up. I'm going to split the money with you, of course."

"He's been using you all," Ida said. "He's no better than a simple conman."

"Or con-girl?" Punch said to her with disgust. "You're no better than he is."

"That's not true," she said. "I never—"

"You never what?" Punch whipped around to face her. "Lied to me? Lied *about* me? You told Mr. Loor I was a traitor and a spy, that I was going to leave the Anti-Delugists for Preanne. You accused me of throwing your friend off the ship! You'll stop at nothing to get what you want."

"You left me to drown in a prison cell!" Ida countered. "No one in your household even bothered to respond to my letter begging for help—let alone try to stop my execution!"

Punch's anger deflated slightly. "What letter?" Before Ida could answer him, he suddenly fell face-first into the sand.

Loor stood behind him with a large piece of driftwood in his hand.

41

Punch lay unconscious, and Loor lurched toward Ida. Loor's blond hair, dark with rain, stuck to his forehead, and he gave her a toothy grin. He swung the driftwood in his hand like a club.

Ida had known Loor was a mean and deceitful man; she'd had no idea he would turn violent. She needed to escape from him quickly.

She jumped up. "You lying weasel!"

"You underworld harpy!" he snarled. He swung at her head.

She bobbed to the left.

He swung again and caught her upper arm with the wood. She yelped at the pain but didn't fall. He tried to hit her again, but she scampered away. He might be bigger and stronger, but she was faster.

Her satchel was several yards away, and she needed her sharp rocks. She made a dash to grab it, but just as she picked up speed, Loor thrust the wood in front of her ankles. She tripped over it and hit the sand hard.

Groaning, she rolled over. Her whole body hurt. Was she bleeding?

Walking over, Loor loomed over her. His eyes gleamed with delight. "Punch was right, you know. We're very much alike."

She spit sand from her mouth. "No we're not."

"You make the best of every situation, just like me. And you always make yourself number one, just like me." He circled her until he'd cut off her escape route toward the city. She was backed up to the water and had no place to go.

"You move from one con to the next, wondering where you'll find your next chump," he continued. "You've built your life on lies."

She was beginning to feel nauseated. Was he right? Were they similar?

"Your little story about being a girl who can't age is not half-bad." He lowered the driftwood, leaning on it like it was a cane. "With a little guidance, you could use it to make quite a bit of money. How about you stop acting like a brat, and let me be your mentor?"

Was he insane?

"I've seen how you treat your mentees." Ida pointed to Punch laying on the ground.

"Punch is a good boy, but he's always been a bit too idealistic. You, on the other hand—you are ruthless. You're a more appropriate apprentice."

Ida's head was muddled. She hated this man, yet she'd never had anyone call her out so bluntly in her life. It was horrifying and, yet, sort of liberating. "I don't like you," she said. "I don't like how you manipulate people."

"You don't care a lick about the people here. All you care about is yourself."

"That's not true."

"Every single step you've taken has been for your precious cure."

"No, I . . . I . . . " Was he right? Did she only care about herself? When the explosions had occurred, she'd only thought about the loss of the Treatment, not about the loss of the flood, or the sadness of the people here. Every interaction she'd had since she'd arrived in the Unfinished City had been about becoming sixteen. She'd not intentionally told anyone the *whole* truth about her actions or motives—not Dunkin, nor Vernon, nor Momma.

She then remembered seeing Dunkin floating, unmoving in the water. How her knees had turned to jelly. She couldn't remember the last time she'd known such fear. Wait . . . she could. It was when her friend Fargus had been under the control of the Master, and she'd thought he might be lost to her forever. She'd been ready to give up her life to save him. And hadn't Vernon Lyon and Momma just freed Ida from prison, risking arrest themselves?

Loor was wrong. Ida did care about people. And they cared about her. She narrowed her eyes. "Just because your life is a big fraud doesn't mean mine is!" She charged him, swept her leg, and struck the piece of wood he was leaning on. While he recovered his balance, she grabbed the driftwood from the ground. She swung it at him.

He laughed.

She swung harder and hit him in the knee. He stopped laughing.

Grabbing her wrist, he wrenched the wood from her easily and tossed it aside. He placed his large hands around her tiny neck. With horror, she realized he was dragging her to the water.

"I guess we won't be working together," he said.

"Wait!" she cried, beating on his arms.

"You claim you can't age!" he said. "Let's find out if you can die!"

When they were a foot into the bay, he plunged her head

down. Her eyes, nose, and mouth filled with sea water. Her lungs burned like fire. She had no air. She thrashed her legs and arms but nothing helped. He was a grown man, and she had the strength of a twelve-year-old girl.

Her hands felt around the sand beneath her. They chafed against rocks and shells. She wrapped her fingers around the largest object they could find, whipped her hand out of the water, and swung as hard as she could toward Loor's head.

He howled and released her. She burst out of the water, gasping for breath. She looked down to discover she was holding half of a brick. The second explosion must have blown pieces of the mill all the way to the shore. Lucky for her.

Blood trickled down Loor's forehead. He looked angrier than ever as he lunged for her.

"Careful," she said, jumping back. "Salt water will really make that cut sting." She stepped deeper into the water.

He followed her.

What was her plan? She couldn't out-swim him.

She still had the brick. She held it up, ready to hurl it at him, when noises came from the beach.

The townspeople were marching along the walkways, headed for the harbor. They were hollering, "Loor!" and "It's the Anti-Delugists!"

"I think someone may have noticed your dam," Ida said.

Loor looked at the mob, and then scowled at her. "They'll blame you as much as me. You destroyed their statue. Why not their flood?"

"They've already sentenced me to death. What more can they do? You on the other hand—you might not even make it to the jail."

As several people climbed down the ladder to the beach, Loor was unable to hide the fear on his face. "I believe I'll leave you to them." He splashed out of the bay and fled in the direction of the cliffs.

"You'd better run, you chinless worm!" she yelled after him, shaking her brick.

She waited for the crowd to follow him, but to her dismay, they kept marching toward her. She ran out of the water. The last thing she wanted was to return to her prison cell.

Fig. She had to do something about Punch, who was still unconscious on the ground. If the crowd got to him, they might tear him apart. Kneeling, she spoke in his ear. "Punch? Are you okay?"

No answer.

"We have to go. I really need you to wake up."

His hair had blood on it, but he didn't seem to be actively bleeding, which was a good thing. However, she was concerned he wasn't answering her.

"I know you didn't try to kill Dunkin. And I'm sorry I told Loor about Preanne. It was a jerk thing to do. Now GET UP."

He had sand all over his face, making him look very young and helpless. He moaned. She found this encouraging. He spoke softly, and she leaned in to listen. "An apology from you would shock anyone back to life."

She rolled her eyes. "Can you walk?"

"Maybe." He gave her a wide-eyed look. "Did Mr. Loor hit me?"

"Yup. He walloped you good, and then he tried to feed me to the fish. Give me your hand."

She helped him sit up. He was *heavy*. With great effort, she tried to yank him up to standing. She was wondering if she could roll him across the beach when she heard a voice behind her.

"Don't move a muscle, missy."

She froze. She knew that voice. It was Sergeant Punctal.

42

Ida turned around to see that the plump sergeant was at the fore of almost a hundred furious townspeople. Many of the men and women held pick-axes.

"I can explain," Ida said.

"No need!" Sergeant Punctal said, outraged. "We saw the catastrophe from our homes. You and the boy blew up two buildings and made a levee. I would say drowning in a prison cell is too good for a monster like you!"

"It wasn't me!" Ida cried, and then, moving protectively in front of Punch, she revised her statement. "It wasn't us!" Mr. Loor had used Punch just as he had used her, and Punch didn't need to suffer for it. She said, "It was Mr. Loor, the Anti-Delugist! He ran off not ten minutes ago. If you head for the cliffs, you can catch him!"

"Maybe you made them all do it, with that dark magic of yours," said a woman, whom Ida recognized as the baker.

"I don't have any magic. I'm just a girl—an innocent girl!" For once Ida wished this were true, that she really were twelve and that she'd never swindled anyone or told a lie in her life.

"Please. I would never stop the flood. I want the flood more than any of you could possibly imagine!"

"Why?" Guiseppe Farnucci the glassblower asked suspiciously.

She decided she had nothing to lose by being honest. "Because I need the Treatment. I want to age and be normal like all of you!"

A voice came from the back. "Friends and neighbors! Please! Listen to me!" Ida's heart fluttered with hope as she recognized the voice as Dunkin's. "You must listen to Ida! She is telling the truth." He pushed his way to the front. "The very first time I met this insolent girl she asked me about the Treatment. It is all she cares about. She would never do anything to endanger her chances of trying it."

"Thank you, Dunkin." She cleared her throat. "But I do care about more than just the Treatment. I care about you and Momma Dunkin and Mr. Lyon, and all the people here who want the flood."

"This is all poppycock!" Sergeant Punctal yelled. "There is the dam and here are the perpetrators. Case closed!"

"The girl didn't make the dam," a crusty voice said with certainty. Vernon Lyon stepped forward, and several people moved back. He was an intimidating presence. "In fact, she helped me look for a dam early this morning, so we could tear it down. I hope you will take my testimony as the final word on the matter."

"Why should we?" Sergeant Punctal asked, hitching up his belt.

Vernon stepped up close to the officer, towering above him by a good foot. "Because I'm the only person here who has survived the Treatment and seen Aquacious! And I swear on her name that this child had nothing to do with that dam."

A murmur ran through the crowd. Most people knew the

legend of Vernon Lyon seeing Aquacious, but no one had ever heard him speak of it. They were gobsmacked.

The sergeant could see that the crowd was now on Vernon's side. "Either way, Mr. Lyon, she confessed to removing the head of Aquacious and must be returned to jail. And that boy sitting over there is clearly an Anti-Delugist. He will be arrested as well."

"Punch is innocent!" Ida said.

The sergeant looked at Vernon with an arched eyebrow. "I suppose now you are going to tell me that the boy is an angel who feeds the poor in his free time?"

Vernon did not find this amusing. "No. I'm going to tell you that we have a bigger problem than this girl or that boy. We only have two hours to destroy the dam."

The crowd shouted in agreement. "Hear, hear!" "Let's get moving!" "We're wasting time!"

"Will you be lending us a hand, officer?" Vernon asked. "Or will you be spending your time at the station guarding two adolescents?"

Sergeant Punctal glared at Vernon. "I will, of course, be helping with the dam. However, if I have any difficulty tracking these criminals down later, I will hold you personally responsible."

"You do that," Vernon said with a snarl. He turned to the townspeople and said loudly, "I know that some of you are hanging onto the small chance that the dam won't hold, and that the flood will get through, but I'm not satisfied to wait and see, and you shouldn't be either! I think we should split up—half of us can head to Skimmer's Point and the other half to the Greenhorn Peninsula. We'll try to take it down from both sides."

The crowd cheered.

"Let's go!" Vernon cried.

43

The townspeople divided themselves up, and Vernon was soon headed to the Point with a rowdy horde, while a large group carrying picks and shovels headed south.

In the chaos of the separation, Momma had emerged from the crowd. Ida was delighted. "I am so happy that you were not too close to the fires," Momma said, embracing Ida.

"I'm so sorry about the dam," Ida said. "I wish I'd seen it coming."

"We all missed it," Dunkin said.

Momma said, "At least you got out of that terrible prison."

"Thanks to you!" Ida said.

"No, no. Not at all," Momma said, blushing with pride.

"Excuse me for one minute," Ida said. She walked over to Punch, who was kneeling in the sand with his hand on his head. "You okay?" she asked him.

He nodded. "I can't believe those people didn't tear me apart."

"I think you have Mr. Lyon to thank for that."

"That was astonishing. I thought he was a fanatic who hated all Anti-Delugists—why did he help me?"

Ida had been surprised herself that Vernon didn't want Punch arrested. She thought of the boy Vernon had lost. "I think maybe he has a soft spot for young people." She offered him her hand. "Can you stand?"

"I think so." He grabbed her hand and allowed her to help him up.

"We're going to help tear down the dam. Want to come?"

He blinked at her in surprise. "I don't, uh, think I'd be welcome."

"You're an able-bodied young man. Besides, maybe you know something about the construction that will help us."

"If you're sure."

She nodded. She wasn't actually sure at all that he would be welcome, but she did feel like every person was needed. She and Punch joined Dunkin and Momma and the four of them followed Vernon's group that was headed north.

As they walked, Ida asked Momma, "What will happen to the city if the flood doesn't happen?"

"Our city will become like every other city," Momma said sadly. "People will only care about work and money. They will not stop to chat with their neighbors or laugh with their children. No one will live to be one hundred and fifty anymore. People will work themselves into an early grave."

Ida didn't know what to say. This was a very grim prediction.

"I am sorry about your Treatment," Dunkin said. "I know your heart was set on it."

"How much time do we have left?" she asked, not ready to give up yet.

"The flood will arrive at noon," Momma said.

"Let's walk faster," Ida said.

When they reached Skimmer's Point, they saw men and

women standing on the shore hacking at the dam with their pick-axes. Occasionally a person would chip away some stone or cement, but the more people pulled at the hair, the more it seemed to tangle and knot. Ida felt like she was watching miniature people caught inside an enormous hairbrush. They would never remove it all in time for the flood.

"This is hopeless," she said.

Punch look pained. "This is exactly how it was supposed to be—impossible to destroy in one day."

Dunkin shuddered. "That disgusting hair looks like thousands of mice in the water."

"If only," Momma said. "We could make mice swim away."

"Your 'dark powers' cannot make the dam magically disappear?" Dunkin asked with a sad grin.

Ida wished she could laugh. If only she *could* make things disappear.

A thought was trying to noodle its way to the front of her brain. What was it? Something about mice . . . and making things disappear. She tuned out everyone's words to concentrate. What was her mind telling her? Mice disappearing . . .

The school! The teacher in the school in Reek had made an entire mouse disappear using, what was it? Um. "Caustic soda and water!" she blurted.

Dunkin frowned in confusion.

"Caustic soda and water can eat through almost anything, right? If it can dissolve a mouse, why not hair, wood, and flour?" Her heart pounded with excitement.

Punch's brow furrowed as Momma tapped her chin.

"I use caustic soda to clear our clogged drains," Dunkin said. "It definitely eats through hair."

Ida ran to find Vernon Lyon. He was running an assembly line of workers who were pulling chunks of stone out of the water.

"Mr. Lyon!" she cried. "We could use caustic soda to dissolve the dam!"

He continued to wave along his workers. Without looking at her, he said, "Lye?"

"No. Caustic soda!"

"Sodium Hydroxide," Vernon said. "It's all the same thing. That's strong stuff, kid. I use it to strip paint."

"Exactly! Maybe it's strong enough to destroy a dam!" Ida said, growing more excited.

Lowering his arms, he met her eyes. "Interesting."

"I think so," she said, smiling.

Vernon grunted, then hollered at the workers. "Otis Sharples, get over here! And, uh, you, too, Quincy Dupont!"

Two men left their stations and walked over. Vernon introduced one of them to Ida. "Mr. Sharples is our pharmacist," Vernon said. Mr. Sharples was a serious-looking man with spectacles and well-tended muttonchops.

After Vernon had explained Ida's idea to Mr. Sharples, Vernon asked, "How dangerous would it be to put lye in the bay?"

As Mr. Sharples pondered the information, he took off his glasses and slowly cleaned them on his freshly-pressed shirt. Vernon and Ida waited in frustration as he wiped each lens over and over. Finally, he replaced the glasses and said, "As you have noted, lye can be quite dangerous. It's corrosive and eats through many things it comes into contact with. It must be put directly onto the dam, and the application must be performed with great caution. Some of it will inevitably spill into the water . . . " He frowned. Ida braced herself for him to say that this was too dangerous, and that her plan was impossible. "However, the bay is large enough that the sea would dilute any spillage. I do not believe it shall affect our precious sea life. Therefore, I think this plan is . . . sound."

Ida exhaled with relief. "Hot diggity."

Mr. Sharples took off his glasses again. "However . . . "

Uh-oh, Ida thought. *What now?*

"It would take an *extraordinary* amount of caustic soda."

"I imagine that's where I come in." Mr. Dupont, the second man Vernon had summoned, stepped into their circle. He had wavy black hair and a pencil-thin mustache.

"Mr. Dupont makes soap," Vernon told Ida.

"I make specialty scented body bars," Mr. Dupont said with a sniff.

"Yeah. Soap," Vernon said. "How much lye do you have on hand?"

"One barrel—around fifty gallons," Mr. Dupont said. "But I need it for—"

"Terrific," Vernon said. "We'll send men with you to bring it down immediately."

"But I never said—"

"Mr. Dupont!" Vernon said. "If there is no flood, how good will your business be this year, when no one needs to wash off any mud?"

Mr. Dupont's eyebrows rose in alarm. He smoothed his mustache. "I will be happy to donate to the cause." Vernon chose an assembly of burly men and sent them back to the city with Mr. Dupont.

Ida clapped her hands. "You mean this is going to work? The flood might happen after all?" She was giddy with anticipation.

Vernon grimaced. "I have one more question for Mr. Sharples." Turning to the pharmacist, he said, "Let's talk in private." They walked just out of earshot of Ida, which she found extremely irritating.

A minute later, Vernon returned to her, his face grim. He put his hand on her shoulder. "Mr. Sharples has confirmed my fear. The sea will dilute the water eventually, but it will not be quick enough for a person to submerge in the water at flood time."

Not be quick enough for a person to submerge.

Her brain reluctantly translated his meaning: even if Ida's plan worked, she couldn't do the Treatment.

44

"You're just saying that because you don't want me to do the Treatment!" Ida yelled at Vernon. "You never have!"

"No. I'm not," Vernon said, remaining calm. "Ask Mr. Sharples yourself."

She looked at the fussy man who was still removing an invisible smudge from his spectacles. She hated him. She hated Vernon. She hated everyone.

Why was everyone and everything determined to thwart her?

Maybe there was a different way to destroy the dam. She racked her brain to come up with another idea. One's first idea wasn't usually one's last. Her mind raced, but she was in such a panic she couldn't think of anything except how little time they had left.

She looked frantically at the others. Why couldn't *they* think of something? Why did it have to be her problem to solve?

"We should blow it up!" she blurted. "We'll use the same kind of explosives that Mr. Loor used to destroy the mill and lighthouse!"

Vernon shook his head. "Loor must have bought dynamite in Reek. We don't have time to get there. The lye was your idea, and it's brilliant."

Walking away from Vernon, she stared at the dam and at the citizens working tirelessly to pull it down. For four years, she'd been searching for her cure, going from one wild goose chase to another. The Treatment was the most promising of all the legends she'd heard. Everything she'd endured in the Unfinished City had been about making it to flood day.

Maybe the water would be safe by next year or the year after that, but was she willing to wait here until then? What about the children of Gulm? How would they feel about another year stuck in the wrong bodies?

She was failing those children, sure, but it was time for Ida to admit that, just as Mr. Loor had said, all her actions since she'd arrived had been for her own personal gain. She could tell herself that she had the children of Gulm in mind, but the truth was, she was most concerned about her own cure, her own ability to age and change. If she had to choose between her own cure and theirs, whose would she choose? Did she want to know the answer?

She looked toward her friends. Vernon, Dunkin, Punch, and Momma watched her with solemn expressions on their faces, as if they could read her thoughts. While they and their fellow citizens were fighting for their entire way of life, her friends were sad for *her*.

She'd almost died twice—she'd been sentenced to die in prison, and Loor had tried to drown her. Life was precious, just as Vernon had told her—had yelled at her, actually. She smiled as she thought of him telling her with frustration that he cared about her. It was time that she accepted that her life—even in this body—was worthwhile. She had plenty of time left to make that life mean something.

She sighed. *It's silly to stand here and stew, when the right thing to do is biting me in the butt.*

She joined her friends. "What are you waiting for?" she said. "We need to find a boat so we can spread the lye properly."

Dunkin smiled. "You are an extraordinary girl, Ida. People could learn a lot from you.'

"Oh, yeah? Like how to hide a weapon with a bow in your hair?"

Dunkin laughed. "Among other things, yes." Dunkin embraced his mother. "Momma, it is time for you to go home, fetch Auntie Gertrude, and head for the hill."

Momma clapped her hands together. "You think it is going to work!"

"We must be prepared for anything," Dunkin said.

"Spread the word around the city that everyone should go to the hill like a regular flood day," Vernon said. "We don't want anyone caught in the water."

Momma walked as fast as she could back to the walkways.

"Where can we find a rowboat?" Ida asked Dunkin.

"At the dock," Punch said. "I have a small one I use to fish sometimes." He looked desperate to help in some way. "It's not far if we run."

"Lead us to it," she said.

IDA HEARD SHOUTS AS SHE, Dunkin, and Punch approached the dam with Punch's boat. The rowboat was smaller than she'd have liked, but it was deep enough that a barrel should fit in the bow, which was the important thing.

Vernon told them to put the boat down next to the water on the bayside.

"Good timing," Vernon said. "The lye has just arrived."

In the middle of a crowd, Mr. Dupont stood gazing at a barrel as if he were saying good-bye to a loved one. Ida joined him, curious to see what lye looked like. It was white and powdery and looked as innocent as baby talc.

"Who's going in the boat?" Mr. Dupont asked nervously. People murmured.

"I am," Ida said. "It's my plan, and I will assume the risk."

There was more murmuring about Ida being a child, while other people whispered that she wasn't trustworthy.

She held up her hand to silence them. "I cut off the head of Aquacious. Let me make my reparations by doing this."

They agreed quicker than she expected, but really, who else wanted the job?

"You'll want these, just in case," Mr. Dupont said, handing Ida gloves and goggles. "They'll protect you."

"Who's going to steer the boat?" Dunkin asked nervously.

"Me," Ida said, at the exact moment that Punch said, "Me."

"I made the dam," Punch said. "I should help destroy it."

Ida gave him a steely look. "When that lye reacts with the water it's going to become a burning liquid, and if there are any waves, that corrosive water could slop into the boat. I doubt you'd like to kiss Preanne without any lips."

She stepped past him to the boat. She'd learned that if you really grossed people out, it tended to shut them up.

Punch followed her. "Someone needs to row the boat and keep it stable while you pour the lye. Otherwise you'll tip over and lose a lot more than your lips."

She glared at him. "You can come, but you'll take orders from me."

"Aye, aye, cap'n."

Ida yelled at the men who had brought down the barrel, "Let's get that barrel in the boat, and for the love of Aquacious, be careful!"

Dunkin smiled at her, and it took a moment for her to realize that she'd just mentioned Aquacious. She smiled back and added, "Only an *imbecile* spills lye!"

When the men were finished, Ida climbed into the boat and sat next to the barrel, which was wedged snugly into the bow. She told Vernon and Mr. Dupont, "I'm going to try little bits at a time, so I can get a feel for how powerful the lye is and how much we'll need, in case we need to go back to Mr. Dupont's factory for more."

"But there is no more!" Mr. Dupont cried. "This is my supply for the next six months!"

"Oh," Ida replied. "Then what I meant to say is, 'This will most certainly be enough lye.' Let's go, Punch."

Punch pushed the boat off the sand and into the water. Ida felt the splash as it hit the water. Punch climbed in and the boat began to rock immediately. He placed the paddles in the water to steady them, then slowly turned the boat around and headed for the dam.

The townspeople walked to the edge of the shore, watching their boat glide away.

"Be careful!" Dunkin yelled.

The baker screamed, "Save our town!"

Ida tried to smile at her but found she couldn't. She was too frightened.

45

"Can't you go any faster?" Ida demanded.

"Not unless you want to tip over that barrel," Punch said. "You concentrate on your job, and let me worry about the steering, okay?" Punch breathed heavily as he rowed, paddling faster on one side and then the other, keeping their path straight and gradually closing the distance between them and the middle of the dam.

"This is as close as I can get," Punch said. "I don't want to split the hull on that jagged debris."

Ida had to restrain herself from reminding Punch that he had created that debris.

Seeing the wreckage close-up was disconcerting for Ida. The stones and wood were piled up in a substantial wall, but the wall was not the disturbing part. The hair was like nothing Ida had ever seen, gooped up and knotted in every crevice you could see. Ida shivered with disgust.

She warned Punch that she was going to stand. She rose tentatively, shifting her weight until she felt centered on the seasawing boat. Placing her hand on the lip of the barrel, she was able to balance herself. She took a deep breath and stuck her gloved hand deep into the weightless powder. Grateful there was no strong wind, she scooped out a large handful and threw it toward the dam. She heard a cheer from the shore, but she dared not acknowledge it, lest she lose her balance. The powder faded into the water. She threw more, and, again, nothing seemed to happen. She threw scoop after scoop into the water, feeling like a silversmith fruitlessly feeding a dead fire.

Punch yelled, “Ida! Look!”

The water around them had turned murky. Ida saw a large bubble float to the surface, and then another, and another. The lye was starting to react!

Without warning, Punch grabbed his oars and paddled away.

Ida fell backward onto the hard bench. Irritated, she said, "Where are you going?"

"I don't want that stuff to eat through the bottom of the boat!" He rowed toward the shore but stayed close to the edge of the dam, so Ida could sprinkle the lye as they went.

The water became angry, hissing and spitting. While Punch concentrated all of his energies on keeping the boat steady, Ida became acutely aware of the dusting of lye that had coated her lower arms. One decent splash would turn her skin to fire.

The people on the shore made noises, but this time it wasn’t cheering. They were pointing at the sky, which had turned steel gray. A new wind swept across the bay, tipping them dangerously close to the water. Vernon signaled wildly for them to return to shore: *The flood is on its way.*

“That’s it. We have to go in," Punch said.

Nodding, she scooped as much lye as she dared on the section of dam in front of her. When she was seated again, Punch paddled like mad toward the shore. The waves were growing enormous on the ocean side of the dam—big enough to swallow the boat and the barrel whole. Thankfully, Ida and

Punch were on the calmer harbor side. As the wind grew louder, Ida couldn't hear the people on the shore anymore. She watched as most of them ran toward the city. They were not going to wait to see if the dam held; they were heading for the hill as they did every year.

Dunkin and Vernon waited for Ida and Punch. She was touched by their loyalty. As soon as the tip of the rowboat hit the sand, Vernon lurched forward and grabbed the vessel, pulling Ida and Punch in with as much force as he could muster. Ida flew forward in the boat and was thankful the barrel was wedged in firmly.

"Thanks . . . I think,' she said, thinking of the bruises she would have tomorrow.

Dunkin looked frightened. "We must go! We must reach the hill or we will drown!"

Hopping out of the boat, Punch offered a hand to Ida. She took it and stepped out. "You were right, Punch. I couldn't have done it on my own. Thank you."

"You're welcome. You did a good job."

Dunkin bristled. "There will be time for that later, but now we must go!"

Ida took off her gloves, and Dunkin handed her her satchel. As she brushed off the lye from her arms, she looked at the sea longingly. "I didn't use the whole barrel. Maybe the lye won't affect *all* the water. Maybe by the time the flood reaches the town square—"

Dunkin glowered at her. "You are an obstinate mouse who would steal cheese even if it were inside the belly of a cat! I am small, but I am prepared to pick you up and carry you if I must."

"Me, too," Vernon said.

"And me," Punch said.

She scowled. She'd been carried once by Punch, and it had

been quite humiliating. Lightning crackled across the sky, followed by an ominous boom of thunder. "I'm coming."

They sprinted away from the dam, along the Point. Vernon staggered behind. Punch was the fastest, but he didn't leave anyone behind. The sky turned black, and a hard rain began to fall. After fifteen grueling minutes, they reached the edge of town.

"What now?" Ida panted.

"We can't go through the city. There's no time," Dunkin answered, trying to catch his breath. "We have to go around."

"I know a good way," Punch said.

"Great. You lead," said Dunkin. "I hope Momma grabbed my nicest sponges, or I will be very upset."

Ida felt bad. His sponges were his livelihood. "I'm sure she did, Dunkin. She's very organized."

"Well, what is done is done.'

Let's hope it was worth it. Ida thought.

Punch led them down the beach and up through a park that grew the trees that the city used for its constant construction. As they ran up through the stormy darkness, Ida heard a horrible sound, like elephants colliding. "What's that?" she asked.

"Aquacious save us! The water is here!" Dunkin said.

"That was a wave hitting the dam," Vernon said.

She heard the boom again. Her heart sank. From the sound of it, the dam was holding. The lye had not been enough. She looked back to the bay.

"Look!" she cried. "Someone's on top of the dam!"

They all stopped running.

In a croaking voice, Punch said, "It's Mr. Loor."

Loor was standing in the beating rain with his hands waving in the air. And was he . . . ? Yes, he was *dancing.*

"What's he doing?" Vernon said.

"He has gone mad!" Dunkin said.

"He's celebrating," Punch said, horrified. "He always told us that he would build a dam so strong that he could dance on it on flood day."

"He doesn't know about the lye!" Dunkin said.

Mr. Loor was drunk with merriment. He turned around and wiggled his bottom at the town.

Thunder roared as the next wave hit the dam.

"I have to warn him!" Punch said, bolting back down the hill.

"Wait!" Ida cried. She looked at Dunkin. What should they do?

"Higher, Ida!" Dunkin said. "We must get higher!"

Hot spit in a bucket. Ida sprinted down the hill after Punch. As she slipped on grass and almost fell, she told herself that she was doing this for Punch and not Mr. Loor, that bottom-dweller.

"Punch!" she hollered. "There's no time!"

Soaking and blinded by the rain, she couldn't see Punch, but she could hear him yelling: "Run, Mr. Loor! The dam won't hold! Run!" But Punch was too far away to be heard.

Punch kept running, and Ida kept following him until they were back at the beach. They were still a long way from the Point, and Punch showed no signs of slowing down. A new deafening crash made Ida stop. This one was different from the others—a rupturing sound followed. Water was breaking through the dam!

She watched as Mr. Loor stopped dancing. He finally seemed to realize that something was not right. He looked as if he knew he should run, but couldn't decide in which direction. After hesitating, he ran toward the Greenhorn Peninsula. He had barely taken two steps, when the biggest wave Ida had ever seen came over the dam like an attacking whale. The wave crashed into the harbor, and once the water had dissipated, the dam was no more. And Mr. Loor had disappeared.

Ahead of her, Punch froze.

Ida's mouth hung open. Where had Loor gone? It had happened so fast—surely he couldn't have just been swallowed up?

Louder thunder filled the sky, and then another titanic wave rolled toward them.

She ran forward and tugged on Punch's shirt. "I'm sorry," she said, "but we have to go! The water's *coming*!" She pulled him back toward the hill. He didn't respond. "Punch! The flood!" She pointed at the next wave, which didn't have the dam to impede it. Bigger and higher than the last one, it crashed into the harbor and the water rose onto the beach, almost touching their feet.

This seemed to wake up Punch. He looked at Ida with wide eyes, and without another word, they sprinted back across the beach and toward the park. Ida's legs were heavy and exhausted, but she kept running, fueled by dread. As they raced through the park, she could hear people on higher ground yelling out to them. "Hurry!" they cried.

I wasn't thinking of stopping for a pastry.

She could see people only a few hundred yards away. She shouldn't have done it, but she looked behind her. She discovered a petrifying sight—a wave the size of a mountain had reared up and was seconds away from breaking over the Unfinished City.

She was so awed by the sight that she didn't look where she was going and tripped over a tree stump. She landed with a painful thud. She flopped onto her back and saw the wave break. The water rose and was only seconds from reaching her. Suddenly, she was being lifted and carried uphill. Punch had picked her up once more. "Maybe you won't mind this time," he panted.

"Don't talk! *Run*!" Ida screamed.

He dashed up the hill.

Ida heard a rush behind her and waited to feel the icy water seize them. She imagined her mouth and nose filling with salt water, as the force of the rushing flood mangled her body. Would she drown or be crushed to death? How arrogant she had been to think she could survive this behemoth of nature!

She willed herself to look back, and when she turned her head, she saw that the water had stopped rising. They were out of its reach. The flood now raced out toward the shantytown.

We made it to high ground. We are safe.

Punch must have realized the same thing at the same moment, because, suddenly, his knees buckled, and he went crashing to the ground with Ida beneath him.

46

Having seen Punch and Ida fall, Dunkin ran from the top of the hill to help.

"Great," Ida said, shoving Punch away. "I survive the flood only to be crushed by a smelly bootlicker."

Next to her, Punch lay smiling, too relieved to respond to the insult.

Dunkin grinned. "You are making nasty remarks, so I know you are feeling okay."

Ida checked her body for broken limbs. "I suppose I am."

She stood and looked down at the Unfinished City, watching as the flood mercilessly attacked the city, leaving nothing standing in its wake. The destruction had the same beauty as a fire consuming fresh paper, but this obliteration was on a scale that Ida could never have fathomed.

Punch stood next to her, mouth agape at the sight below. "I've never watched it before—I always refused." He looked around the hill at the gathered crowd. "How can they just watch their lives being destroyed like this?"

"That's the point," Ida said. "These homes and objects *aren't* their lives, just their possessions."

The true lives of the townspeople were not in the city below, but here on the hill, in the form of families and friends. Each year they were reminded of what really mattered in the world, and it gave them peace.

If only Ida could know that kind of tranquility. But she knew, as she watched the water begin to recede back to the ocean and heard the cheers and claps of the people, that by acting on their behalf instead of her own, she had begun to know what real happiness felt like.

The flood water continued to withdraw from the city, leaving the squares, the alleys, and the homes, until it was gone completely, returned to the sea for another year.

Ida turned to Punch. "You saved me, and I'll never forget it."

Punch blushed deeply. "Oh, uh, don't mention it."

Ida stuck her hand out. "You've been a real surprise."

Punch raised an eyebrow, as if he wasn't sure what she meant by surprise—if she were being nice or insulting him, as usual—but he took her hand and shook it.

Many people on the hill waved at Ida. She recognized them as the citizens who'd been on the Point trying to take down the dam. She waved back.

Vernon approached, smiling ear to ear. She'd never seen him happy, and it was an odd look on him. "You did it, kid! You really did it."

"I couldn't have done it without Punch," she said.

His frown returning, Vernon grunted. "I suppose."

"Thank you, sir. I appreciate you giving me a chance," Punch said politely.

"Even morons deserve a chance now and again," Vernon said.

Ida laughed, but Punch did not.

Momma and Auntie Gertrude made their way down to Ida's group. Momma cried uncontrollably as she embraced

Ida, smothering her into her bosom and refusing to let her go. "When Wee arrived on the hill without you, I was sure you had decided to try that *peverakivska* Treatment!"

Dunkin gasped. "Momma! Your language!"

Freed from Momma's clutches, Ida asked, "What did she say?" She was always happy to learn new curse words.

"I would not dare to say, but in Motvian it means something close to 'devil' mixed with 'the cheeks of a pig's buttocks.'"

Ida laughed, wishing she could speak Motvian.

Momma carried a full sack that was almost as big as her, although it seemed to weigh nothing.

"Are those the sponges?" Ida asked.

When Momma nodded, Ida said, "Dunkin is smart to sell something so lightweight."

"Someone his size cannot sell hammers, can they?" Auntie Gertrude said, sneering.

"Wee always thinks ahead," Momma said proudly. "He is my little genius."

"Speaking of little geniuses," Auntie Gertrude said to Ida. "I guess you are stuck looking like a young twerp forever, eh?"

"Uh, yeah. I guess I am." Ida was in no mood to discuss the matter with Auntie Gertrude. She'd had no time to absorb the idea herself.

"What will you do?" Punch asked.

She shrugged. She had no idea.

"You should stay here. You are a hero!" Dunkin said. He gestured to all the townspeople who passed by, smiling and waving at her.

"You could live with us," Momma said. "Wee could add on another room for you."

"Or . . . " Vernon cleared his throat. "You could help me rebuild my house."

"The Anti-Delugists will have to rethink our entire philosophy," Punch said. "You could help us create a new belief system!"

Ida was so touched that she felt something new—she wanted to cry, not because she was sad, but because she was happy.

"Thank you all. I think I need to be on my own for a minute. I need to do some thinking," she told them.

"Of course!" Momma said, backing up. "Give the girl some space!"

"No. You stay here. I'd like to go back down to the beach."

"Do not touch the water!" Dunkin said. "The lye!"

"I'm not an *imbecile*." She smiled. "I'll be back soon."

"We understand," Vernon said.

She made her way down the hill and through the park. The sky was now clear of clouds and as blue as a sapphire. When she reached the beach, she saw that the sea sparkled, and each reflection of light on its surface seemed to be a wink of contentment. The day had become astonishingly beautiful. She inhaled the crisp air, which was charged with the promise of new beginnings. Was every flood day like this? If so, she could understand why it was sacred.

She walked along the harbor, now at high tide.

What should she do now? With the majesty of the sky and sea in front of her, she could imagine taking up one of her friends' offers and staying here for a while.

She knew herself well enough to know that if she were here next year, she'd want to try the Treatment, even after she'd seen how deadly the flood was. Maybe she should just go back through the magic door to see if it took her somewhere with a different cure. What if she searched and searched and still had to return to Gulm empty-handed?

Her stomach sank at the thought of all the other children in Gulm in the same predicament as she. Plus, she'd promised herself she wouldn't search for Fargus and Josephine until she'd cured herself and those children. How long would she have to wait?

As her thoughts became more dispirited and gloomy, she saw something stir in the bay. Perhaps the flood had not finished, in which case she'd better run up the hill again.

The water churned, but not as it had before. This disturbance was only in one area. Soon a small whirlpool had formed, and it moved closer and closer to the shore. Was that possible? Could whirlpools move without getting larger?

When the whirlpool reached the beach, sand blew up and formed a little tornado that whipped grit into Ida's eyes. She threw up her hands, trying to block the wind and sand, worried she might be knocked off the beach and into the tainted water.

When she felt the wind die down and she had her balance again, she blinked open her eyes. She couldn't believe what she saw. The most beautiful girl that she'd ever seen was bobbing in the shallow part of the harbor. She had pale green skin and blue hair, and on her regal head she wore a coronet made of red coral. She glowed like a jellyfish, and resting high between her shoulder blades was a diaphanous purple fin. Most wondrous, from the waist down, she had the body of a seahorse.

Holy mollusks. It was Aquacious!

47

Ida stumbled back, afraid she might pass out.

Aquacious beckoned her forward. "I can't come any closer. You must come to me." Her voice pinged across the water like tinkling bells.

Ida glanced up to the hill where her friends were. Could they see this? She walked as close to the edge of the water as she dared. "You look different from your statue," Ida said, thinking of the grand, matriarchal woman carved in stone.

"I reflect your expectations and desires. If you were a poor man, I might appear to be made of gold."

Ida contemplated that to her Aquacious appeared to be a girl of around sixteen. "I see."

Aquacious winked, causing a pearl to drop from her eye. She caught the pearl in her hand, produced an oyster shell, and placed the pearl inside. She tossed the oyster joyfully into the ocean. "You did well, Ida," she said.

"You know my name?"

Aquacious laughed, and the sound was as if the fish were playing harps. "I know everything that happens in my land."

"Then why didn't you help us save the flood?" The question popped out of Ida's mouth before she realized it was probably rude. She hoped she hadn't given offense.

"The flood has no power if it happens because I want it to. The flood must happen because the people want it to." Her seahorse tail flicked in the water. "These last few years, doubt has been introduced to the townspeople, and, sometimes, when one seagull flies in the wrong direction, the other birds follow it, until they are all lost. If the flood had not happened this year, it would have stopped forever. And I . . ." She looked at the sky. "I would have disappeared with it."

"I'm glad you didn't disappear," Ida said, and she was. This gentle, mystical creature should always be in the world. "Why don't you let yourself be seen? Then everyone would believe in you and the flood."

Aquacious smiled. "If they take me for granted, they'll think they don't need the flood—that I will live among them without it—but I cannot. Their yearly sacrifice feeds their souls, which feeds mine."

This sounded confusing to Ida, but what did she know? Her own background was full of magic and mysteries, and she didn't have an explanation for those. "Thank you for introducing yourself. I feel better about today."

"Of course you do, but I didn't come just to make you feel better. I came to give you a gift."

Ida's every nerve twitched in anticipation of the goddess' next few words.

"You have shown great bravery, and you helped to deliver the flood today, and for that, I grant you your heart's greatest desire." Ida's eyes went wide as Aquacious clapped her hands over her head.

The water surrounding Aquacious lit up as if she were a ball of fire. Light raced around the bay and then disappeared. "When the tide recedes, you will find kelp on the shore. Eat the kelp, and you will grow into your true self."

Ida could barely breathe. "Is there enough—?"

"The kelp is bountiful. You will have enough for your friends."

"I-I don't know what to say. Thank you!"

"Don't waste this gift. And do not forget what you have learned from the Unfinished City."

"I won't. I promise."

The whirlpool reappeared around Aquacious, and Ida sensed the goddess was about to submerge. She wished she could make her stay. "Thank you again! Good-bye!" She waved.

The extraordinary creature sank, and just as her head was about to dunk under the water, she said, "One more thing. About your friend Punch . . . "

AFTER AQUACIOUS DESCENDED, the whirlpool remained. As it spun, it sucked in not only the tide but every last puddle of water within the Unfinished City. Ida watched as tiny rivulets and drops came rushing by and inhaled into the ocean. The mud, which would usually stay goopy and wet all year, dried into hardened clay. Not a drop of dangerous lye-filled water was left for anyone to step in or touch.

As the wind calmed, the whirlpool disappeared. Aquacious was gone.

The shoreline looked as it always did at low tide—littered with clams and kelp. Stunned and overwhelmed, Ida had to shake herself to be sure it hadn't been a dream.

She rushed forward to fill her bag with the kelp—long strips of the slimy, yellow-brown seaweed lay in piles all over the shore. Grabbing the first few strips, she found them hard to separate. The color and gooeyness made her think of snail bodies. *This stuff is magical?*

She hoped her satchel could hold as much as she needed. How many children had there been at the Master's manor? Fifty? A hundred? She couldn't believe she might be able to help them without having to bring them here and subject them to the flood.

She suddenly stopped filling her bag. *I can't take something home that doesn't work. I have to try it first.* Was she ready? Was it dangerous? Would it hurt? Should she do it alone, or did she need other people around?

She chided herself. She'd been willing to drown for this cure, and now she was hesitating? She shoved a handful of kelp into her mouth. It was so slimy, she almost spat it right back out. She forced herself to chew. It didn't taste awful. It tasted like the beach smelled—salty, sandy, and fishy, with just a hint of unbathed sailor.

She made herself swallow.

Then she waited . . .

But nothing happened.

What was the problem?

Ida had a horrible thought: Aquacious never said how long the kelp would take. What if by eating the seaweed she would now begin to age like a normal twelve year old, but the last four years were lost forever?

She let out a large sigh. She was angry at the lost time, and it seemed very unfair, but she could live with it, if from now on she would age normally. The hardest part would be waiting the months or even years until some changes started to appear, but she was used to waiting, and things felt less urgent today than they had yesterday.

She strolled along the beach, collecting more kelp, and wondering what the next few years would bring. For the first time in her life, she felt like she had options. She didn't want to admit it, but the idea was a little frightening. Being obsessed with one thing—like a cure—might be an eccentric way of life, but it did give one drive and focus.

She leaned over to pick up another pile of kelp, when her stomach spasmed as if she might be sick.

Terrific. Aquacious made me eat something poisonous, she thought as she fell to the ground.

Her body shuddered. A current ran through her. It wasn't painful—just a large surge of energy. She saw spots in front of her eyes like she'd stared directly into the sun. The bottom of her feet tickled like crazy. She giggled. And then it was over.

She got to her knees, brushed off the sand, and stood up. Remarkably, she felt fine, great even.

That was weird, she thought. She reached down to pick up more kelp. When she saw her hand, she yelped. Her fingers had grown! Her shirt sleeve was too short!

She looked down to see that all of her clothes were too small. She'd grown at least three inches. She wanted to laugh and cry at the same time. It had worked! Aquacious had done it! Ida had aged!

Kicking off her too-tight shoes, Ida paraded down the beach, admiring her long legs and arms. Wondering about her face, she ran to the edge of the bay and used the water as a mirror. She was surprised. Her face had not changed as much as she'd been expecting, and yet she definitely looked different. Her cheekbones were more defined, her forehead was broader, and her eyes did not seem as large, which took away from the "wide-eyed girl" look she'd always taken advantage of. Her hair had grown by a foot! For four years it hadn't grown one inch!

She plopped herself down on the sand. She laughed and then laughed some more. Here she was—*the real her*—and she could feel it. Even if she'd looked in the water and seen a middle-aged man, she would've been happy—as long as she *felt* like herself. Feeling like herself was the greatest gift she'd ever known, and she hoped everyone she knew got to feel this way.

Thinking of her friends, she hopped up, dying to show them what had happened. She ran up the beach and was almost to the park when she remembered the kelp. She needed to gather as much as possible before the tide rose. Who knew if the magical seaweed would ever be here again?

She sprinted back to fill her bag to the brim.

48

Ida ran up the hill as quickly as she could. By the time she reached the meadow, many of the townspeople were leaving, ready to examine what remained of the city.

She almost ran head-first into Punch.

"Excuse me," he said, moving around her.

"Punch! It's me!"

He looked her up and down. When he got to her face, his chin dropped. "Ida?"

"It worked! I was by the water and suddenly Aquacious was there and she said I did a good job and she gave me magic seaweed and now I'm cured!"

"Magic seaweed? What are you talking about?" He continued to gawk at her.

"Don't be scared. I'm supposed to look like this!"

"I'm not . . ." He straightened up and swallowed. "I'm not scared. I just always thought you were lying about the whole age thing."

Of course he did.

He looked her up and down again. "It's jarring, okay?"

Ida was thrilled to think her transformation was so significant that it was "jarring." She couldn't stop smiling. She took his hand. "Come with me."

She dragged him across the meadow to where Vernon was sitting. Vernon looked at her, looked away, and then looked back again, stupefied. "You've changed, kid."

"Isn't it wonderful?" she said.

"What happened?" Vernon asked with a furrowed brow.

"It was Aquacious, and I'll tell you all about it, but first, I need to make an introduction. Vernon, this is Punch. Punch this is Vernon."

Tearing his eyes away from Ida, Vernon surveyed Punch and scowled. "I already know him. He's is the piss-ant that blew up the light house."

"Yep," Ida said, beaming. "He's also your son."

Punch and Vernon gaped at her.

"Don't go making things up, Ida," Vernon said, standing up. "It's not—"

"It's true!" Ida said. She looked at Punch. "Loor found you in Reek, right? A homeless boy wandering the streets? Vernon's son washed away in the flood thirteen years ago. And I can't believe I never saw it before, but Punch you have Vernon's eyes!" She was giddy.

Punch didn't smile. In fact, he looked nauseated.

"It's true, I lost my son," Vernon said, frowning. "But he's dead. And this isn't funny, Ida."

"It's no joke. Aquacious told me!" As Vernon's eyes widened, Ida said, "You told me yourself that you had no proof that your son was dead."

Vernon squinted at Punch, studying his face like a vexing construction problem. His voice shook as he said, "The day my boy disappeared, he was wearing a green wool sweater and brown pants. His front pocket held a wooden horse that I'd carved for his birthday. His mother wore a pale blue dress, and she would have still been wearing the harness that was supposed to keep her connected to him and me."

Punch had gone pale. He knew the wooden horse well. It had been his only possession throughout his childhood. "If you're my father then . . . then . . . what's my real name?" He held his chin up defiantly.

"Theodore was my son's name. But his mother and I, we called him Theo."

Punch's whole body seemed to crumple. His lip trembled. "I haven't heard that name in a long, long time."

"*Thunder and lightning*." Vernon sat back down on the grass with a thud. Eyes filling, he said, "And your mother . . . ?"

Punch shook his head. "She, uh, didn't make it."

Vernon put his head in his hands and sobbed. "All this time you were right here."

Punch looked defiant. "Why did my mother take me into the flood?"

Vernon's face fell. "We both did. We were trying to save your life. You were very, very sick, and you were going to die, so your mother and I decided to try the Treatment. But the flood overpowered us, and you and Delia were washed away. I lost everything . . . "

"My mother died because of me?"

"No. She died because of me, because I wasn't brave enough to release my harness before she did. She was the bravest, most beautiful woman you could ever meet, and you should be proud to call her your mother."

Punch sat down next to Vernon.

"I'm so sorry, Theo," Vernon said. "I'm so sorry I didn't find you sooner."

"You didn't know," Punch said, putting his arm around his father.

"Now that is a beautiful thing!" Ida said. "Aquacious really knows how to deliver."

Vernon wiped his eyes. "You saw Aquacious?"

"Down by the ocean."

"She gave Ida magic kelp that helped her age," Punch said, laughing.

"Don't laugh!" Ida said. "It's true."

"You look like a proper young lady," Vernon said, smiling in approval.

She stuck out her tongue. "Yuck. Don't ever call me 'proper' again." Opening her bag, she showed them the seaweed she'd gathered. "Now I can help the kids back home."

Vernon's smile disappeared. "So you're leaving?"

"I'm sorry, Mr. Lyon. I can't tell you how much it means that you wanted me to stay. Most people find me to be sort of a . . . a . . . "

"Large pain in the rump?" Vernon offered.

She grinned wickedly. "Yeah. It's been nice to feel wanted for a change."

"It's good you want to help out those other kids," Vernon said. "And when you're finished, you can always come back here if you want. You and Punch can be brother and sister if you like!"

She looked at Punch, and both of them blushed.

"Uh, no thanks," Punch said. "I'm not interested in being related to a lying, thieving brat." He produced a dazzling smile.

"And I'm not interested in being related to a stubborn, suck-up pea-brain." She smiled back.

"I no longer understand young people," Vernon said.

"Do you think Mr. Loor knew? About you and me?" Punch asked Vernon.

Vernon's brow furrowed. "I don't know how he could have. I didn't like the man, but I will always be grateful that he took you off the streets."

Punch looked out at the sea. "Did you see him get swept away?"

Vernon nodded. "I'm sorry things had to end that way for him."

"Me, too. I don't really think he meant any harm."

Ida tried hard not to roll her eyes. Mr. Loor had meant *plenty* of harm to her. But the man was gone. There was no need to besmirch his name further now.

Vernon put his hand on Punch's shoulder. "We'll build a nice memorial for him."

"That would be nice."

Vernon looked out at the bay and whispered, "Do you think Aquacious is still down there?"

"She seemed to disappear with the tide." Ida was curious about something. "How did Aquacious look when you saw her?"

Vernon smiled dreamily. "She looked like the creator of all things big and small. She was gentle and sort of reminded me of my mother. Why? How did she look to you?"

Ida was fascinated. "The same." She thought she would let Vernon keep his dreamy ideal.

"She was very generous to us this year," Vernon said.

Ida was amazed by Vernon. Other men might be angry that Aquacious had known who his son was and not revealed him until today, but Vernon had decided to see it all as a glorious gift. Ida would try to follow his example. She would never lament the years she had been stuck at twelve. Instead, she would forever celebrate the day when she had been rewarded for helping her friends.

Punch continued to talk to Vernon about a memorial. "What kind of material—"

A shrieking voice interrupted them. "Is that you, witch-girl?"

Ida turned to see Ms. Neely standing with her hands on her pointy hips, as angry and unpleasant as ever.

49

"Looks like you've been up to some frippity-froppery-hocus-pocus to me!" Ms. Neely yelled to everyone on the hill. "Look at this freak! She's just what I said she was: a monster who should be locked up!"

Ida searched the faces around her, wondering if the people were going to turn on her once more. She was tired of explaining herself.

"Is there a policeman here?" Ms. Neely yelled. "I think we'd all feel safer if this evil spirit were no longer loose on our streets." She dove toward Ida. Vernon and Punch stepped forward to block her, both looking ready to fight. Ida was grateful, but knew the men wouldn't strike the older woman.

"Who's a freak?" a new screeching voice said.

Dunkin and Momma had heard Ms. Neely's yelling and headed over. Marching beside them and waving her cane like a sword was Auntie Gertrude. When Gertrude reached Ms. Neely, she yelled like she wanted to be heard in Reek. "Ms. Neely, you like to frighten children! You make your living out of being a tattle-tale and a bully! If that does not make you a freak then I do not know what does!"

"I am the head truant officer of the—"

"I do not care if you are the mayor of my butt. Your schemes almost cost this girl her life, and if she had died, then we would have had no flood. I think you owe her and the entire town an apology."

Ms. Neely went red in the face. "I have no intention—"

"Even better. Then get out of our city and never come back."

Cheers and whoops came from everyone on the hill.

Ms. Neely stood as tall as she could, lifted her chin, and opened her mouth to speak.

"I said, 'Get!'" Gertrude said, raising her cane.

Incensed, Ms. Neely marched down the hill without another word.

Ida laughed and laughed. "That was great, Auntie Gertrude! You really told her!"

Dunkin, Momma, and Gertrude all gaped at the new Ida.

"I never liked that woman," Auntie Gertrude said, "but she had one thing right—you have been up to *something*."

Ida explained the miracle on the beach, still unable to believe it herself.

Momma clucked her tongue. "What a miraculous day!"

"You have no idea," Vernon said, putting his arm around Punch.

"Maybe you should give Wee some of that seaweed," Auntie Gertrude squawked. "It is about time he grew up, too!"

"Auntie Gertrude, you just said that no one likes a bully!" Ida said.

"It is different when it is someone in your own family, because—"

"No. It's not," Ida said, studying Dunkin's pained expression.

Gertrude pondered this. She asked Dunkin, "Wee, have I ever hurt your feelings?"

Dunkin stroked his beard. "I, uh, well, yes, Auntie. You have a very sharp tongue."

Gertrude looked shocked. "In Motzia, that is how we show love. I am sorry if I offended you."

Now it was Momma's turn to be shocked. She had never heard her sister apologize for anything.

"Thank you, Auntie. I am touched," Dunkin said. "Now can we please get back to the very important fact that Ida saw Aquacious! I need to hear every last detail, please. Especially the colors. I would like to do a fall line of sponges based on her skin tones."

Ida proceeded to tell them again about her rendezvous, leaving nothing out this time.

WHEN ALL THE questions were finally answered, Ida announced she wanted to go back to the beach to collect more seaweed before the tide returned. Her friends were too exhausted to argue. Dunkin was the only one who made a comment. "I thought you had a bag-full."

"I do, but I want to have extra. I'll find a second bag to fill."

He gave her a funny look, and as she waved goodnight to them all, she suspected that Dunkin had known she was lying. She knew it was time to leave the Unfinished City, and she couldn't bear the thought of saying good-bye to everyone—the sentimental hugs, the promises to return, the proclamations of sadness and grief. She'd decided she would rather just disappear. They knew how she felt and vice versa. Why get all emotional about it?

She walked alone to the bottom of the hill and, instead of approaching the beach, she headed into the city. The ladders and walkways had been destroyed, so she walked along what had been a mud path. The sun was setting, creating a sherbet sky streaked with crimson and rose. She felt like Aquacious had created an extra-beautiful sky that night just for her, but that was arrogant. It was for the entire Unfinished City.

She stood staring at the sunset for longer than she meant to, thinking of her journey home and what it meant to never see her friends here again. Next thing she knew, her feet were leading her back down the path and up the hill. Her friends were on their way home, walking and chatting. They stopped in surprise.

"Was the seaweed gone?" Punch asked.

Ida looked at the ground. "Okay, chumps. Here's the deal. I was going to leave town just now, and maybe that wasn't very nice, but it's time for me to go, so if you want to say good-bye, this is, uh, the time, because I don't know when or if I can come back." She looked up.

Dunkin and Momma looked stricken. Punch appeared confused, and Vernon was as non-plussed as ever.

Gertrude rolled her eyes. "Make up your mind, already."

Ida smiled, realizing she might grow up to be a lot like Gertrude.

"Come here, child." Momma pulled Ida into an enormous hug, smothering her in her scent of gravy and citrus. Ida told herself to remember this smell.

Punch, who was acting a bit shy, offered her a handshake. Ida wanted to spit in her hand first, because she thought it would be funny, but she didn't. She decided it would be childish, and she was no longer a child. They shook hands, looking each other straight in the eye.

"Hilly will be heartbroken you've left," Punch said. "So will Mrs. Gauge, Mrs. Brown, and everyone else."

Ida knew she'd miss them in her own way—even the annoying twins. "Tell them I said, 'Goodbye,' and 'Thank you for taking me in,' and tell Hilda she should go back to talk to that baker kid, and she can have my green dress with the ruffles to wear when she does."

"She's been trying it on while you were away," Punch said. "She'll be delighted."

Ida felt a thrill knowing she wouldn't need the dress again. "If I never see a ruffle again, it will be too soon."

Punch laughed.

Ida turned to Vernon. "I might have recognized Punch from his smile, if you ever smiled, Vernon."

Vernon grunted in response, then grinned guiltily. "I think I'll be smiling a lot more now. Thank you, Ida, for everything."

"I'm so happy for you."

"I'm so happy for *you*."

Now only Dunkin remained. He looked at her with teary eyes. Ida wagged a finger at him. "Don't you start. You're becoming more like your Momma every day."

He removed a handkerchief from his pocket and blew loudly. "Yes. It is true. We Motzians are very sentimental."

"Thank you, Dunkin, for everything—"

"You will come back to visit, right?" he asked.

The question she'd been dreading. "It's a complicated journey. I hope to make it again someday . . . " She had needed the Treatment the last time the door brought her here, but would a need to see friends convince the door to bring her back? She truly had no clue, and not knowing if she would ever see Dunkin again filled her with sorrow. "I really hope to visit again. I'll miss you." *Proclamations of sadness and grief.* Just like she hated.

"I will miss you, too, friend. Life has been so much more interesting with you here."

"Continue to travel, try new foods, and keep buying mysterious hats," she said with a wink.

He winked back. "Of course."

Waving good-bye, she walked down the hill once more,

hurrying so no one would notice the tears threatening to fall. The apricot sky had turned gray, which was good. Ida wanted the cover of darkness for her journey home. She didn't need any townspeople witnessing her stepping through a magic door.

Her mind turned from her good-byes to the next momentous step she must take. Would the door take her where she needed to go?

50

How long had it been since Ida had first arrived in the Unfinished City? It felt like years, but it had only been one month. Each moment, she grew more excited to return home.

Without the walkways, the trip to the middle of town took more time than usual. Ida couldn't imagine how long it would have taken in thick mud. Using the hills and the sea as her guides, she found the approximate area where she'd first arrived. Luckily, most citizens were still on the hill or checking on their homes. The business area was deserted.

She searched for her landmark—the sign for the Farnucci Brothers' Glass Blowing Shop. She looked everywhere but couldn't find it. Panicking, she realized that, of course, the flood would have washed it away. *Peverakivska sign,* she thought.

She studied what remained of the buildings, which was little. Ahead on her left, she saw a brick smokestack which was the only standing section of what had been a large structure. She walked to it hopefully. Much to her relief, she saw broken glass. This was the chimney of a furnace for a glass blowing shop!

She walked away from the chimney until she was as far away from the shop as she remembered being on her first day.

After triple-checking that no one was around, she reached into the outside pocket of her satchel and pulled out her two watches. One had gotten cracked—probably when Punch fell on her—but it still worked, which was all that mattered. Holding a watch in each hand, she observed the second hands closely. She walked in small careful circles like she had at the Institute and gradually made those circles larger.

On her third revolution, she saw the clock hands flutter, and then, in an instant, one watch was one second behind the other. Her heart raced, as a sudden breeze whipped through her long hair. She blocked out her surroundings and concentrated on where she needed to go: *I need to go to Gulm. I need to help the children of Gulm. Will Fargus be in Gulm? What about Josephine? Josephine wouldn't be in Gulm. Josephine went home.* Concentrate, Ida! *Think about Gulm, not Josephine!*

A bang filled the air, followed by a blinding flash of light. Ida fell through darkness, struggling for air. She told herself not to panic, that the journey had felt this way the last time—a terrifying fall that might last forever.

When she landed it was with an awkward thunk that knocked the wind out of her.

When she could breathe normally again, she looked around. She couldn't see anything in the pitch-black space but felt that the surface beneath her was wood. Standing, she felt for her satchel—it was intact and still hanging across her body.

Holding her hands out in front of her, she walked toward the meager source of light, which, thankfully, turned out to be a door. She opened it nervously, letting in a flood of sunshine. The illumination revealed she'd landed in a shed full of gardening supplies and tools.

She stepped outside onto a beautiful green lawn lined with rose bushes, azaleas, and a huge, gorgeous tomato plant. She didn't spend much time scrutinizing the yard, because she was busy staring in amazement at the enormous farmhouse that towered above it. She'd never been here before, but she'd heard about it in infinite detail years ago from Fargus. This was Josephine's house.

Ida was madder than a slapped-at hornet. She was supposed to be in Gulm! She needed to help the children there. This was her own stinkin' fault. If she'd concentrated on Gulm and not started to think about Fargus and Josephine, she wouldn't have ended up here.

She sighed. What should she do? Did Josephine even live here still? Years had passed. Maybe Josephine had moved.

Fig and turnips. Ida had to check at least.

She approached the house with trepidation, relieved that her feet in the grass made no noise. If strangers lived here, she wanted to depart unnoticed.

Getting as close as she dared, she peeked into a window.

Sunlight cascaded into a cozy kitchen that centered around a round table with a gingham tablecloth. A porcelain teapot was perched on the table, along with two cups of steaming tea and a plate of cookies that looked fresh out of the oven. Seated at the table was an older man, around Vernon's age, with salt-and-pepper hair, brown eyes, and thin lips. And next to him sat Josephine!

She looked so different. She wore boyish dungarees, but nothing could hide the fact that she was becoming a pretty young woman. Her hair, once so curly and wild, had grown into long soft waves. Her face had lost its baby fat, narrowing to accentuate a strong jawline. Her amber eyes sparkled as she chatted with the man, and at one point, she burst out laughing.

Mesmerized, Ida realized she'd never seen Josephine truly content before. All their time together had been under dire circumstances, and Josephine had usually been nibbling nervously on her hair, frowning in confusion, or rolling her eyes at Ida's stubbornness. Ida smiled to herself, feeling nostalgic for their adventures together. She couldn't wait to find Fargus, too.

Ida heard a teacup shatter on the floor. Josephine was staring straight at her. Ida grinned and waved. Josephine tilted her head, confused.

"It's Ida!" Ida said. "Let me in!"

Eyes as wide as saucers, Josephine hopped up and leapt for the back door. She unlatched it for Ida, who strode into the kitchen as if it was something she did everyday. "What's up, farm-girl?"

Josephine was still in shock. "Is it really you?"

"In the flesh." Ida took a little bow.

"You look so beautiful!" Josephine said, touching Ida's long hair.

Ida shooed her away. "More importantly, look at this." She held out her newly long arm and flexed her muscle.

Josephine stared at her, mouth agape, for another few seconds, and then she threw her arms around Ida, squeezing her tight. "I'm so happy to see you! I can't believe you're really here!"

Ida smiled. It felt good to be so welcomed.

"You aged! Did you find a cure?"

"It took ages, like four years, and believe me, it was no picnic. But I am exceedingly clever at most things, as I'm sure you remember. Now I am completely cured and can age like any normal nincompoop." Ida swaggered over to the table, sat down, and popped an oatmeal cookie into her mouth. As she chewed she said, "I thought I should say hello before I headed to Gulm." No need to reveal she was here by accident. "I'm going to help the kids there. I've got something that can cure them, too." She patted her bag.

"That's fantastic!" Josephine said. "I've always felt so awful for all of them."

Taking a second cookie, Ida focused on the old man. "And who are you?"

"This is my father. And . . ." Josephine gave the man a questioning look, and after he nodded she said, "He is also, uh, Fargus."

Ida choked on the cookie and then guffawed. "Uh. Right. And I'm the Princess of Cauliflower."

"I'm serious. This is Fargus Dudson, the boy you grew up with." Josephine proceeded to explain how she thought she had only traveled to a different world when she went to Gulm, when in fact she'd also traveled to a different time.

When she was finished with the bizarre explanation, the man said, "It's all true, Ida."

"Can I have some water?" Ida asked.

Josephine grabbed a glass from the cupboard and filled it at the tap. Ida chugged the whole thing, buying herself time to think. She was inclined to believe these two were bananas. But the more she considered what they'd said, the more she had to admit their story wasn't any crazier than what she'd just experienced.

She studied the man more closely, observing that he had the same hard brown eyes as the boy she'd known. She raised an eyebrow. "Prove you're Fargus."

"When I was nine you and I stole a tin of raisins from Kitchen Maggie. You replaced them with mouse droppings."

"I'm feeling a bit ill," Ida said.

"So am I," Josephine said. "That's disgusting."

Ida wasn't ill because of the mouse turds. She felt ill because no one knew that story but Fargus.

"Drink more water," Josephine said.

"It's wonderful to see you," the man, Fargus, said. "I have always worried about what happened after you left me."

After you left me. How could this old codger be the little boy who was two years younger than her? "How long ago did we part ways in your, uh, time?"

He had to think a minute. "More than fifty years. Maybe fifty-three?"

"More water, please." She waved her glass at Josephine, who took it and returned to the sink. "How long have you been back?" Ida asked Josephine.

"Four years."

The same amount of time since Ida had left Gulm. At least she and Josephine seemed to be living on the same timeline.

"How about I make dinner, and we can explain it all to you?" Fargus asked.

Ida put her satchel on the floor and pulled her chair closer to the table. She needed to hear every last detail.

51

The three of them spent the next four hours eating, talking, and reminiscing. Ida couldn't remember the last time she'd eaten so well or laughed so hard. Hearing her childhood escapades explained in this older man's voice was just bizarre, but she soon grew accustomed to it and felt as if she had her best friend beside her once again. He did an impression of Stairway Ruth that almost made her fall out of her chair. She responded with her impersonation of Kitchen Maggie and the voice was so perfect that Fargus got a cramp from laughing.

Josephine watched them entertain each other with awe and delight in her face.

When they had stopped laughing for a moment, Ida asked him, "What have you been doing since you got back?"

"Improving the town, mostly," Fargus said.

"Father changed the laws so people don't have to wear gloves anymore, and he used his money to build new parks and a bigger school. And this year we're opening a huge library. Father is building it right next door so we won't be so isolated from the rest of town and—"

"Have you been using the door?" Ida interrupted.

"No," Fargus said sharply.

"Why not?" Now that Ida understood that the door involved time travel, the possibilities were endless. "Josephine, you said your mom died a long time ago. You could go back and save her! And Fargus, you could go save your parents. No one you love has to die!"

Fargus gave her a sad smile, and it was so familiar that Ida's heart contracted. "Anything we change could threaten Josephine's very existence, and I can't have that. One tiny alteration to the past and maybe she wouldn't be born. No matter how much it hurts, we have to leave the past as the past."

"And if I want to go save my parents?" Ida said, her voice rising.

"If they'd lived, you never would have come to the Institute. You and I would never have met. And I very much doubt that Josephine and I could have defeated the Master without you."

Ida took this in. It was all so confusing. "So am I meant to go help the children of Gulm or not?"

"I can't tell you the future," Fargus said. "All I know is that it's very dangerous for you to mess with the past."

She absorbed this disappointing news.

"I hope you'll stay with us for a while." Josephine sat at the edge of her seat. "I want to hear more about your adventures."

"You're welcome here as long as you like," Fargus said. "We have lots of room, and it would make us both very happy."

Josephine nodded with enthusiasm. "You'd be family."

"That sounds really nice." And it did. The last time Ida'd had a long-term home was at The Institute, and it had been a dreary place run by nasty crones. She could barely remember what it was like to live in a real house with a family. She was so tempted to stay that she had to jump up immediately. "I need to go. I have to get to Gulm."

Josephine and Fargus were startled. "Now?" Fargus said.

"Haven't they waited long enough?" She grabbed her bag.

"We haven't had dessert yet," Josephine said.

Grabbing the plate of remaining cookies, Ida dumped as many as would fit into the outside pockets of her satchel. "That'll do."

"Uh, okay," Josephine said, looking to her father for help. "Do you need anything else? Water? Uh, clothes?"

Ida looked down at her mud-splattered garments. Next thing you knew they'd have her taking a hot bath and sleeping in a comfy bed, and then she might never leave. "Nah."

Fargus grabbed something from the window sill. "Take the claganmeter."

She examined the device in his hand. She'd seen it once, bundled in cloth, but never unwrapped. It was bigger than she'd imagined, nearly a foot long. Made of brass, it had one long cylinder with a time piece at each end. Very simple and elegant.

"I don't think so." She handed it back to a surprised Fargus. "I have watches that work fine, and you might need this one day."

"I already told you—"

"If something goes wrong in Gulm . . . " She hesitated, not wanting to admit her secret fear. "If I go through the door and I end up in the wrong time, like maybe the Master is still in charge, I would feel better knowing that you and Josephine have a way to get there."

"How would we know you were in trouble?" Fargus asked.

"You'll know that something went wrong if . . . " She struggled to come up with an answer, and then thought of something simple and perfect. "You'll know that something went wrong if I don't come back here tonight."

"Tonight?" Josephine was startled.

"Get that bed made," Ida said. "When I leave Gulm again,

I plan to tell that door to bring me right back here, right now. Got it?"

Josephine and Fargus both nodded but looked nervous. They seemed a lot alike now. *Weird.*

Fargus put the claganmeter back on the window sill. He'd known her long enough to know that there would be no changing her mind. "We'll walk you to the shed."

"No." She smiled. "Because I'm going to be right back, remember?"

They agreed to say good-bye in the kitchen.

Ida tried to give them quick hugs but each insisted on a prolonged squeeze. Ida pretended she hated it, but she was filled with warmth and satisfaction as each embraced her.

Finally, she exclaimed, "Bye, you lunkheads. Go run me a hot bath!"

She dashed out the back door without looking back. As she crossed the lawn, she was struck again by its calm and beauty. Josephine and Fargus had really created a nice life for themselves. And if everything went right, she could be a part of it.

She felt lighter and happier than she had during dinner. She realized she felt better because she'd admitted that she was worried about the Master. She'd always thought that the best feeling in the world was to feel smarter and braver than every person in the room. She thought the secret to life was to always be one step ahead of everyone. She was slowly beginning to understand that admitting you needed help was very important in life, and that when people truly cared for you they would listen and give you reassurance. If need be, they would give you the help you asked for. Knowing friends were there for you was the most satisfying feeling of all.

This revelation irked Ida a bit. She liked being right, and in order to learn this nugget of wisdom she had to admit she'd been wrong, but at least she didn't have to say it *out loud* to anyone. Josephine, Fargus, Dunkin, Punch, Momma,

Vernon—they were all people in her life that she loved and trusted. As she thought about them being on her side, she felt an opening in her chest, as if a dam were coming down and water was finally flowing through.

She threw open the door to the shed so enthusiastically that she nearly pulled the creaky door off its hinges. She pulled her timepieces out of her bag and stepped inside. "Okey, dokey. Let's get this done."

EPILOGUE

Nowadays, if one asks the people of Gulm about the night Ida Dorrington came home, one will get many versions of the story. Some will say she arrived with the Brothers, riding one of them bareback and howling at the moon. Some will say she was a ghost who floated along the cobblestones, while others will claim she was human but had hair made of seaweed. The part they can agree upon is this:

The townspeople were in their beds, most of them sleeping soundly. The children, the ones who had lived with the Master, been buried with the Brothers, and lost their ability to age, were not sleeping well. They spent their days enjoying their families and friends, relieved to be home, but at night, with only their thoughts to occupy them, they always began to think about their lives—their alternate lives—in which they had grown up as they were meant to. They would float out of their bodies mentally and imagine their adult selves walking, talking, marrying, having children, and growing old.

They never spoke to each other about these late-night fantasies. They guessed that the other children had them, too—but speaking about them might seem like ingratitude.

And weren't they happy to be home? To be safe? To be rid of the Master, at last? So they continued with their restless nights, becoming more lonely and isolated from each other every day.

The night Ida returned, Ned Mosley was wide awake. Nowadays, he was always awake at 3am to bake bread with his stepmother, Beatrice. He and his father, Morgan, had once been the town sweepers, but four years ago the streets had seemed to start magically cleaning themselves. Every morning when they arrived on Main Street, every cobblestone had already been swept and shined. After two weeks of this unexplained gift, Morgan announced it was time to find a hobby.

Beatrice, Morgan's new wife, was a surprisingly good baker. Ned had tried his darnedest to keep disliking her, but every morning, as he sank his teeth into the most delicious breads, cinnamon rolls, and sticky buns you've ever tasted, he found it more and more difficult to resent the woman. Ned was the one who had suggested they start a bakery. It had been a success from day one, and they were barely able to keep up with the orders for fresh breads and cookies.

He was pulling twin loaves of pumpernickel from the oven when he heard a bell tolling. "Do you hear that?" he asked Beatrice.

She stopped working. "Sounds like the tower bell."

"At this hour?" he said.

"Maybe Angus has finally cracked," Beatrice said. The town's bellman had always been eccentric.

Outside the door, a child hollered. Beatrice's eyes widened. Given the history of the town, a child out of his bed at night was an eerie event.

Putting down the bread, Ned raced to the door with Beatrice right behind him. When he opened it he saw little Georgie Starch knocking on the door next to theirs.

"Thomas, come out! It's here! It's finally here!" Georgie cried.

"What's here?" Ned asked, but Georgie was running to the next door, knocking and yelling the same thing: "It's here! Wake up! It's here!"

Ned and Beatrice followed the boy, as did everyone he awoke.

He eventually led the crowd to the church on Main Street where a girl stood on the steps. Her long black hair blew in front of her face as she yelled at the gathering crowd. "I have come with the CURE for the lost children of Gulm! I took it myself, and I know it works! Make a single-file line, and I'll hand it out as quickly as I can!"

"Who are you?" an old man asked.

The girl smiled, thrilled that no one could recognize her. "My name is Ida Dorrington. Together with my friends Fargus and Josephine, we saved you from the Master."

People gasped. Everyone knew the story of the children who had appeared, destroyed the Master, and then vanished.

Ida! thought Ned. He couldn't believe she was back. He looked around, wondering if his old friend Josephine were here, too.

Beatrice whispered to Ned, "You helped save the children from the Master, too."

Ned shrugged. No one seemed to remember that he'd been at the manor that day as well, but he didn't mind. He couldn't explain everything that had happened, and he certainly couldn't tell people where his friends had disappeared to, so the fewer questions the better.

Children lined up in front of Ida at once. She opened a satchel slung across her chest and pulled out a strand of something that Ned couldn't make out. Ida gave the strand to the first child in line—Philippa Parker, who looked around ten. Ida whispered in Philippa's ear. Philippa scrunched up her face, and then ate the strand.

The whole town seemed to hold its breath while they

waited for something to happen. Ida yelled, "It takes a minute, okay? Next!"

Ida passed out five more strands, and each time the child looked sick as they chewed. Word spread that they were eating some sort of brown seaweed. As time passed, people murmured that it must be a hoax, and some were wandering home back to their warm beds. All of a sudden, Philippa dropped to the ground with a squeal.

Her family gathered around in alarm, but Ida said, "It's fine. She's fine."

Philippa shuddered and twitched, and right in front of everyone's eyes, she grew two feet taller. Her nose elongated, her face expanded, and her hair grew so long it reached her ankles. Philipa giggled and stood up. "Why are you all staring?" Surprised at the sound of her richer, deeper voice, she glanced down. "Oh." She laughed more. "How wonderful!"

Soon all the children were dropping to the ground, convulsing briefly, and becoming their adult selves. Jackie Crisp shot up to almost six-foot-five, like his father the window washer. Wilbert Francis became hairy from his head to his knuckles, while Gerhart Thorne became as bald as a peeled onion. He grinned as everyone patted his new shiny dome.

Rosetta Collins, who had a face full of freckles and monstrously large teeth, transformed into a breathtaking beauty. Gertie Parsons went from chubby to willowy, and Pauline Alexander went from pencil-thin to thick and hearty. No matter what kind of transformation occurred, it happened with laughter—giggling seemed to be a necessary part of the metamorphosis—and, except for bald Gerhart, everyone grew hair that reached to the ground.

Ned looked around frantically for his aunt Lucy, who was one of the lost children he'd rescued from the Master's manor. She was thirty-four years old, but she still looked eleven. Despondent when he couldn't find her, he told Beatrice he was going home. He sprinted to their house in the alley of Mary Lynn Lane.

He had to bang on the door for five minutes before anyone came to the door. When Lucy finally answered, Ned explained the situation, and despite Lucy's skepticism, she and Morgan dressed quickly and returned with Ned to Main Street.

A crackling energy filled the night. The children who were now adults who'd been cured were running around to show off their new selves. The children waiting in line for their turn were giddy with anticipation, whispering about what they might look like. The rest of the townspeople were dizzy with wonderment and happiness.

"The line is there, Lucy," Ned said, pointing. "Go join!"

Lucy, suddenly shy, asked Morgan. "Shall I?"

"Of course you should, silly girl! I mean, if it's what you want."

"I want it *too badly*. I'm terrified of being disappointed again."

"You won't be disappointed. I promise," Ned said. He hoped he wasn't promising too much, but everything he'd seen that night indicated that the kelp would work on Lucy just as it had on the others.

She got in line.

Ned felt like he aged twenty years himself waiting for her turn. At long last she reached the front, and Ida gave her a strand of the kelp. Lucy took it and ate it without prompting. She smiled at Ned and Morgan, as if they were the ones that needed support.

She returned to them, and the whole family held hands silently while they waited. After five minutes, Lucy's body twitched, and she dropped to the ground. Ned felt alarmed, hating to see her fall over, but he knew it was part of the process. Lucy laughed as they watched her arms and legs grow, her torso elongate, and her flaxen hair lengthen and become dark brown. When she was finished, she stood and brushed herself off.

Morgan, tears flowing down his cheeks, declared, "You look like Mother!"

Lucy's mouth popped open. "That's not very nice."

"In the best possible way." He hugged her. "You're beautiful!"

Ned hugged her next, amazed that her body was now the same size as his. "Aunt Lucy."

"Who's going to fetch me a mirror?" she asked, grinning.

"Let's run back to the house!" Beatrice said, and the two of them dashed off. Lucy had to hold up her hair so she wouldn't trip on it, which made Beatrice twitter like a schoolgirl.

Only one of the lost children was still a child: Ludwig Hill. He hid behind his mother's legs. He looked to be only four or five, but like the others, he was probably closer to thirty years old.

"Your turn, Ludwig!" Rosetta Collins said.

"I don't want to go," he said. "And you can't make me."

"There's nothing to be afraid of. We're all fine," she said, pointing to all the grown children.

"I'm not afraid . . . I . . . I don't want to grow old."

The crowd went quiet.

Ida was still at her spot on the steps. "No one will force you to eat the kelp. And no one can force you to grow old. If you prefer yourself the way you are, so be it."

Ludwig was visibly relieved. "Thank you." Taking him by the hands, his parents led him home.

"Ladies and gentlemen!" Ida announced. "I hope you enjoyed the show as much as I did, and I hope you will appreciate your adulthoods. If you don't, then, uh, there's not much I can do. That's life."

People blinked, unsure how to respond.

Ned clapped his hands for her, and slowly everyone began

to applaud. Soon the crowd was whooping and hollering in Ida's honor. People clamored around her, patting her on the back. Mothers smothered her with kisses and hugs. A few of the younger men looked ready to propose.

"Thank you everyone," Ida said. "I've done what I came to do. It's time for me to go."

She descended the steps as people protested.

Ned approached her with shyness. "Do you remember me?"

"Uh, sure!" she said.

"Do you really have to leave so soon?" he asked. He had a lot of questions for her.

"I have a hot bath and a soft bed waiting for me," she said, smiling hugely. "But it was great to see you!" She marched away from the crowd.

Disappointed, he yelled after her, "If you see Josephine, tell her I said 'hello!'"

She didn't turn around, but she waved and shouted, "You bet, Ted!"

"NED!" he yelled after her.

She waved again, and he hoped she'd heard him.

He shook his head in disbelief at the entire night. Was this all really happening, or had he fallen asleep at the bakery and this was some crazy fantasy?

A celebration began that Ned was sure would go on all night. People set up tables and brought out food and wine. Musicians fetched their instruments. Couples danced. A barber pulled out his scissors, offering free haircuts to those that wanted them. Angus rang the bell over and over.

A toddler waddled around the party. When he reached the steps of the church, he crawled up happily. His hand landed on a stray piece of seaweed. He was shoving it into his mouth, when a stooped old man shambled over. "Oh no you don't, boy!" He scooped the child into his arms.

Ned recognized the old man. It was Mr. Seaworthy! Which meant that the toddler was . . . Ned felt ill. That adorable little boy was the Master! And he'd almost eaten a piece of kelp that would have made him into an adult again. A cold sweat dotted Ned's brow.

Ned told Mr. Seaworthy, "Take that child away from here."

"He's not hurting anyone," the old man said. "He thought it was candy."

Ned spoke quietly through clenched teeth, not wanting to make a scene. "I don't care if he thought it was spun gold. Get him out of here, *now*."

Ned shuddered as Mr. Seaworthy walked away, the toddler in his arms. The old man had smiled apologetically, but Ned could swear that the child had smirked at him.

TWO HOURS LATER, Ida stepped out of a hot bath. She would have stayed in the tub longer, but her fingers and toes were turning pruney. *Like Ms. Neely's face*, she thought with a wicked smile. After drying off with a towel, she put on pajamas that Josephine had lent her. They were soft and pink and had matching slippers. Normally, Ida would make fun of such a girly ensemble, but not tonight. The fabric of the pajamas made her feel as if little bunnies were nuzzling her.

Wiping the mist off the bathroom mirror, she studied her new face. How long would it take for her to stop gaping at herself? Months? Years? She combed through her hair, enjoying its clean smell and marveling at its length.

She opened the bathroom door, allowing the steam to escape, and entered the guest room, which Josephine and Fargus were calling *her* room. The bed wasn't huge, but it had a white feather comforter a foot high. Mushy pillows were piled at the top, and a powder blue throw blanket was folded neatly at the bottom. Books were stacked on a bedside table and filled the shelves that lined the room.

Ida gave a squeal as she ran and jumped onto the bed, squashing the comforter and causing the mattress to groan.

A concerned voice came from downstairs. "Everything all right up there?" Fargus asked.

Ida giggled. How strange that he was now the adult in the house, worried about her safety. "Yes!" she hollered. "Everything is wonderful!"

Climbing into the bed, she slid underneath the comforter. She tried to yank up the sheet, but it wouldn't budge. She pulled harder. It would only come up as high as her knees. The truth of the situation dawned on her—Fargus had short sheeted her bed!

"*You're a conniving pile of cowplop*!" she shrieked.

Deep laughter filled the house. "And you're a *squid nibbler*!" Fargus yelled.

"Better *a squid nibbler* than *an old-man lice-train*!" Ida yelled back.

Ida could hear Josephine howl with laughter, while Fargus hollered, "Go to sleep, you *two-faced turkey waddle*!"

Ida decided that this one time she would let him have the last word. Chuckling, she remade the bed. She climbed back in and closed her eyes, ready to have the best sleep of her life.

ABOUT THE AUTHOR

Carolyn Cohagan began her writing career on the stage. She has performed stand-up and one-woman shows at festivals around the world from Adelaide to Edinburgh. Her first novel, *The Lost Children*, is a middle grade fantasy which became part of the Scholastic Bookclub and was nominated for a Massachusetts Children's Book Award. The first book in her YA dystopian trilogy, *Time Zero*, won eight literary honors, including the 2017 Readers Favorite Award and the 2017 International Book Award. In 2020, she and her mother, painter Lynn Cohagan, collaborated on the *Creative Writing Journal: Clever Prompts for Clever Children*. Carolyn is the founder of Kids With Pens, a creative writing organization in Austin dedicated to fostering the individual voices and offbeat imaginations of kids ages 8-15.

Book One, *The Lost Children,* is available on Amazon.

To receive Carolyn's monthly newsletter containing what she is watching, reading, listening to, and writing, go to www.carolyncohagan.com

ACKNOWLEDGMENTS

I would like to thank Claire Campbell for exchanging pages of writing with me throughout 2020. You kept things moving forward with this book when nothing else in the world was moving at all. I also want to thank my mother Lynn Cohagan whose enthusiasm for this story never waned. Thank you to my husband for speaking with me very seriously about the architectural feasibility of my absurd plot.

I'm grateful to former teacher Elizabeth Petty for reading *The Lost Children* to her third graders every year and to her former students Charlotte and Jane Whitaker for investing so much in my characters. Thank you to my early readers Drea Clark, Maxine Hopkins, Hester Kamin, Elisa Todd Ellis, Sam Suguira, Lori Levy, and my goddaughter Violet Yingling.

I also need to thank my editor Andrea Eames who found the time to work with me despite having a one-year-old squidge. As always, thank you to the Loma Linda Fellows for your support as friends, women, and fellow writers. I can't wait to see you in person again and howl at the moon.